ROGUE GHOSTS
& OTHER MISCREANTS

ANNETTE MARIE
ROB JACOBSEN

dark owl
fantasy

Rogue Ghosts & Other Miscreants
The Guild Codex: Warped / Book Three
By Annette Marie & Rob Jacobsen

Dark Owl Fantasy Inc.
PO Box 88106, Rabbit Hill Post Office
Edmonton, AB, Canada T6R 0M5
www.darkowlfantasy.com

Cover Copyright © 2021 by Annette Ahner
Cover and Book Interior by Midnight Whimsy Designs
www.midnightwhimsydesigns.com

Editing by Elizabeth Darkley
arrowheadediting.wordpress.com

ISBN 978-1-988153-61-2

MORE BOOKS BY ANNETTE MARIE

STEEL & STONE UNIVERSE

Steel & Stone Series

Chase the Dark

Bind the Soul

Yield the Night

Reap the Shadows

Unleash the Storm

Steel & Stone

Spell Weaver Trilogy

The Night Realm

The Shadow Weave

The Blood Curse

OTHER WORKS

Red Winter Trilogy

Red Winter

Dark Tempest

Immortal Fire

THE GUILD CODEX

CLASSES OF MAGIC

Spiritalis

Psychica

Arcana

Demonica

Elementaria

MYTHIC

A person with magical ability

MPD / MAGIPOL

The organization that regulates mythics and their activities

ROGUE

A mythic living in violation of MPD laws

ROGUE GHOSTS
& OTHER MISCREANTS

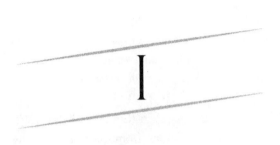

I

"THIS IS MY NIGHTMARE," Lienna gasped.

Swirls of orange light danced across her dilated pupils, her brown eyes wide and her glossy raven hair reflecting the flashing neon radiance coming from all directions. Her left hand closed convulsively around the strap of her satchel, knuckles white with tension.

I frowned. "It's … a carnival."

She flinched as a heavyset man bumped her on his way past, two squealing kindergarteners in tow. "It's sticky and loud and it smells like—"

"Like deep-fried gym socks?"

Her throat bobbed as she swallowed her stomach down. "That's putting it nicely."

She wasn't wrong. Even for a traveling carnival, the odor was unusually pungent. Some genius had decided to bring this corn dog festival to Vancouver in late January, the drizzliest season imaginable, so the whole thing—rides, games, cotton candy, and all—was housed inside an old warehouse in Burnaby. Hence the immersive "aroma."

My partner's eyes scanned the crowd. "At least there aren't any"—a finger tapped her shoulder, and she turned with a squeaky gasp—"*clowns.*"

The finger belonged to a tall Pennywise lookalike, with thick white face paint and dead eyes. The clown loomed over her, his jaws opening inhumanly wide to reveal double rows of shark-like incisors. A wet gurgle bubbled out of his gaping throat.

I'd seen Agent Lienna Shen frightened before. We'd been through some dicey situations, from springing a deadly booby trap in my former boss's secret lair, to fighting off demons and electrifying assassins, to surviving a sinking ship full of ultra-nasty baddies in open ocean.

But I'd never seen anything close to the unvarnished terror that splashed across her face when faced with Bozo the Belligerent, viscous saliva hanging from his teeth.

She reeled back and shoved her hand into her satchel for a weapon. Before she could ram a stun marble down the clown's throat, he disintegrated into gray dust that blew away in a nonexistent breeze.

Lienna froze, then looked around wildly as though the clown might've teleported behind her.

"So, it's true," I mused.

Her gaze snapped to me. "What?"

"You're afraid of clowns."

"That was *you?*"

The fact that my involvement was only *now* occurring to her—and not, say, when the clown's jaw had dislocated like the bug-spewing mummy from the classic Brendan Fraser adventure flick—was stronger confirmation.

"I've suspected it ever since I noticed you avoid the old Ronald statue outside the local McD's," I confessed. "Now I know for sure."

Releasing her satchel with jerky movements, she shot me a fiery glare. "Remind me to strangle you as soon as we're back at the precinct."

She pushed into the bustling crowd, leaving me to rush after her.

"Oh, come on," I said. "You can do better than that."

"Do better than what?"

"Strangle me? That's a boring, human-style threat."

She spun to face me so suddenly that a harried mom with a toddler in one hand and an extra-large popcorn in the other had to do some nifty sashaying to avoid her. "How about I cut off your fingers, fashion them into an artifact to suppress your dumbass warps, and make you wear your own desiccated digits as a tiara?"

I grinned. "Much better! I was worried I'd rattled you with Chuckles."

She resumed her trek toward the games area, where blaring whistles and shrieking bells added to the din. "I'm not rattled. Although your warps are getting better."

Letting the compliment pass unacknowledged, I homed in on the more important issue at hand. "I assume there's a traumatizing clown experience in your past. What was it? A birthday party gone wrong?"

"No."

"Did somebody make you watch the original *It* miniseries as a child?"

"No." Stopping, she nodded toward a booth squished between a closed pretzel stand and another throwing game. "There he is."

The booth was narrow and deep, with a wall of multi-colored balloons at the far end. The man running it—a greaseball with mutton chops and an ill-fitting vest—handed three darts to his victim, a teenage boy trying to impress his date. Unsurprisingly, the boy failed in his trio of attempts at popping a balloon.

Yeah, Mutton Chops was the guy we were looking for.

Lienna nudged in close as passersby flowed around us. "Did you see how the darts moved?"

"I was too focused on those disgusting chops. He looks like Peter Stormare dressed up as Wolverine."

She kept her focus on our target, skipping the eye roll she no doubt wanted to toss my way. "I don't think he has claws, but he *is* a telekinetic. The complaint claims he's cheating his customers. No one ever wins at his booth."

"In other words, he's saving entire *dollars* on balloon costs."

This time, she fired off that eye roll. "The problem is he might expose magic to the general public."

I gazed around the noisy, odorous Festival of Fried Food. Maybe once I retired from the MPD, I could open up my own carnival booth. Psycho warping on the cheap. I'd be like a one-man holodeck from *Star Trek*, at least until I got busted for threatening the secrecy of magic, not unlike our dart-dealing target.

Lienna interrupted my daydream by tugging on my jacket sleeve. "We need to get closer to confirm he's using magic."

"And without him noticing us." I surveyed the area again, then looped my arm around her waist and drew her against my side. "Ready?"

Her eyes widened. "Ready for what?"

"We can't just stand there and stare at him, can we?" Grinning, I pulled her with me. "But we *can* stand there while I teach my beautiful girlfriend how to throw."

"*Girlfriend?*"

I marched her toward the telekinetic's neighboring game, that classic throwing challenge where you have to knock six stacked milk bottles off a table with a baseball. We got in line behind a couple a few years younger than us. The scrawny guy made a big show of winding up before throwing. The baseball soared right past the milk bottles without touching a single one.

"Kit," Lienna growled under her breath, trying to surreptitiously tug my hand off her waist.

I leaned down, bringing my mouth to her ear. "Mr. Mutton Chops won't look twice at a couple on a date. How else can we observe him at close range without tipping him off? Think of it as an undercover operation."

She considered that, then one side of her mouth curled into a smile. "Fine. But I already know how to throw."

"You think you do, but—"

"If you say I throw like a girl, I'll start on that finger tiara right here and now."

"I was going to say, even though you fire off those evil little marbles like a friggin' howitzer, you've got the accuracy of a drunken mosquito in a hurricane."

She scowled. "I am *not* that bad."

I handed a couple of bills to the booth operator, a lady sporting a green pantsuit from the eighties and a perm from the seventies. She handed me three baseballs.

I tossed one to Lienna. "Prove it."

Lips pressed thin, she took the ball and lined herself up in front of a stack of milk bottles. She took a deep breath, cocked her arm back, and launched the ball like a missile. It hooked left, clipped a milk bottle, and veered at the pantsuited carnie, who ducked to avoid a concussion.

"Watch it," the woman squawked. "You don't win anything by knocking *me* over!"

Lienna muttered an apology, then gave me a narrow-eyed glower like this was all my fault. "Let me try again."

"Be my guest," I replied, handing her another baseball.

She wound up once more and the projectile cut left a second time, missing the milk bottles by an inch and smacking harmlessly into the tarp behind them.

Glower deepening, she folded her arms. "You can do better?"

I stepped in beside her, positioned my feet, and hurled the ball. It crashed into the bottles, sending five of them off the table. One stubborn son-of-a-dairy-container remained standing.

"Since when do you have such a good arm?" Lienna asked grouchily.

"I did some sportsing as a kid. I even helped coach a church baseball camp for a couple summers as a teenager."

A snort escaped her. "I'm sorry, what? They let *you* in a church?"

"It was Gillian's idea."

"Oh? Who is Gillian?"

"She was ..." I trailed off, not wanting to delve into my bittersweet memories of Gillian at an overpriced carnival game in the middle of a warehouse that smelled like the inside of Ghost Rider's unwashed jockstrap. "Just someone I knew back in the day."

Lienna prodded my shoulder. "C'mon. I wanna hear about your ex-girlfriend."

"She wasn't a girlfriend." I handed Captain Pantsuit another bill in exchange for three more baseballs. "Why don't you tell me about your clownophobia? Did little Lienna stay up too late reading about John Wayne Gacy?"

"It's called 'coulrophobia' and no."

"I thought for sure that was it." I tossed her a ball. "We need to fix your hips."

Her eyebrows shot up. "Excuse me?"

"When you throw, your body naturally rotates, so if you stand like this when you throw"—I faced the table of milk bottles square on, imitating Lienna's stance—"you'll hook it to the left."

I placed my hands on her hips, slowly twisting them to the right until her body was perpendicular to her target. Then I moved my left hand down her lead leg. "Point your toe at your target."

She didn't move, her stare oddly vacant and her lips parted slightly.

"Lienna?"

"Hmm?" Her eyelids fluttered, focus returning to her gaze. A faint flush tinged her cheeks. "Huh?"

"Point your toe."

"Right." She pivoted her heel to point her foot at the milk bottles. "Now what?"

"Now throw."

She reeled her arm back and let the ball fly. Her throw was more or less straight, hitting the bottom bottles and toppling half the stack.

"Hell yeah!" She tossed her arms in the air in celebration and spun around to face me—not realizing how close I was standing. We collided and I grabbed her upper arms before she could fall backward, pulling her into me.

Our eyes met, faces inches apart—then she hastily stepped back. I released her arms.

Clearing her throat, she faced the milk bottles again, made a show of lining up her foot the way I'd instructed, then flicked a pointed look at the balloon booth, which we'd so far been completely ignoring.

Right. Our job.

Our jobs were important. In fact, Lienna's career was so important to her that she wouldn't risk it on any "unprofessional" behavior, such as having a romantic fling with her partner.

It was her choice, and I wasn't holding it against her. My crush was my own problem. All I could do was pretend real hard that I didn't think about her naked more often than was strictly professional.

While Lienna practiced with her remaining baseballs, I struck up a casual conversation with the pantsuited carnie, my attention drifting toward the neighboring booth. Mutton Chops smiled greasily at a fresh trio of teenagers as they handed over their hard-earned part-timer pay for a handful of darts.

I watched as every throw veered into the balloon-less spots on the board, even when it involved physics-defying flight paths.

As I refocused on my "date," Lienna hurled her final ball. It crashed through the bottom row of bottles, shattering the centermost one and sending the rest toppling. My eyebrows quirked. The only way that bottom bottle could have broken was if its base was glued to the table.

Lucky for Ms. Pantsuit-and-Perm, we only investigated *mythic* frauds.

"Congratulations," the carnie said with a false smile. "Which prize would you like?"

She gestured at the stuffed animals hanging from the top of the stall. My hand jumped into the air, finger pointing at the only possible choice: a hot pink unicorn the size of a chubby corgi with squat little legs and a sparkly, rainbow-colored horn.

"No thanks," Lienna said, pushing my arm down. "We can't carry it."

"You won so you get a prize." The woman tugged the unicorn down and held it out insistently.

I scooped Sir Sparkles the Joy Bomb out of the woman's hands and hugged him tightly to my chest. His beady eyes bulged and Lienna's brown eyes rolled.

"We have a job to do, remember?" she muttered out of the corner of her mouth.

"And we can go ahead and do it now," I replied with a chipper grin. "Mutton Chops manipulated every throw for his last three customers. He's one hundred percent guilty."

Nodding, she marched to the next booth, taking the place of the dejected teenagers who'd walked away empty-handed. The milk-bottle lady was busy sweeping up broken glass, and no other customers were within earshot of the balloon booth.

Mutton Chops opened his mouth to start his welcome spiel, then choked when my partner flashed her badge.

"Agent Shen," she said. "This is my partner, Agent Morris."

I sidled up beside her, still hugging my new best friend. "You can call me Kit."

"*Agent Morris* and I received a tip that you're using magic in front of humans. That's a violation of—"

"I ain't using magic," Mutton Chops interrupted aggressively. "You can't prove nothing."

Ugh. Even his voice was greasy.

"We don't need to prove anything," I said, smoothing Sir Sparkles's mohawk-like mane. "We witnessed it with our own two peepers, so we can testify against you. Great, huh?"

He smiled meanly, twirling a pair of darts in his hand.

"As I was saying," Lienna said, reaching into her satchel, "you're under arrest for violations of—"

Mutton Chops opened his hand, and the two darts launched at her as though fired from an invisible slingshot.

I swung Sir Sparkles into their path, and the darts sank harmlessly into his thick, huggable tummy.

The greasy telekinetic grabbed a fresh handful of darts and hurled them at us the old-fashioned way, while simultaneously diving toward the back of his booth. Sir Sparkles took another one for the team, then Lienna and I vaulted over the counter.

Our target had vanished behind the tarp that formed the booth's rear wall, and we shoved through it to find him escaping down the narrow gap between booths in a weird sideways shuffle. His natural grease must've been helping him slip through.

We gave chase. At the end of the cramped corridor, he whirled around and flung a shiny dagger at us with the full force of his telekinesis.

Lienna and I dove for the floor. The dagger flew over our heads as I landed on Sir Sparkles.

What? Of course I hadn't *abandoned* him.

We leaped up again, but Mutton Chops had already disappeared. Racing out of the corridor, we burst into the bustle of the carnival. Innocent entertainment-seekers swarmed in every direction, and I rose onto my tiptoes, trying to spot the armed and stabby psychic scam artist. I couldn't see him, but he could only have gone left or right.

Lienna and I exchanged swift glances, then she sprinted right and I sprinted left.

My route carried me toward the warehouse entrance. If Mutton Chops was trying to make like Harrison Ford and play fugitive, the exit seemed like an obvious choice. I bobbed and weaved through the throng of exiting people, searching for a glimpse of Mutton Chops. There were many greasy heads for my eyeballs to sift through—but only one with those fugly face whiskers.

They were like an eyesore beacon, calling my gaze to them as he shoved past a young couple and charged outside.

I picked up speed, using Sir Sparkles to punch through the double doors and into the gloomy January weather. Rain had dampened everything outside, the wet haze shrouding the city.

Mutton Chops raced for the back of the parking lot, where a chain-link fence separated it from a railroad. The pavement was slick, but I managed to close the gap by the time he reached the fence.

"Hey, dickhead!" I called as I skidded around the bumper of a silver Prius and held the unicorn's pincushioned belly aloft. "You left a few darts in my new friend, and I thought you might want them back."

Mutton Chops turned around with a slimy sneer and retrieved another nasty-looking dagger from his vest. This scammy, side-burned slug bucket was going to try to stab me—or Sir Sparkles—again.

It was time to end this shit.

I focused on his puny brain and created my trusty Split-Kit warp, hot pink unicorn included. Real me slipped to the side, invisible to his mind, while the phony me stared the rogue runaway down.

Mutton Chops hurled the knife at my chest. The actual blade passed through thin air and punctured the Prius's rear tire, but as far as the telekinetic was concerned, it had hit me square in the sternum.

Blood oozed down fake-Kit's blue t-shirt. "Is that all you got? You think one little knife can stop me?"

Fake-Kit added extra grit to his stance by dropping a fake Sir Sparkles to the ground and stepping on his plushy head.

From his vest, a wide-eyed Mutton Chops grabbed a trio of darts and fired them off in unison at my warp. They hit their mark: one in my stomach, one in my left leg, and one in my cheek. The real darts landed—you guessed it—in the side paneling of that poor Prius.

Fake-Kit laughed darkly. "Bull's-eye!"

"What the hell are you?" the scam artist gasped, rifling through the inner pockets of his vest for another weapon—but he was fresh out.

"I am he who can't be killed," my warped self crowed. It was a little dramatic, but, hey, I was having fun.

Although my fun was beginning to paint me into a corner. Fake-Kit's Jason Voorhees impression had Mutton Chops pressing himself against the chain-link fence in pants-wetting fear, but the warp couldn't do much else. Meanwhile, I was too busy maintaining the warp—which was extra complex with the flying knives I had to incorporate—and keeping an eye out for carnival goers to get close enough to take him down with my flesh-and-blood fists.

"Lie facedown on the pavement with your hands behind your back, you sniveling dung heap," fake-Kit snarled.

Unfortunately, Mutton Chops was either too scared or not scared enough, because he whipped around and scrambled up the wet, slippery fence.

Keeping fake-Kit alive and well—with his sinister sneer fully intact—and my real self invisible, I dashed after the escaping telekinetic. He swung one leg awkwardly over the top of the fence.

And that's when a small marble pinged off the post three inches to the left of Mutton Chops.

Ah, Agent Shen was here.

Behind me, she was simultaneously cursing her aim, pulling another stun marble from her satchel, and sprinting closer. As she wound up again, I ducked out of the way.

Her second throw caught him in the left shoulder. The greasy carnie seized up and keeled over, slamming heavily onto the pavement. I pounced on his prostrate body, rolled him onto his front, and pulled his arms behind his back. Not that he was offering any resistance, but better safe than sorry.

Lienna slowed to a stop, standing over us. She pointed at the dart-peppered unicorn plushie tucked under my arm. "Really, Kit? You should've left that thing behind."

"And you should've pointed your toe."

She rolled her eyes and passed me her handcuffs for Mutton Chops's wrists. We made such a good team.

2

WE DROPPED OFF Mutton Chops at the intake desk, where he'd get booked into a shiny new holding cell to await official charges—probably a bevy of misdemeanor fines steep enough to make him rethink that whole "increased profits versus exposing magic to humans" decision he'd made. The MPD's approach to controlling delinquent behavior was straightforward and surprisingly effective: hit them in the wallet.

Breaking mythic laws went hand in hand with mean fines, and MagiPol didn't mess around when it came to collecting. Just ask my bank account.

With our culprit in lockup, Lienna and I headed back to our desks to complete the absolute bestest part of our job: paperwork. Yay. When I'd been promoted to field agent two months ago, I'd hoped to escape the sea of documentation I'd been swimming through as an analyst, but it turned out paperwork never ended. Ever.

The bullpen greeted us with a buzzing hubbub of busyness. Usually, it was more of a hushed murmur, but the last week had been more exciting than usual. Every agent on the payroll was pulling overtime to cope.

"Where are the rogues from the Sea Devils incident?"

The impatient voice preceded Brennan Harris, a senior agent with lots of clout in the precinct and the second-most pretentious demeanor of anyone in the building. He marched past a row of cubicles as he pushed his wire-framed glasses up his nose.

"They're next for processing." His gravelly boom cut through the bullpen's chatter. "Why aren't they here?"

"They're, uh—" Vincent Park rushed after him, cargo shorts flapping as he struggled to balance a stack of folders while reading from the topmost one. "They're still at the correctional center for holding."

"Have them transferred here for—"

"Lockup is almost full," Vinny blurted, his stack tipping sideways. "We're holding the rogues from the Pandora Knights attack here, and—"

Harris whirled on the younger agent. "I thought Agent Wolfe was processing them."

"His team isn't finished yet."

"Check with him. We need them out of here. Then get to work preparing for the next round of interrogations. Pull the rogues' files and verify the incident reports. I expect the Submission of Criminal Charges forms prepared and on my desk by tomorrow morning." He tugged his suit jacket straight. "I'm going for a coffee."

With that, Harris swept away, leaving a slack-jawed Vincent clutching his folder stack.

I stifled a grin as I waltzed past him. "Hope you have an extra pair of arms in those pockets, Vinny."

He drew himself up with a self-important sniff. "Agent Harris and I are the lead agents in the largest incident of organized rogue violence since—"

"Harris is the lead agent," I corrected. "You're his analyst."

"I'm his *partner*. I passed my field exam three days after you, Morris." He eyed the pink plushie cradled in the crook of my elbow, then smirked. "Is that the dangerous criminal you got off the streets today? A stuffed animal?"

"This bad boy? He's a dangerous artifact that could eviscerate your soul with a poke of his horn."

"It's a toy."

"A *dangerous* toy that I need to get to processing," I said, following Lienna, who'd breezed past us with an air of exasperation. Turning, I walked backward so I could grin at Vinny. "You know what it's like. You've led your own cases— oh wait, you haven't."

"I work the *big* cases."

"Keep telling yourself that, bud."

"Kit!"

At Lienna's irritated call, I gave Vinny a smirk and hurried after her. We zigzagged past more harried agents, all rushing from desk to desk as they tried to scale the avalanche of work that'd hit our precinct this week.

Rogues never considered us poor MagiPol agents when they plotted violent takeovers of the city's criminal underground.

Lienna and I took shelter behind the flimsy walls of our cubicle. As she dropped into her chair, I tucked a slightly worse-for-wear Sir Sparkles into the corner behind my monitor. My desk was cluttered in a very specific manner with souvenirs from all my cases—a business card from a mage who'd told me I looked like a young Nathan Fillion, a golf ball from a sting operation at a driving range, and a strangely hued feather I was certain had come from a dark fae but that Lienna claimed was a seagull feather covered in grape juice. My partner's desk, by comparison, was hyper-organized in a way that clashed magnificently with her bohemian fashion sense.

In unison, we turned toward the file on our desk—the complaint about Mutton Chops, whose actual name was Berkeley. Time for that paperwork.

"We got the short end of this stick," I muttered, sitting down and flipping the folder open. "Not that I'd ever admit that to Vinny."

Lienna glanced my way. "What do you mean?"

I waved around at the bullpen. "Half the precinct is working overtime because a dark-arts sorceress from Russia activated her 'evil mastermind' mode, attacked Vancouver's toughest combat guilds, and tried to seize control of the city's black market from all other criminal syndicates!"

"Why do you sound so excited?"

"Because it's *awesome*." I grinned unrepentantly. "It's like an entire season of *Peaky Blinders* crammed into four days of real life. A city-wide power struggle between crime families? Guilds banding together to stop it before they could be annihilated? And the best part is the evil Russian sorceress wasn't taken out by a guild or the MPD, but by Vancouver's most notorious rogue."

She shook her head. "That's not a good thing, Kit."

"No, but it was super badass." I flopped back in my chair. "Our homegrown rogue went all Walter White and was like, 'No way is this import sorceress taking over *my* turf,' and—"

"What's your point?" she interrupted with a poorly suppressed smile.

"It sucks we aren't working on it too."

"We did tag those two rogues who escaped the first wave of arrests." Shrugging, she tapped the open folder for the telekinetic. "With so many agents working on the aftermath of all that, someone has to pick up the slack. It's actually a vote of confidence from Captain Blythe."

I cast a skeptical look at our inbox—not the digital kind but an old-fashioned plastic basket where a stack of folders awaited our attention. Lienna and I had spent most of our agent partnership working on follow-ups for other cases, investigating tips and complaints from the hotline, and handling arrest warrants for low-level crooks who hadn't shown up for summonses or trials. She was right that our caseload and the urgency of those cases had increased by several degrees over the past week, but I wasn't convinced it was because Blythe had faith in us.

"Well," Lienna said on an unenthusiastic exhale. "We should start our report for today's arrest. Describing the suspect's capture will be interesting."

I poked the power button on my computer, firing it up. "Meaning what?"

"You used magic in public."

"How else was I supposed to stop the guy?"

"Not in public, that's how." She woke up her computer and logged in. "The whole reason we arrested him was for exposing magic to humans. You're lucky nobody saw you."

"I only targeted his mind. No one else could see a thing."

"But people *could* see the telekinetic throwing things around with *his* mind. We have to set a better example."

As I scrunched my face, her phone chimed.

"I'm just saying"—she dug her phone out and looked down at the screen—"we could've found another way to—oh."

"Oh what?"

She blinked at her phone. "Captain Blythe texted me."

Blythe, texting? I'd never once received a text from her, probably because the written word couldn't accurately convey her unflagging disdain for my particular brand of charm.

"She ... she wants us to meet her for dinner."

It took a moment for Lienna's words to sink in, then I blurted, "She's been abducted!"

"Huh?"

"It's a call for help. She can't let her captors realize what she's doing, so she sent an innocuous message to tip us off."

Lienna typed a quick reply. "Can you imagine someone kidnapping Blythe?"

"No," I admitted. "But I can't imagine a friendly social visit over sushi either."

"Not sushi. It's a Lebanese restaurant." She rose to her feet. "Only one way to find out what's up. Let's go."

I hastened after her, fully on board with this change of plans. Best case scenario, something dastardly was afoot. Worst case scenario, I got falafels. Either way, no paperwork today. Win, win, win.

BLYTHE'S MYSTERIOUS dinner invitation brought us to a restaurant tucked into the bottom floor of a condo building on the corner of Richards and Davies. The weather was still overcast and damp, making everything seem extra bland.

Lienna parked Smart Car III at the curb half a block away, and I patted the roof appreciatively as I shut my door. After the tragic deaths of our last two smart cars back in November, this one had become our trusty four-wheeled steed, and while still clownishly minuscule, it included a backseat, which came in very handy when transporting criminals to the precinct. We didn't have to strap them to the roof rack anymore.

The restaurant's interior was dimly lit by soft orange lamps that reflected lazily off the white plastered walls. Delicately carved arches separated the various sections, and the whole place smelled of citrus and grilled spices.

Bypassing the hostess, we ventured into the dining area. Blythe was easy to spot; not only was she alone at a table for four, but she was the only person in the entire establishment who was scowling.

I glanced around covertly. No sign of her kidnappers ... yet.

"Captain Blythe," Lienna said with a cautious smile as we approached the table. "Thank you for inviting us to—"

"Were you followed?" the captain barked.

I redoubled my efforts to spot a suspicious face among the crowd of happy diners.

"No?" Lienna said uncertainly.

Blythe pushed her chair back. "Then let's move."

"Move where?"

Ignoring her subordinate's question, Blythe swept away. I snagged a piece of her untouched flatbread, scooped it through the accompanying hummus, and stuffed it in my mouth before following Lienna. Blythe power walked through a staff-only door at the back, cut through the kitchen to the surprise of the busy cooks, and led us out the rear exit into an alley.

"What's going on?" Lienna muttered as I caught up to her.

I grinned. "No idea."

"Again, why do you sound so excited?"

Our captain led us through the alley, across the street, and into a sandstone apartment building. Skipping the intercom panel, she unlocked the security door with a key.

We piled into the elevator and Blythe selected the eighth floor.

"Have you guys seen the movie *Devil*?" I asked as the creaky cables pulled us upward.

Blythe stared unwaveringly forward, while Lienna closed her eyes in a way that implied she was wishing I'd lose my voice like a certain mermaid.

"It's an M. Night Shyamalan flick," I rambled. "A bunch of people are trapped in an elevator while a mysterious bad guy slowly kills them off."

The captain didn't flinch. Lienna shook her head mutely.

"But I'm sure that won't happen to us," I said as the elevator came to a halt and the doors slid open. "See? Safe and sound."

Blythe's destination was apartment 808. Unlocking the door with another key, she wordlessly ushered us into a plain, one-bedroom suite. The empty white walls and mousy carpet matched the building's boring exterior. Instead of the usual living room furniture, two cheap folding tables were lined up end to end, their surfaces covered in stacks of paper, folders, two binders, and items stored in clear plastic bags. Cardboard boxes occupied the rest of the space.

"Was this all a trick to get us to help you move?" I asked as we congregated in the middle of the room. "I can think of a dozen agents back at the precinct who are better suited to lifting heavy stuff than me and Lienna."

"I'm not interested in your lifting abilities, Agent Morris," Blythe answered. "As you may recall, I am perfectly capable of that on my own."

"Then what's with the covert-message, sneaking-through-back-doors meetup?" I asked, my neck aching at the reminder of her telekinetic powers. Mutton Chops's dart-tossing didn't hold a candle to Blythe's psychic strength.

"This"—she waved around the room—"is Shane Davila's apartment. *Former* apartment, I should say."

"Dr. Bunsen Honeydew?" I exclaimed.

Both women gave me a questioning look.

"That famous bounty hunter you brought out to the farm murder," I clarified. "Short, bald, glasses. Looks like a Muppet."

The captain's stare turned withering.

The "farm murder" was an innocuous way to describe an investigation Blythe had assigned to us a couple of weeks ago where a Jane Doe's body had been recovered. It had involved a quaint countryside ranch north of the city, where one dark-arts master had obliterated the property of their archnemesis, a fellow dark-arts practitioner.

At least, that was my working theory. We hadn't gotten far in the investigation before the big "evil sorceress takeover" thing had derailed all non-urgent cases.

Interestingly, the captain had insisted the farm investigation stay off the books … kind of like this covert meeting.

Blythe picked up the largest stack of folders and slapped the top one like it'd personally insulted her. "Mr. Davila's interest in the farm incident was spurred by the bounty he was chasing: Varvara Nikolaev."

My eyebrows rose. "As in the evil Russian sorceress who made her hostile-takeover bid last week?"

"With her death, Mr. Davila has moved on to other bounties, leaving all this behind." Blythe's gaze cut between us. "And now you will use his work to catch a different rogue who abducted another victim this morning. A teenage boy. Agent Vigneault started the investigation, but I'm assigning you two to it."

Something dastardly was indeed afoot, but not in the fun way. The abduction of a teenager instantly got my hackles up.

Lienna tugged on a string of beads in her hair. "If Agent Vigneault already started the investigation, why are Kit and I—"

"Because neither your investigation nor the evidence in this room will reach the eyes or ears of anyone else at the MPD," Blythe stated flatly. "You and Agent Morris will report directly to me. Involve a single other soul in what you are investigating and I will have your badges and your heads. Do I make myself clear?"

"Exceptionally," I muttered. "Minus the whole secrecy business. Why can't we tell anyone about this?"

"Those are your orders, Agent Morris. Catch this bastard, and I'll worry about the rest."

Okay, then. "Those are your orders" must be police-speak for "because I said so"—a phrase I'd heard often from a wide variety of delightful foster parents. Both phrases, whether uttered by an abusive douchebag named Dwayne or the captain of the magic police, were meant to stifle independent thought.

Blythe's version wouldn't work on me any better than Douchey Dwayne's had.

She extended her pile of folders and dropped them in my unsuspecting arms. "The case is yours. Don't screw it up."

I was surprised by how heavy the Leaning Tower of Paperwork was, but, more importantly, I was thrown off by seeing Blythe willingly give up a pile of folders. It felt like a queen handing over her scepter.

Wait … did that mean …?

"I'm the captain now," I whispered to myself.

Thankfully, Blythe didn't hear me and continued giving instructions. "Focus on the rogue, not the kidnapping. Find him and you'll find the boy."

"But who's the rogue?" I asked, hefting the folders. "And what does Shane's investigation have to do with him?"

"Do you recall what was so unusual about the farm incident, Agent Morris?"

"It was a brutal power play between two dark-arts practitioners who clearly hated each other." My eyes popped in realization. "And Shane was hunting the Russian sorceress! She must've been one of the two rival rogues from the farm!"

Lienna sucked in a breath. "Does that mean the other rogue, the one we're supposed to bring down, is actually—"

"—the Ghost," Blythe finished for her. She flipped open the top folder of the stack I now held, pulled out a photo, and handed it to Lienna, whose stunned gaze zoomed across the image.

"Also known as the Crystal Druid," the captain continued grimly. "He has the largest individual bounty of any rogue in Vancouver and over three hundred felony charges against him, and he has evaded capture for the past eight years. Five days ago, he killed Varvara Nikolaev. This morning, he kidnapped a boy."

Lienna dragged her attention off the paper and we both stared silently at our captain.

Blythe's cold stare offered no mercy. "His name is Zakariya Andrii, and you two will bring him in—dead or alive."

3

AS THE APARTMENT DOOR closed behind Blythe, I dumped myself into the single chair. The stack of folders almost toppled out of my arms.

"Okay, let me get this straight," I said. "Earlier this month, Blythe brings us out to a farm that's been, like, ninety-three percent destroyed by some very nasty sorcery. We meet Shane, the spherically skulled bounty hunter, who's on a mysterious job that turns out to be Varvara Nikolaev and her dastardly plot to take over Vancouver. Now she's dead and we're supposed to use all his investigative work to capture the rogue who killed her. And that rogue is the Ghost, the single nastiest dude in the city who was nicknamed for his ability to vanish without a trace."

Lienna was already searching through a cardboard box, which so far contained objects like a watch, a football-sized eagle sculpture made of glass, and a used napkin, each in a sealed plastic bag.

"Oh, and we can't tell anyone about it," I added. "That about sum it up?"

"I guess so," she muttered, opening the next box. "Some of this evidence must be related to the Ghost. Shane would've been investigating them both since the Ghost and Varvara were enemies."

"Do we know anything about the Ghost, aside from the farm incident, his stabby treatment of rival rogues, and the fact he's a kidnapping shitbag?"

"Well, we know *that*." She pointed at the photo Blythe had handed her, which was now resting on one of the many boxes.

Reluctantly rising from my chair, I deposited the folder stack on the table, picked up the photo, and—

Holy Adonis, that face! The photo looked like an outtake for a cologne model's magazine shoot, except instead of selling you the sweet musk of rugged spice and sex appeal, this brooding dreamboat was selling a renegade brand of seething anger and ... well ... sex appeal.

The man was in his mid-twenties and had fair skin, short tousled hair that was either very dark brown or black, and a jawline designed to make men jealous and women swoon. The photo was a candid shot of the subject glaring in a smoldery way at something off in the distance, a dark alley behind him.

"*This* is the Ghost?" I shook my head, bemused. There was no agent in the precinct who hadn't perused the notorious rogue's case files at least once, including me, and I hadn't seen any photos before now. It wasn't like I would forget a face like that if I had.

Opening the folder that Blythe had pulled the photo from, I found a printout of the Ghost's bounty from the MPD archives. There was no name or photo. Seemed like Shane Davila hadn't updated the bounty listing with the results of his investigative work.

I tapped a finger on the only useful information besides the two-mile-long list of criminal charges: the guy's mythic class.

"'Spiritalis, druid,'" I read. "And 'Arcana, alchemist.' Di-mythics aren't exactly common. How much fun do you think we'll have taking down a druid-alchemist?"

Lienna looked up from her box. "Are you going to help me? Or are you going to stare at his photo all day?"

"It's hard not to. Seriously, this guy looks like the love child of Matt Bomer, James Dean, and an evil version of those dudes who stand shirtless outside Abercrombie and Fitch stores."

Leaving her to the boxes, I dove into the stack of folders Blythe had given me. The first one contained info I could find in the MPD archives: the Ghost's bounty listing and thoroughly unilluminating profile, along with case files for all the semi-recent attempts to arrest this guy, from agents' to bounty hunters' to entire guilds'.

The second folder contained Agent Vigneault's preliminary investigation into the kidnapping this morning, most of it recorded via scribbled notes on lined paper. Just after nine a.m., a librarian at Arcana Historia, a scholarly guild in downtown Vancouver, had witnessed a man in a hooded black coat abduct a fourteen-ish-year-old boy from the library's front steps. He'd dragged the kid into an alley where he and his victim had vanished into thin air. Sounded rather *ghostlike*, didn't it?

Until someone reported the boy missing, we had no way to identify him, aside from a black leather bracelet, which he'd dropped in the struggle. The bracelet, inside an evidence bag and clipped to the report, had a rune-engraved band, making it an artifact of some kind. So we knew the boy was a mythic, and that was it.

The next few folders contained Shane Davila's investigative work, which I knew because they were covered in the sort of small, neat printing only a Muppet would have. I flipped through the first folder, which detailed artifact thefts attributed to the Ghost. The list took up dozens of pages.

"Not exactly environmentally friendly, Dr. Honeydew," I remarked under my breath. "What do you have against computers?"

The deeper I delved, the colder I felt. Theft, blackmail, murder—all expected activities for a dangerous rogue—but one folder was devoted entirely to missing persons reports. Yeah, plural. That boy's abduction this morning wasn't the Ghost's first teen-napping rodeo.

I flipped through Shane's notes. Nasrin Anwar, age thirteen. Jasper Briggs, age seventeen. Nadine River, age sixteen.

"They're all teenagers," I said, louder than I'd meant to.

Lienna glanced up from her latest box, which contained a collection of books. "What?"

"The Ghost's victims—they're all kids."

I kept flipping endless pages, counting until I hit the final one. There were thirty-two missing kids in here. *Thirty-two.* A simmering warmth rose up my neck. What kind of monster preyed on children? The documents Shane had collected included missing persons reports and case files, some from the MPD and some from the regular ol' VPD. The Ghost didn't limit himself to mythic kids.

The papers I held crunched as my hands clenched into fists.

Lienna stepped away from her cardboard archeological dig to put a hand on my shoulder. "You okay?"

I held up a victim profile. "Kristy Huang, age fifteen. She wasn't reported missing for almost a month, not until a volunteer at the soup kitchen she usually went to noticed she hadn't been around. That was two and a half years ago and nobody's done shit to find her."

Lienna squeezed my shoulder. "Once we catch this guy, he'll never touch another kid again."

"Yeah, because I'm going to mulch both his hands."

She winced. "You know, it's a lot scarier when *you* make threats like that."

Still seething, I glanced at her. "Huh?"

"You can actually do that sort of thing. In an instant."

"You mean reality warping?" I slumped back in the chair. "Not likely. I have more faith in Kevin James winning an Oscar than my ability to pulpify anyone's hands."

She prodded a spatula encased in an evidence bag. "You could always practice. I can help. If you want."

My temper flared, and I forced myself to take a long inhale. She'd brought up reality warping every couple of weeks since I'd last used the nebulous ability to transform a grappling hook into an anchor, drowning a demon and saving her life. What she didn't know—what I'd hidden from everyone—was that I'd lost all my magical powers for forty-eight hours afterward.

It'd been the single most terrifying two days of my life, and I fully intended to never, ever repeat the experience. Next time, my powers might not come back, and I couldn't risk that. No more altering the fabric of the universe for me.

Forcing myself to focus, I set Shane's victim profiles aside and collected the other papers scattered over the table.

"Why don't you help me sort through all this?" Lienna suggested. "Maybe we can make sense of it together."

"I'm going to keep looking for stuff about the victims. Maybe I can learn something."

"Captain Blythe said we should focus on—"

"I don't give a shit what Blythe said," I snapped. Damn it, the anger hath returned. I took another calming breath. "This is our case now. We'll do it our way."

"Okay," she said neutrally.

I shuffled through the loose pages, trying to decipher Shane's tiny handwriting, then scoured the room for anything else of the paper variety. Just when I thought I'd found everything, I spotted a handful of papers abandoned in an empty box like they'd been discarded. Rescuing them, I skimmed the contents.

Three more victim profiles, but these were different. None were at-risk youth. They were adults with jobs and families: an officer at the Vancouver branch of M&L, an international bank that doubled as a guild; an up-and-coming mage in the International Association of Elementaria; and the GM of a small Arcana guild in Surrey called Cantrix.

Strange. Unlike the missing teens, these abductees hadn't vanished unnoticed. Shane had printed big, fat MPD case files on their disappearances. I recognized the names of several experienced agents who'd led the investigations, as well as a handful of guilds that'd tackled the bounties. And also unlike the teens, whose disappearances spanned years, all three adults had vanished in the past month.

A frustrated groan from my partner interrupted my perusal of the cases.

"I just don't know what I'm looking at," she huffed, dumping an armload of evidence back into a box.

"Those are books," I informed her.

"Thanks, Sherlock." She hefted a bag containing a pair of women's runners. "Nothing is labeled. It's just a bunch of crap, half of it in plastic bags."

I pointed at the shoes. "I recognize those. Shane found them at the farm. He had his grubby psychic paws all over them."

"His—of course. He's a psychometric." She waved the shoes. "He didn't need notes for all this junk. He could 'see' each object's history just by touching it."

I skimmed the boxes and their nonsensical collections of items. "Wanna bet he was organizing the stuff in different boxes based on what he got from his psychic reading?"

"Sounds plausible to me." She puffed out a breath. "You know what this means, right?"

"Going into a public bathroom must be a nightmare for Shane?"

"It means we need a psychometric." Fishing her phone out of her satchel, she woke the screen. "We don't have any with the precinct, but there must be one in the city."

"I used to work with one at KCQ."

Lienna looked up. "Do you think they'd talk to us?"

"I doubt it."

"We should try."

I suppressed a smirk. "You want to hold a séance?"

"What?"

"I'm pretty sure he was one of the unidentifiably charred bodies they found in the building's wreckage."

Her lips thinned. "Very helpful, Kit."

"There's got to be another one in the city, right?"

"Hopefully." She returned her attention to her phone, tapping on the screen. "There are a few, but one just moved to Italy and two others are members of sleeper guilds."

"You're telling me there isn't a single functional, touchy-feely mythic registered in the entire city?"

"Just one." She held up her phone to show me a profile. The brunette woman in her early thirties looked harmless enough until I spotted her guild.

"Oh, come on," I groaned. "There isn't anyone else?"

"Not unless you want to drive four hours out to Kamloops."

Well, that settled it. We were paying another visit to the Crow and Hammer.

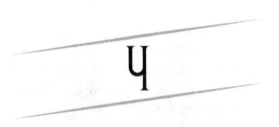

THE CROW AND HAMMER was my second least favorite guild in the city. Numero uno was the Grand Grimoire, thanks to a fondness for hellish demon pets that I most definitely didn't share.

My dislike of the Crow and Hammer wasn't entirely reasonable. Yeah, they had a bad reputation among the MPD and, sure, they'd obliterated my previous guild. But my old boss Rigel had mostly had it coming, seeing as he'd taken a Crow and Hammer member hostage. And as a lifelong outcast, I kind of appreciated that this place was a haven of misfits, former rogues, and ex-cons. I couldn't even complain about the GM, who'd given me and Lienna a key hint that'd helped us crack a case—and served me a delicious adult beverage.

But I still didn't like them. Just a gut feeling, I guess.

It was pushing eight p.m. when Lienna swung the guild's front door open, allowing a rush of light and noise out into the chill evening air. The last time we'd visited the guild's pub, it'd been abandoned except for a feisty bartender and the GM, but not this time.

As we stepped inside, a hush fell over the nearest tables and spread across the room until it reached the bar at the back. I didn't see the redheaded bartender, but two dozen unfamiliar mythics, ranging from barely legal young adults to beefy tough-guy types to elderly off-beat ladies, filled the tables—and they all stared at us with hostility.

Weird. Most mythics couldn't pin me and Lienna as MagiPol agents at a glance. We must've been giving off real-deal law-authority vibes tonight.

Or maybe it was the box I was carrying, full of random items in evidence bags.

"Good evening," Lienna said as she flashed her badge at the room. "Is Darius King in?"

Silent glaring answered her.

It took two guild officers, an awkward five-minute delay, and a lot of dark mutters and furtive glowers from the watching members before Lienna and I were ushered up to the third level of the guild and into an office where none other than the Crow and Hammer's sort-of-terrifying guild master awaited us.

Darius King didn't *look* terrifying, not at first. A well-dressed man in his late forties or early fifties, he exuded cool competence and quiet authority. But behind his amused gray eyes were cutting intelligence and beguiling charm, which he used to manipulate anyone and everyone who put themselves in his crosshairs.

At least, that's the impression I got when he had waltzed conversational circles around me and Lienna the last time we'd tried to interrogate him.

"Good evening, Agent Shen, Agent Morris." He smiled as he assessed us. "You're working late."

"Crime doesn't sleep," I quipped, balancing my cardboard box of evidence on my hip. "Also, a teen boy was kidnapped this morning."

Darius's gaze sharpened. He gestured at the plush chairs in front of his desk. "Then take a seat and tell me what you need."

I set my box on the floor, then dropped into the chair, relieved to get off my feet. Lienna perched on the chair beside me.

"Mr. King," she began. "We were hoping to use the skills of your assistant guild master. She's a psychometric, right?"

"She is. What do you need her for?"

I pointed at my box. "Some or all of this stuff is connected to the kidnapper, but we don't know what or how because Shane Davila is the one who collected it all."

"Mr. Davila … I see."

Lienna's eyes narrowed. "You're familiar with him?"

"We've had encounters," Darius replied with a mysterious little smile. "My guild worked with him to stop Varvara Nikolaev's attacks last week."

"Did you run into the rogue known as the Ghost at any point?" Lienna asked. "There were several rumored sightings of him in the twenty-four hours leading up to Varvara's death."

The GM steepled his hands on his desk. "Do you suspect the Ghost of abducting your victim?"

"The kidnapping matches his MO, and a witness reported a man fitting his description." Lienna leaned forward in her chair. "If you've seen the Ghost, Mr. King, now would be the time to tell me."

Ah, so Darius's smooth evasion hadn't slipped past Lienna either. I waggled my eyebrows knowingly at the GM, letting him know he couldn't play us as easily as he had last time. We had two whole months of additional field experience now.

His lips curved up. "Did you read my report, Agent Shen? I detailed how one of my combat teams witnessed the Ghost killing Varvara on the night of the rogue altercation."

"I did," she admitted.

"Then there you have it." He picked up the phone on his desk. "Allow me to call my AGM and see if she can come in tonight."

Two rounds for Darius, zero for the home team.

Ten minutes later, we found ourselves outside the GM's office and in a large communal area on the second floor. It was currently abandoned, but the long tables, computers, whiteboards, and corkboards all showed signs of in-progress work that'd probably be picked up again on Monday.

I poked my box of evidence grumpily. "I can't believe he gave us the runaround again."

Lienna flopped back in her chair. "And just like last time, he definitely knows more than he's letting on."

"He knows something about the Ghost," I agreed. "But I don't think he's hiding anything about the kidnapping. He didn't like hearing about a kid in trouble."

Lienna nodded. "The boy's been gone for almost twelve hours, though. Why hasn't anyone reported him missing?"

"If he's anything like this shit stain's other victims, he's probably part of the foster system or a runaway or something."

"Runaway, maybe, but he's a mythic, so he wouldn't be in the human foster system. The MPD has their own system for orphans and abandoned kids."

A mythic foster system? That was news to me. How different would my life be if I'd ended up there instead of the human version? Would that have been possible? I had no idea if either of my parents had been mythics. Arcana, Spiritalis, and Elementaria powers were hereditary, but Psychica was the only class known for "spontaneous" development of magical abilities.

I was still brooding over the past when a quiet throat-clearing interrupted me. A woman stood in the doorway near the stairs, a wool coat wrapped around her curvy form and her hair tied into a messy bun.

"Agent Shen? Agent Morris?"

"That's us," Lienna said quickly. "You must be Clara. Thanks for coming out so late."

She hurried toward us. "Of course. Darius said your case is related to a missing child."

"A kidnapped boy." I gave up my chair for her and circled the table to sit across from the two women. "How good is your psychometry?"

"Um." She sank down beside Lienna and unzipped her coat. "My job is mainly administrative, so I don't use my magic often. I'm not sure how much help I'll be."

Lienna offered an encouraging smile. "Anything you can tell us about these items will be greatly appreciated."

She handed the first object to Clara, who opened the evidence bag and took out a charred chess piece. We couldn't bring everything from the apartment, but I'd grabbed the box containing the women's runners. The broiled farm was our best lead; the Ghost was either the owner of the property, or its destroyer.

Clara gently cradled the cooked rook and rolled it back and forth in her hands, closing her eyes to concentrate.

"It was … in a fire. Obviously." She chuckled in a self-conscious way. "I can see the shape of the man who owned it. Tall. Muscular."

"Anything else you can tell us about him?" I asked.

"Ah, well …" She coughed. "From what I can see, he's … quite handsome."

So, the statuesque douchebag who kidnapped kids and weakened knees with his smoldering, evil intensity was the farm's owner. Which I'd already suspected.

"Is it an artifact?" I queried, gesturing to the rook.

Clara shook her head. "Just a regular chess piece."

While Lienna rummaged through the cardboard box for the next bag, I pulled out my phone. Before we'd left Shane's apartment, I'd snapped photos of the profiles he'd created for the Ghost's victims. I studied the first one, then logged into the MPD archives and typed in the teen's name to see if his case had been updated since Shane had printed his notes.

Lienna elbowed me in the ribs and hissed, "Quit scrolling IMDB and pay attention."

"I'm not on IMDB." I flashed her my screen. "I'm working."

Clearly annoyed, she swiveled back to Clara, who had pulled the women's shoes from a bag. The psychometric stiffened.

"What is it?" Lienna asked. "What do you see?"

Clara hastily set the shoes down. "The last person to wear these shoes was … upset."

"Upset about what?"

"I can't tell. All I get is a sense of emotional distress. What's the next item?"

Lienna squinted at the psychometric, then put the shoes away and handed her a bag with the kidnapped boy's leather bracelet in it. Clara confirmed a boy around thirteen or fourteen with medium brown hair owned it but couldn't offer more than that. She didn't get a read on the kidnapper; he must not have touched the bracelet.

I returned to my phone and the victim profiles. There was a pattern I was missing, or some other connection between the kids. And what about the three adults? They'd pinged on Shane's radar, even if he'd cast them aside. I just needed to figure out why.

While I ruminated on the possible connection between mythic foster kids, a small-time GM, an officer in an international guild, and a prodigy mage, Clara gave another item some shut-eyed attention. It looked like an oversized acorn with strange runes etched into its sides. She held it in her right hand while the fingertips of her left caressed its surface.

"It's changed owners several times. I see the same man as before—the handsome one. He gave it to a young woman. I think she sold it to a different man, but I can't see him clearly."

I was only half-listening to her murmurs about what she saw in the artifact's past until I noticed her face scrunch up as though she'd gotten a whiff of something reprehensible.

"… most recent owner was a strange person," she was saying. "A thin, pale man with long dark hair and beady eyes. He's smiling and it … it looks sort of"—she contorted her mouth as though trying to replicate the expression—"pointy?"

I snapped to attention. "Does he look like a Corey Feldman Minecraft avatar?"

"I don't know what that means."

Lienna must've been on my page, because she was hastily typing something into her phone. She turned the screen to show Clara. "Is this the man?"

Clara's mouth popped open. "Yes! How did you know?"

"We've run into that cuspidate creep before," I told her, then looked at my partner. "What do you think Faustus Trivium is up to these days?"

5

A FOOD TRUCK, it turned out, was what Faustus Trivium was up to these days.

As much as I'd hated pausing our investigation for paltry things like eating and sleeping, Lienna and I had called it quits after leaving the Crow and Hammer last night. We'd been forced to wait for morning—and for certain people to answer their phones—to discover our pal Faustus's current whereabouts.

I'd last seen him back in June during that exciting period of my life when I'd been on the run from MagiPol after escaping Lienna's custody. I'd helped rob Faustus's restaurant, and long story short, Lienna and I had faced him and his goons in a free-for-all battle where he'd tried very enthusiastically to kill me.

Since then, he'd spent a couple of weeks in holding until the Judiciary Council had decided to levy a hefty fine against him and send him into a rehabilitation program.

Despite working inside the MPD for over seven months, I still didn't understand how the Judiciary Council made decisions. Whether you got a slap on the wrist, a swift execution, or a financially crushing penalty was an utter crapshoot.

Faustus was lucky to have escaped lockup with his head still attached to his shoulders, but his financial hardship had cost him his restaurant—a greasy diner that gave a bad name to both dining and grease. As part of his rehabilitation, he was now gainfully employed at a food truck called Jumpin' Jigglies.

The name did not inspire confidence that Faustus's culinary tastes had improved.

We tracked down Jumpin' Jigglies just before noon on Hastings near Burrard, and Lienna parked Smart Car III down the block from the food truck. I stretched my legs as I stepped onto the sidewalk. It felt good not to have my knees tucked under my ears.

"*Killer Klowns From Outer Space*," I said, shaking out the tension in my hamstrings.

Locking the car, Lienna joined me on the sidewalk. "Am I supposed to know what that means?"

"It's a sci-fi horror-comedy from the eighties about aliens who look like clowns. I thought maybe you caught a rerun on TV when you were up too late as a toddler."

She shook her head with a smirk. "Nope."

"You sure?"

"I never watched much TV as a kid."

Clearly, Lienna and I had led very different lives as children, and I didn't just mean the whole "foster kid who didn't know he was a mythic" versus "Arcana prodigy and daughter of a famous MPD agent" thing.

As we headed toward the food truck, I noticed a distinct lack of customers nearby. Vancouver, as the west coast hipster capital of Canada, had a love affair with food trucks. Strolling through downtown, you could find people lining up for everything from gourmet Japanese hot dogs to overpriced lemonade to vegetarian BBQ.

But no one seemed interested in Jumpin' Jigglies.

Then I saw why.

The truck's exterior featured a wraparound mural dedicated to creepy crawlies: ants, grasshoppers, cockroaches, spiders. If it had more than four legs and could be swatted with a newspaper, it was featured in the artwork.

My throat closed in protest. "Do they serve …?"

"Insects," Lienna finished, scrunching her nose up.

The menu on the side of the truck boasted an eclectic offering of entomological entrees. There was a beetle burger, a cricket corn dog, and something called termite tahini that I tried not to imagine.

And there, inside the truck, looking as bored as a teenager at the opera, was Faustus Trivium. He was, if it was possible, skinnier than I remembered. Even his shoulder-length black hair, which clung to his strangely geometric face, seemed thinner.

Without looking up, Faustus greeted our footsteps with a dry recitation. "Welcome to Jumpin' Jigglies. What would you—"

His eyes landed on me and he froze.

"Hey, FT," I said cheerily. "How's the bug business treating you?"

Faustus's face morphed into an ugly, triangular sneer. "Kit Morris. I wondered if I'd ever see your face again. Have you come for seconds?"

"Oh, man, I don't even want firsts," I replied, eyeing the industrial, stainless steel refrigerator behind him.

Lienna stepped forward. "Mr. Trivium, we need to ask you some questions."

"And why would I answer your questions?"

"You don't have a choice."

He pointed at a small sign in the corner of the truck's window. "Says here I have the right to refuse service to anyone for *any* reason."

"Faustus, seriously," I said emphatically. "We are not—and I mean this in every way your insectile brain could possibly imagine—we are *not* here for the food."

Lienna nodded in curt agreement. "We're here for information."

"Information about what?"

Lienna reached into her satchel and pulled out the plastic bag containing the acorn artifact. "This."

Faustus squinted. "Where'd you get that?"

"It's evidence in an investigation."

"You stole it from the MPD?"

I shot Lienna a confused look, which she reciprocated.

"We *are* the MPD," I told him.

"You?" He gave a twitchy shake of his head. "You're a KCQ conman."

"Times have changed, FT." I pulled my badge from under my jacket and waved it at him, its chain jangling. "You went into rehabilitation and I got a job."

His sneer returned. "A job? I'll be free long before you will, Kit."

Lienna wiggled the evidence bag pointedly. "This artifact, Mr. Trivium. Where did you get it?"

"I bought it. Why does it matter?"

"Who did you buy it from?"

"A man."

"The Ghost?" I asked sharply.

Faustus stared at me, his dark eyes narrowed to slits—then he snatched a cast iron frying pan from the grill and hurled it at us. We sprang out of the way and it landed in the middle of the road.

The food truck's door banged, and its buggy chef bolted down the sidewalk.

"Son of a bitch," I muttered and took off after him, Lienna right behind me. Faustus veered left up a wide staircase that led into a brick courtyard surrounded by a bunch of small businesses. How was this scrawny bastard so fast? Did a diet of ladybugs and caterpillars turn you into Usain Bolt? Maybe I should've ordered a cricket corn dog.

"Stay with him," Lienna called from behind me. "I'll try to cut him off. And no magic!"

Way to take the fun out of a classic cops-and-robbers foot chase, Agent Shen.

Faustus scurried between two buildings that might have been a real estate office and a pizza parlor. Or maybe a law office and a Japanese fusion restaurant. They were kind of a blur as I blew past them at full speed.

Another staircase took us up one more level. I charged up the stairs three at a time, then lunged at the top, grabbing for Faustus's ankle. I missed by an inch.

Shoving back onto my feet, I sprinted after him into a concrete corridor between two buildings. Faustus barreled past rows of metal doors toward the street—and his escape.

Just when I thought I would lose him, Lienna, in all her ass-kicking glory, stepped out in front of the stringy-haired douche nozzle.

Faustus tried to shove past her, but she delivered a brutal hip check that would've made any NHL enforcer proud. Faustus careened over her like a rag doll on a string, bounced off the concrete wall with his feet higher than his head, and crumpled to the ground with a pathetic, "*Ungh!*"

God, if I weren't already crushing on her, that would have done the trick.

I jumped on the fallen creep, grabbed his shirt, and dragged him back into the corridor. Finding the closest doorway, deeply recessed in an alcove, I shoved him into it.

"Shouldn't we bring him in?" Lienna asked.

"Captain's orders, remember?" Bringing a suspect into the precinct would raise a whole bunch of questions we weren't supposed to answer. I cast her a quick wink and added in a whisper, "How about a little good cop, bad cop?"

As Faustus attempted to push past me, I grabbed him by the collar and forced him back down onto his skinny ass with as much action-hero gruffness as I could summon.

"Get your hands off me," he wheezed.

"Make me, you cowardly shit cricket." I kicked his ankle, my shoe connecting with something bulky hidden under his pant leg. "Oh wait, you can't. Those pesky rehabilitation restrictions, eh?"

The MPD wasn't naïve. They didn't toss convicted criminals into their rehabilitation programs and walk away. Goons like Faustus got the equivalent of a tracking anklet attached to their legs, except it wasn't for tracking. It was an abjuration spell that worked just like the MPD's handcuffs, suppressing the wearer's magic.

"I'll make this easy for you, Faustus," I growled. "I'm going to ask some very simple questions. If you don't answer them, my lovely colleague will remove your lungs and make balloon animals out of them."

Faustus looked more confused than scared, which was not the response I'd been going for. Maybe the balloon animal bit had undermined the threat. Lienna, on the other hand, looked more alarmed than I'd expected.

Oh, yeah. Balloon animals ... clowns. My bad.

"Look," Faustus said, trying and failing to project cool composure. "I don't know anything about ... *him*. I just bought an artifact, that's it."

"From the Ghost."

"No! From a different guy."

"Oh really. Then why'd you run away?"

"Because talking about the Ghost is dangerous."

I shoved him into the metal door. "Not answering my questions is dangerous too."

He smirked. "What are you going to do, Kit? Illusion me to death?"

"I've been informed that I'm not supposed to use my magic in public." I focused on his mind and reached behind my back with my free hand. "But I don't need it to make a sniveling larva-licker like you talk. This knife will work just fine."

I pulled my hand from behind my back with a dramatic flourish. My fingers were curled around insubstantial air, but according to Faustus's bug-riddled brain, I held an eight-inch bowie knife, not unlike the ones Mutton Chops had been tossing around at the carnival. Just bigger.

I was tempted to make a Crocodile Dundee joke, but the timing wasn't right.

"Kit …" Lienna muttered in a low tone, eyeing my empty hand as though she too could see my scary murder blade.

"Tell me what you know," I snarled, "or I'll start remodeling your creepy-ass smile, Joker style."

Faustus's stare was glued to the dagger, his face so white he could've passed for a poorly decorated snowman. When he didn't speak, I pressed the non-existent blade against his ribs. His entire body flinched. I had to concentrate to make the sharp pressure of the knife tip as realistic as possible.

"Wait, wait, wait!" he squealed. "What do you want to know?"

"Where did you get the artifact?"

"Like I said, from an artifact seller. *Not* the Ghost."

"And what does the artifact do?" I asked, poking him harder.

"Kit!" Lienna hissed.

"I don't know!" Faustus cried. "Nothing, probably. I bought it a few months ago. The seller said it could control fae, but I don't even know if it works. I never tried it."

My partner crossed her arms. "You're not supposed to be dealing in artifacts anymore. That's a violation of your parole."

"I—I know. That's why when that agent came around asking questions a couple of weeks ago, I turned it over to him."

"Agent? What agent?" I demanded.

"Agent Smith. He was a short man … bald … wearing glasses."

That could only be Shane Davila. Was he allowed to pose as an agent? And had he really gone all Hugo Weaving with that "Agent Smith" nonsense? That was the best he could come up with? Agent Henson, Agent Cantaloupe, Agent Rapscallion III. Be creative, Shane!

Refocusing, I glared at Faustus. "Did *Agent Smith* ask about the Ghost?"

"Yes, but I told him the same thing. I don't know anything about the Ghost."

I gave the halluci-knife a twist, and Faustus yelped. "Don't lie to me."

He squirmed, futilely trying to escape the pain. If any of this had been real, there'd be serious blood coming out of his side, but I didn't add that to the warp; I was too focused on creating the sensation.

"I think that's enough," Lienna said firmly.

She was really playing into this good cop/bad cop dynamic.

"Not yet," I barked aggressively. "Where did you meet the Ghost, Faustus?"

"I didn't! I've never had anything to do with him, but the seller claimed the artifact used to belong to him. That's it, I swear!"

"Who's this seller?"

"His name is Brad. I don't know his last name. He's a regular at the market."

"What market?"

Faustus panted with pain and fear. "You know … the flea market."

"*Flea* market? You're shitting me."

"Lots of mythics use the flea market to buy and sell artifacts." He swatted desperately at the blade, but he couldn't smack away the hallucination, so I kept it in place. "Brad never misses it. He'll be there."

"You better not be lying," I growled.

"I'm not! Brad is a seller. He'll have a booth. Th-the market is open every weekend, isn't it? Just go s-see him!"

The last bit came out in a quivering gasp, and I took a closer look at him. Snot glistened on his nose and tears swam in his eyes as he cringed away from the non-knife I was not actually sliding between his ribs. His chest heaved with panicked breaths.

I pulled the fake knife away from him, and he clamped a hand over his side, sagging against the wall. "What does Brad look like?"

"My height," Faustus said hoarsely. "Heavyset. In his forties, with a brush cut and thick eyebrows. His stall display is mostly jewelry. He keeps the artifacts under the table."

I grunted. "And where is his stall at the market?"

"The layout is always different. You'll have to look for him."

Fixing a cold stare on him, I ran a finger across the knife's bloody edge, which to Lienna must have looked like the stupidest game of charades she'd ever seen.

To Faustus, however, it was effectively menacing. He recoiled, clutching his side more tightly, too panicked to realize he wasn't bleeding. "That's all I know, Kit, I swear. That's it."

As I debated whether he was being truthful, Lienna's hand landed on my shoulder. She pulled me backward.

"Thank you, Mr. Trivium," she said as I rose to my feet beside her. "You've been very helpful."

"As if I had a choice," he muttered, half whimpering, half vicious.

Smirking, I raised my knife in salutation—and let the warp fade.

His eyes widened in realization, and he jerked his hands away from his side, gawking down at his unblemished jacket.

"Get back to work, slacker," I told him mockingly. "There's probably a whole flock of pigeons waiting in line for some housefly hummus."

With that, I strode away. Lienna hurried after me, and as we headed for the street, Faustus yelled shrilly, "Kit, you bastard! You'll pay for that!"

I snorted as Lienna and I rounded the corner and joined a sparse stream of pedestrians. We only got a dozen steps before she took my elbow and pulled me into the empty doorway of a clothing store. I turned to face her, expecting her to launch into an analysis of Faustus's information.

"What the hell were you doing?" she snapped.

Rocking back on my heels at her tone, I said warily, "Good cop, bad cop? You play a surprisingly convincing softy."

"More like good cop, raging psychopath!"

I angled my head, reassessing her expression. "Why are you so angry?"

"You crossed a line. The MPD has methods for interrogating informants. You learned them. Proper ways. *Ethical* ways."

"We both know that cutesy interview crap wouldn't have worked on him."

"We *don't* know that."

"Well, I do," I huffed. "So what if I scared him? That asshole tried to kill me. *Twice.* I could've stuck a real knife in him and it would've been less than he deserved. Besides, you can't argue with the results."

"Just the means."

I threw up my hands. "What does it matter, Lienna? This case is off the books. We don't have to report our methods."

She stepped back, her eyes wide. Her expression abruptly hardened. "Don't cross that line again, Kit."

I grimaced. "Fine. No more pretend knives."

"No more pretend torture," she added. "Pain is pain, whether you inflict it with a knife or with your mind. It felt the same to him."

My grimace deepened as discomfort twisted my gut, but I shrugged it off, remembering the gleeful way Faustus had ordered my death at his restaurant. I wouldn't feel guilty for giving him a dose of harmless payback, and that aside, we'd needed his information.

"Which way to the car?" I asked.

"This way."

I followed her down the sidewalk. She took a right at the intersection and suddenly, we were on the same block where we'd parked. So *that* was how she'd gotten ahead of us. Faustus and I had taken the most roundabout route possible.

She stopped beside the smart car and pulled out her phone. She tapped on the screen for a moment, then announced, "Three hours."

"Huh?"

"The flea market closes in three hours. That's how long we have to find this 'Brad' person."

And if we didn't, we'd lose our only lead. We'd be back at square one, with no chance of finding the unknown teen before he vanished forever like all the Ghost's other victims.

6

THE GOOD NEWS: it was Saturday, meaning the flea market was open.

The bad news: it was Saturday, meaning the flea market was a madhouse.

Lienna and I wove through the meandering crowd, the din of voices and footsteps pressing in from all sides. Unpleasant mustiness clogged my nose, but at least it wasn't "deep-fried gym socks at a traveling carnival" unpleasant.

My partner surveyed the claustrophobic jungle of booths and grungy peddlers. "How are we going to find Brad?"

"How are we going to find *any* mythics?" I peered around a woman in a leather vest with dreadlocks down to her waist. "We can't just ask, can we?"

Lienna frowned. "Maybe we should've brought Faustus with us."

"Hard pass on that idea. I'll try asking."

I cautiously approached the closest vendor: a hunched-over dude in a toque, hawking a medley of chains and car parts. His merchandise was piled haphazardly on a rickety wooden table that he watched over with a lazy eye, a flask gripped tightly in his hands.

"Excuse me," I began with a friendly smile. "I'm looking for a jewelry seller called Brad. He's a regular around here."

The man glowered silently.

"So, any idea where I can find Brad?"

More mute glaring.

I backed away like a lost hiker retreating from a hungry grizzly bear and rejoined Lienna.

"We can scrap the 'asking for directions' idea too," I muttered.

"Maybe we can find Brad ourselves. This place isn't *that* big."

Not that big compared to what? The Forbidden City?

The tightly packed booths stretched almost to the ceiling, making it impossible to get a clear idea of the layout. We wandered from aisle to aisle, dodging milling shoppers, none of whom actually seemed to be buying anything. Not that I could blame them when half the booths were selling the decades-old contents of their relatives' attics. The rest were selling bizarrely specific and alarmingly strange paraphernalia.

I unintentionally slowed to stare at a booth packed with hand-carved bottle openers in the shape of various genitalia, then hastened to catch up to Lienna. We pressed farther into the labyrinth, scanning for a middle-aged mythic selling jewelry.

"Is there an end to this place?" I muttered. "Or is it like a modern-day Swamp of Sadness, and we'll be trapped forever in a boundless pit of overpriced junk unless we can summon enough hope to—"

Lienna pressed her fingertips to her temples. "Kit, focus."

"Okay, okay. I'll try asking for directions again."

I approached a pot-bellied vendor with a gnarly mustache, who readily answered my query—but he spoke like he had a mouthful of thumbtacks and I couldn't make out a single word.

"We're getting nowhere," Lienna said as I returned from the mumbler's table.

"Yeah." I scanned the crowd for someone more articulate, but instead, I spotted a familiar figure weaving through the masses. "Maybe we need a friend to show us around."

"A friend? I don't think—"

"Come on!" I took off at a quick jog, my gaze locked on a tall blond woman with a pompadour haircut. She adeptly navigated between the shoulder-to-shoulder patrons, her poofy hair moving deeper into the crowd.

Before I could lose her, I targeted her mind and warped a giant red STOP sign a foot in front of her face. She came to a screeching halt, momentarily taken aback by the materializing octagon, then spun around and squinted through the bustling throng.

Our eyes met and I gave her a friendly wave.

The tall blond marched back toward me with a dirty glare plastered on her mug. I couldn't tell if she was annoyed, genuinely pissed off, or if that was her standard face, which usually fell somewhere on the anger spectrum.

As she got closer, I grinned. "Hey, Vera. How's it—"

She grabbed my arm and yanked me around the corner, dragging me into one of the few semi-quiet spots, nestled in a dead space between two booths. Lienna chased after us.

"What the hell are you two doing here?" Vera growled.

I shook off her grip. "I'm surprised you didn't see us coming."

"I only get visions of imminent danger, not imminent annoyance." Her gaze snapped to Lienna, and she added in a more neutral tone, "Agent Shen."

"Hello, Vera," Lienna replied politely. "Shopping?"

"Some assholes dropped my RPG launcher and grappling gun into the ocean, so I'm looking for replacements."

I peered around at the array of junk for sale. "Who in here sells *that*?"

"I doubt any of these booths are licensed for weapons," Lienna added.

Vera narrowed her eyes. "I guess I'm wasting my time, then."

Painfully awkward silence fell. Lienna and Vera had worked together to save my life a couple of months ago, but they hadn't bonded over my non-death. Being on opposite sides of the law remained a sore spot for them.

Vera tossed a furtive look over her shoulder. "If you two are gonna make a scene, I'm gonna peace out."

"Why would we make a scene?" I asked.

"It's what you do. You wouldn't be here unless you were planning to bust someone."

"We can't bust any mythics if we can't find them," Lienna complained, half under her breath. "How do you tell mythic and human sellers apart?"

"You don't know?" Vera snickered. "Came prepared, I see."

My eyebrows rose. "But you do know, I'm assuming. Care to share your wisdom?"

"For a price."

Lienna took half a step forward. "The MPD doesn't—"

"What price?" I interrupted.

"I just told you what I'm in the market for."

A rocket launcher/grappling hook fun-pack? As much as I loved the thought of Smart Car III's trunk being packed with firepower, the MPD didn't even give field agents real guns.

"How about a beer?" I offered.

She gauged me for a long moment, then gestured for us to follow her. "Come with me."

Marching out of the gap between booths, she wound between shoppers for two dozen paces, then veered toward a stall run by a grizzled old woman with a glass eye. She wore a long black robe and reminded me of a witch. Not the real type of witch but the Hans Christian Anderson, push-children-into-an-oven, "double, double toil and trouble" type of witch.

While the witchy lady showed off a collection of creepy ceramic figurines to a mildly horrified mom and daughter, Vera nodded to the top corner of the booth where a square of fabric the size of a sticky note had been pinned. Stitched onto it was a black spade.

"Mythic booths always have a spade on display somewhere," Vera informed us. "You have to tell the seller what kind of magic you're looking for. Ask for a king of spades if you want Elementaria. Queen of spades is Spiritalis. And ace of spades is Arcana. Jack of spades means anything magical."

Ah, the good ol' SPADE acronym. Easiest way to remember the five magical classes. "What about Psychica and Demonica?"

"No one's hocking demon shit at a flea market. As for Psychica"—she shrugged—"I don't know. Psychica artifacts aren't really a thing."

Tell that to the psychic-magic-amplifying wand I'd accidentally destroyed by turning it into a snake. Then again, that'd been made with sorcery, so it was technically Arcana.

The mom-daughter duo retreated, and the witchy old lady turned toward us. "Looking for anything in particular, dearies?"

Vera jabbed her elbow into my kidney.

"Uh," I stammered breathlessly, my side throbbing, "do you have an ace of spades?"

She smiled, showing three missing teeth. "Sure do, handsome."

Reaching under her table, she pulled out a metal case and flipped the top open, revealing an assortment of rune-engraved artifacts ranging from coin-sized talismans to shiny daggers.

I leaned toward Vera and whispered, "Is this what you come here to shop for?"

She answered with a stony glower that warned me to shut my big mouth.

Lienna looked over the case with a frown, then pointed at a leather choker. "Is that what I think it is?"

"I don't know what you think it is," the woman croaked. "But with the right incantation, it'll turn your boyfriend's brain into putty."

My eyes bulged.

Lienna's frown deepened. "This artifact breaks, like, eight laws."

The old woman snorted. "Who the hell do you think you are? The MPD?"

I guided Lienna away from that petrifying box of Arcana toys. "I don't think this is what we're looking for. Let's keep moving, shall we?"

The woman leered at me as we retreated quicker than her last customers had.

Vera dusted her hands together. "You're all set. I'm out of here."

"Wait!" I caught her elbow. "We're looking for a specific seller. Or, actually, we're looking for a rogue who might be dealing with a specific seller."

"What sort of rogue?"

I took out my phone and pulled up the picture I'd snapped of the Ghost's photo. "Do you recognize this guy?"

Vera pursed her lips in appreciation. "Hell, no. I'd remember a jawline like that."

"He's hot, right?"

"I'd put that photo up as a poster above my bed."

Lienna rolled her eyes at us. "We need to track him down. He's a serial kidnapper."

Vera smirked. "If you need bait, I'd be willing to—"

"You're not his type," I cut in. "You're too old."

Her nose scrunched up. "Ew."

"Yeah. Most people know him as the Ghost. Have you—"

She slapped her hand over my mouth. "Did you say *the Ghost*?" she whispered with a frantic look around. "Christ, do you lunatics realize who you're talking about?"

I pushed her hand off my face. "More or less. Scary, slippery, ghostly."

"People who talk about him too much disappear. You don't wanna mess with this dude."

"I *do* want to mess with him," I countered firmly. "He abducted a kid yesterday. I'm going to take him down."

She shook her head. "I don't know anything about him. In fact, I actively avoid knowing anything about him."

"How about a jewelry vendor named Brad?"

"Brad?" Her discomfort morphed into a ferocious grin. "You're here for that shitbag? Now *him* I'd be happy to help you bust. Come on."

She zoomed off again, and Lienna and I rushed after her. Now that I knew what to look for, I spotted small black spades on more booths, all pinned, taped, painted, or stitched in plain view but otherwise inconspicuous.

Vera guided us through the maze, taking turn after turn until I doubted she knew where she was going. Finally, she halted in front of a booth filled with jewelry, clothing, and other assorted knickknacks. A middle-aged dude with a thick neck and a brush cut stood protectively over his wares, his jaw dotted with stubble and thick eyebrows nearly covering his gaze.

Vera bared her teeth at him. "How's business, pal?"

The vendor appeared equally displeased. "Vera …"

She reached across his table, grabbed the front of his shirt, and yanked his face close to hers. "No names, dumbass."

He jerked back with a scowl. "Don't get your panties in a twist. And for the last time, I'm not refunding anything. That was a fair sale. I can't guarantee magic I didn't make."

"It wasn't even magic! It was a goddamn rock!"

I shouldered in front of Vera before she could beat Brad's ass. "What've you got for sale today?"

He squinted suspiciously at me.

"Jack of spades," I added.

Grunting, he pulled a wooden box out, set it on the table, and opened it to reveal six small drawers that swiveled out into a wide display of jewelry. "All artifacts. Or did you want to see potions?"

"Potions," Lienna said quickly.

Her request made sense, seeing as our di-mythic phantom was an alchemist as well as a druid. However, I wasn't paying much attention as Brad heaved a second case onto the table—I was too busy peering at one of the necklaces in his jewelry collection.

Attached to a shiny black chain was a transparent gem shaped like a teardrop, with a frozen flame encased inside it. A piece of gold wire spiraled around the jewel, three tiny cobalt marbles hanging from the bottom.

It seemed so familiar. I must have seen it before, but where?

I took my phone out of my pocket and pulled up my photos of Shane's victim profiles.

Mercury Tibayan. The Elementaria prodigy from the IAE was a bright-eyed twenty-year-old with shaggy hair hanging off her forehead. In her photo, she wore a white tank under a baggy plaid shirt—and around her neck was the teardrop pendant.

7

"WHAT'S THAT?" I asked, accidentally speaking right over
Lienna as she fished for information about Brad's alchemy
sources.

"Huh? Which one?"

I pointed at the teardrop necklace.

He flipped the pendant over and checked the sticker on its
reverse side. Pulling open the black curtain that served as the
booth's backdrop, he dug around for a second, then returned
with a battered notebook and opened it to a long list of
numbers and descriptions.

"Protection spell," he revealed. "Defensive Arcana. Shields
against most minor elemental attacks. Asking two grand. Good
price for something like this."

I tried not to gawk. "You're selling it for two-thousand
dollars?"

"That's what I said." He glanced at Vera, who was glowering at him with her arms crossed, then back at me. "You buying or not?"

Flashing him an impish smile, I slipped my arm around Lienna's shoulders. "That depends on my girlfriend. What do you think, sweetie? Do you like it?"

Lienna huffed. "We're not playing this game again, Kit."

"I *really* think you should look at it. It's just like the one Mercury had."

"Who?"

Brad and Lienna were both giving me the same partly annoyed, partly confused look. I widened my grin and gave my partner a small squeeze. "Oh, you remember Mercury! *Shane* told us about her yesterday."

"Oh?"

She was starting to catch my drift, but she'd hardly looked at the victim profiles. Time to refresh her memory. I threw up a quick warp in front of her: my best imitation of Mercury's photo with the words "GHOST VICTIM" emblazoned above it. Lienna nodded, so I zoomed the warp in on the pendant and changed the caption to "IDENTICAL."

"Right, I remember now," she said hastily. "It's so pretty. Where did you get it?"

"My sources are reputable," Brad replied. "You might've seen the design before, but it holds a one-of-a-kind spell."

Lienna's mouth tensed. We both knew his source was the Ghost. The kidnapping scumbag was hocking his victims' possessions.

Slipping away from my arm, she pulled out her MPD badge and flashed it. "We have some questions for you, Brad."

His eyes bulged, then fury contorted his face. He raised his hand and fire ignited over his fingers. "Keep walking, MagiPol."

Great, an angry pyromage surrounded by a crowd of humans and a garbage dump's worth of highly flammable crap.

"We can't do that, bud," I said calmly. "We don't care about you, your booth, or whatever you're selling. We just need to know who—"

The flames whooshed higher and he swung his arm back like he was winding up for a discus throw.

Before he could barbeque my face, Lienna whipped a stun marble at him. It hit him square in the chest and he dropped in a heap—but his collapse didn't go unnoticed. Several curious shoppers stopped to stare. Lienna hurriedly scooted around his table and dragged his limp form into the back of his booth.

I smiled reassuringly at the rubberneckers. "Someone hit the sauce a bit too early today. He just needs to sleep it off."

With a mixture of expressions ranging from sympathy to judgmental derision, they all quietly shuffled off in search of whatever niche rubbish they were interested in.

"Man the booth," I told Vera as I hurried to help Lienna. The two of us hauled him behind the black curtain. The dark nook was only about three feet wide, hemmed in by neighboring booths and a concrete wall.

I pushed the pyromage up against the wall, and Lienna pulled his arms around the sturdy pole holding up the back of the booth and cuffed his wrists. The abjuration spell in the handcuffs would ensure he didn't start any more fires.

With Brad secured, Lienna produced a small capsule from her bag. Holding it under his nose, she crushed the capsule between her fingers and the faintest wisps of purple gas lifted into his nostrils. His eyelids fluttered, then snapped open.

"What ... what the hell did you do to me?" he demanded hoarsely, jerking his arms against the pole. The handcuffs rattled.

"Nothing permanent," I answered. "As long as you tell us what we want to know."

He glared up at me. "You two think you're tough, huh? I'm not scared of you."

"Are you scared of the Ghost?"

Brad paled, answering my question. "He scares everyone."

I straightened my shoulders. "Not me."

"He should. No one crosses him. You never see him coming, and even if you did, you couldn't stop him."

"Sounds like fun," I lied through my toughest Robert De Niro-esque grin. If the Ghost's rap sheet weren't intimidating enough, the way he terrified every mythic we talked to was downright alarming. "Why don't you tell us where to find him so we can play?"

"You're not gettin' shit from me."

I maintained my grin. "You say that now, but I can be quite persuasive."

Lienna grabbed the back of my jacket and tugged. I looked over my shoulder at her.

"No knives," she mouthed silently.

"No knives," I promised as I turned back to the cuffed pyromage. Pretending to pull something small out of my pocket, I held it up. "Do you know what this is?"

Brad scowled at the brown seed the size of an almond. Including Lienna in the warp so she'd know I wasn't brandishing any weapons, I dropped the fake seed on the floor and ground it under the heel of my shoe.

"It's something I picked up from an old friend," I continued, "who dabbles in botanical Arcana."

"That's not a thing," Lienna muttered just loud enough for me to hear.

"Do you like plants, Brad?" I asked.

He shifted his weight uncomfortably. "What?"

I lifted my foot, and the seed sprouted a little green stem. Then another. And another. A whole tangle of vines burst outward like one of those National Geographic time-lapse videos. The searching tendrils crawled across the floor—directly toward Brad.

"It's looking to feed," I told him. "It's carnivorous, like the Venus Fly Trap, except it prefers larger prey."

I paused, partly for dramatic effect and partly to concentrate on the warp. The plant swelled in size and rushed toward Brad's feet. He tried to scramble away but couldn't get far.

"Plants don't eat people," he growled, pressing into the pole.

"No?"

One of the acid-yellow flowers that had bloomed at the end of a vine rose up like a snake about to strike. Then it pounced and latched onto his leg. Brad squirmed and kicked, but the flower stayed plastered to him as more vines slithered around his feet and over his ankles. I made sure he could feel the pressure of their tight—but not painful—constriction.

"What ... what ..." Brad gasped in horror. He thrashed around, trying to escape the herbaceous entanglement. "What's it doing?"

"I call it *vegetis metamorphosis*," I answered in extremely fake Latin.

"Also not a real thing," my partner chimed in, too quiet for Brad to catch.

I let the warp grow further, winding its weedy vines up his knees and onto his thighs.

"*Vegetis metamorphosis*," I repeated, "is the process of human to plant transformation. Within a couple minutes, you'll become Treebeard the Ent, although you won't be able to walk or talk because my flowered friend here will have consumed your flesh and bones. All that will be left is your mind."

Brad wrenched on the pole he was cuffed to. "Get it off me!"

"Kit," Lienna murmured in warning.

I made the vine crawl up his chest. "In a few hours, I'll plant you in my backyard and watch you grow into a majestic, albeit ugly, tree—a new species which I will name the Giant Bradwood. Your consciousness will live there, entombed in bark and leaves, until I chop you down for lumber. And even then, fragments of your tortured soul may endure, raging silently in immortal agony, while I—"

"Make it stop!" he gasped as the vines curled up his neck and poked at his mouth. He strained away from them, the tendons in his neck stretched taut.

Lienna grabbed the back of my jacket again. "Kit, stop!"

"Only if you tell us what you know about the Ghost," I told Brad.

He twisted wildly to keep the vines away from his mouth. "He comes through a couple of times a month. Usually selling, but sometimes looking for specific stuff to buy for his clients."

"When did you last see him?"

"I—I don't know. M-months ago. He doesn't—"

"That's a lie, Brad." Which I knew, because he had Mercury's necklace, and she'd vanished three weeks ago.

The curtain behind me rustled and Vera stuck her head in. "You're making too much noise," she hissed. "Someone called security. They'll be here any minute."

"Can you keep watch for—"

"I'm getting the hell out of here. Last thing I need is a dead Brad on my résumé. Adios, mofos."

"Dead?" the pyromage croaked as Vera ducked back through the curtain and, presumably, as far away from the booth as she could get in the next ninety seconds.

I swung back toward Brad. "If you take much longer, I won't be able to save you from your floral fate. When did you last see the Ghost?"

His eyes bulged as the vines tickled his ears. "Today! He was here today! Picking up an artifact I sourced for him."

"What artifact?"

"A scepter.

"You mean like a big rod that a king carries?"

He nodded fervently. "Four feet tall. Heavy. Arcana artifact. I never found out exactly what it does."

"Where did he go after picking up the scepter?" Lienna asked.

Brad panted, his head bobbing side to side to evade my warp. "If I tell you, will you get this off me?"

"You bet, Brad," I said cheerfully.

Beyond the curtain, a loud, authoritative voice ordered people to stand aside. Our time was up.

"The Red Lily. Saw the invite when he paid me. It's for tonight. He's probably taking the scepter to a client there."

"The Red Lily?" Lienna repeated.

"*Yes!* Now get this off me!"

"A promise is a promise." I snapped my fingers and the warp vanished. As Brad gaped in shock, I turned to Lienna. "Time for us to vanish too."

She uncuffed Brad from the pole and touched her cat's eye necklace. "*Ori menti defendo.*"

I invisified us as the last word left her mouth, and a moment later, a uniformed security guard flung the curtain open.

Leaving Brad where he was, I pulled Lienna past the guard, then we sped away from the crowd that had gathered around Brad's booth like a flock of squawking magpies.

8

"WHAT DO YOU KNOW about the Red Lily?"

The question floated out of the bathroom just off Lienna's living room, the door open wide enough to allow her voice to escape but not enough for me to see inside. Something clattered against the counter.

I was reclined on her sofa, still stunned at my luck. Considering the firm boundaries Lienna had established between our work and personal lives, I'd resigned myself to the fact that I would never score an invite, no matter how innocent, to her home.

Her single-bedroom abode felt bigger than it was thanks to the open-floor design and a neat lineup of houseplants adorning the windowsill, beyond which was a view of the busy street below. The bookshelf beside the TV was stuffed full of Arcana textbooks and a single Shen family photo.

"Kit?" she prompted. "The Red Lily?"

I grabbed a sleek black remote and turned the TV's volume down a few notches. *Casino Royale* was playing, and Bond, James Bond, was currently at the poker table, ordering his famous martini. What better way to get in the mood for our next operation while I waited for Lienna?

"Not much," I called back. "It came up a few times in my old guild. Rigel, my GM, moved in those circles."

"What sort of circles?"

"Rich, morally bankrupt circles." I tapped the remote on my knee as I watched Le Chiffre reveal his hand: a full house. "The Red Lily is a hoity-toity casino with a few mythic-exclusive levels. *Really* exclusive. From what I heard Rigel say, it's geared for pleasure, but a lot of business happens there too."

Something in the bathroom made a spritzing sound. "It's not farfetched that the Ghost would deliver the scepter to his client there."

"Nope. And if Brad was right that the Ghost has an invite to something special happening tonight, he'll probably hang around long enough for us to catch him."

"The only problem is that *we* don't have invites."

I flashed a grin toward the bathroom even though she couldn't see it. "Which is exactly why we're dressing up."

My makeover was already complete. We'd stopped at my place and I'd pulled a garment bag from the back of my dinky closet. In it was a simple black suit way outside my usual clothing budget and custom-tailored to fit me. Rigel had paid for it a few months into my internship so I could blend in at events while subtly manipulating his targets. It was also one of the few outfits I'd stuffed into my carry-on when attempting to flee the continent.

I straightened my cobalt-blue tie—a color that complemented my eyes, or so I'd been told—then checked the time on my phone. Lienna had been getting ready for an hour now.

"I can make us invisible," I added as Bond confided in Vesper about his poker-winning strategy on the screen, "but not indefinitely. And casinos are always full of cameras. Lots and lots of cameras. That's a problem for me."

"Sounds like you're speaking from experience."

"I've never tried my hand at Danny Ocean-ing a casino, if that's what you're implying." I smirked. "But I have done a lot of cheating."

A moment of quiet from the bathroom. "Cheating?"

"That's how Rigel found me." My eyelids hooded as I thought back. "A foster kid with a juvie record, no high school diploma, and no job experience doesn't have many opportunities for gainful employment. And living on minimum wage is impossible in Vancouver."

At least, living in better conditions than "utter squalor" was impossible.

"I needed money to survive, and since casinos are so good at cheating people out of their cash, I got good at cheating them. It wasn't hard to fool the dealers, but the cameras were a problem."

"You don't have a high school diploma?"

No longer muffled by the bathroom door, Lienna's soft voice was clear and close. I opened my eyes—and my jaw dropped.

Agent Shen had transformed. A tight red dress hugged her curves, the shiny blood-red fabric glittering wherever the light touched it. Thin straps left her shoulders nearly bare, and the hem stopped a few inches above her knees, showing off her slim, firm legs. The scoop neckline revealed far more of her skin than I'd ever seen before.

She'd twisted her long hair up into an elegant coil and replaced most of her usual collection of eclectic jewelry with a pair of simple diamond earrings, leaving only her cat's eye necklace resting just below her collarbones. Aside from her hair, she must've dedicated most of her prep time to her makeup. It was more than just the smoky eyeshadow and red lips that perfectly matched her dress; her face appeared more angular and mysterious somehow.

I couldn't have warped a more beautiful vision.

Only when she cocked a hip and folded her arms in a sassy way did I snap out of my daze. Leaping to my feet, I tugged my jacket straight and cleared my throat.

"You look amazing."

Amazing? That was the best I could do? My vocabulary could put Vizzini to shame, but at the moment, I couldn't produce a single synonym for "dumbstruck idiot."

She peeked at me through eyelashes that hadn't been nearly that thick and sultry an hour ago. "You look pretty good yourself."

I grinned like a dumbstruck idiot.

Pressing her hands together, she seemed to give herself a shake. "Why don't you have a high school diploma?"

"Huh? Oh." I blinked, too dazzled to think straight. "Never took my final exams. I completed all the coursework up to twelfth grade, but I ran away when I was sixteen, so ..." I shrugged.

Her eyebrows arched, surprise silencing her for a moment. "Why did you run away? And from whom?"

"My foster parent passed away, and I didn't want to go into a group home. I didn't fit in with other people like that. Humans could tell I was different, even when I wasn't messing with their minds." I gave another quick shrug. "Anyway, are you ready?"

"Not quite." She hurried back into the bathroom, leaving the door open. Grabbing a bottle of hairspray, she thoroughly doused her head, eyes squeezed shut. "Did you say something about Rigel finding you at a casino?"

Dropping back onto the sofa, I chuckled. "Yeah. I ended up at a high-stakes poker table with him. He figured out I was swapping my chips and confronted me at the bar afterward. I expected him to pick a fight with me, but he asked what kind of magic I was using to cheat. I almost did a full-on spit take at him."

She disappeared into her bedroom, then returned carrying a pair of strappy black sandals with low heels, a shimmery black purse, and her satchel, which bulged with what I assumed was a change of clothes for after our casino mission.

Sitting on the sofa beside me, she pulled a sandal on. "How did Rigel figure out you were cheating? If he could guess, so could the casinos, right?"

"He guessed because he knew magic existed. I don't think the casinos ever figured out what I was doing, but they all eventually noticed I was winning too much. It didn't matter, though."

"Why not?"

"I always used a halluci-bomb to change my appearance. The only people who could possibly see I was cheating were the security guys watching the camera feeds. But if they ordered the six-foot-tall young guy with short brown hair to be tossed, no one could find him on the floor."

She blinked at me. "That's … ingenious, but also nefarious."

"One of my better brainwaves."

"Hm." She wiggled her foot into her second sandal. "If you were gambling to make ends meet before your KCQ internship, does that mean the MPD is your first legitimate job?"

I thought about it. "First since I delivered papers as a twelve-year-old."

She carefully placed her sandaled foot on the floor, staring down at it as though questioning everything she knew about shoes and/or feet. "Do you like it?"

"Like it?" My brow furrowed. "I don't think it's as simple as 'like' or 'dislike,' but I like working with you."

Still not looking at me, she let out a slow breath.

I ducked my head, trying to catch her eye. "What's wrong?"

"It's just …" She shook her head. "The Red Lily is connected to one of the most powerful mythic crime families in North America, so we have to be careful. No pretend knifings, no torture plants—"

"Torture plants? I didn't hurt Brad. You said I couldn't do the knife warp again, so I came up with the next best thing."

"How was slowly morphing a man into an immortal foxtail fern 'the next best thing'?"

"It was the first idea that popped into my mind."

"Why is breaking the law always your first idea?"

I faltered, unable to respond.

She pushed to her feet and stared down at me, beautiful and fierce. "You did it again, Kit. You crossed the line. That shit you pulled is illegal."

Illegal. That wasn't exactly a compelling word to use against me. As I'd just casually revealed, I'd spent many years wading through the fruitful pools of illegal.

But was she right? Had I gone too far?

"I got the job done," I retorted. "What else were we supposed to do? We couldn't take him to the precinct to interrogate, not with Blythe's orders. Was I supposed to hold him there indefinitely while he refused to answer our questions?"

"We could've come up with a different strategy."

"Like what?"

She bit her lip. "Just … something else. You can't torture people."

"I did not hurt him," I said, tersely emphasizing each word. "No pain. None. How is that torture?"

"It's psychological torture."

"It wasn't *real.*"

"But it could have been!" She shut her eyes as though she didn't want to look at me. "What if you had reality warped instead?"

That was it. It clicked. This wasn't about MagiPol policy. It wasn't even about Brad's mental health or the trouble we could get into.

It was about me.

"I wouldn't do that," I said quietly. "Even if I could do it on command, I wouldn't. Come on, Lienna. You know me better than that. You know I'm not capable of that."

"Do I?" she whispered.

Her question speared me in the gut. We'd been through hell together—we'd battled demons, escaped near-death situations, and done so much paperwork it could be classified as a human rights violation. She'd seen me at my lowest and my highest.

If she didn't know me after all that ...

I had no idea what to say. My mouth hung loose like a fish at the bottom of a boat that was still alive but had given up ever returning to the water. Pushing to my feet, I picked up the garment bag for my suit, which now contained my street clothes. "We should go. We have a Ghost to catch."

"Yeah," she agreed, not meeting my eyes as she passed me, her purse and satchel in her arms and her blood-red dress shimmering.

ON MY BUCKET LIST of agency things I wanted to do before my inevitable death in a Smart Car-related disaster was a whole sub-list of secret agent awesomeness. Using a shoe-phone to call for backup, saving a dignitary from an assassination attempt at a fancy opera, casually opening a hidden bookshelf door to reveal a secret room full of insane weapons, state of the art computers, and expensive whiskey.

And, of course, sneaking into a casino run by a terrifying cartel while on the hunt for a dastardly, untouchable outlaw.

The Red Lily took its name seriously as far as the décor was concerned. The carpet, walls, and much of the interior were swathed in shades of deep red. Slashes of gold added a sumptuous richness that treaded the gaudy line without crossing it. Lily-shaped patterns created a dizzying design on the floors and ceiling, where grand chandeliers hung.

The casino was owned and operated by the Miura family, which was an offshoot of the Yamada Syndicate, a mafia-like organization that pretended to be a legit international guild just well enough that the MPD didn't want to piss them off—or drive their whole operation underground. But their façade of respectability didn't make them any less dangerous, especially for unwelcome MagiPol agents snooping around one of their establishments.

With Lienna's hand tucked in the crook of my elbow, I paused to take in the familiar sights and sounds—the chatter of conversation, sporadic outbursts from the slot machines, and the gentle whoosh of money being sucked straight from the patrons' pockets.

Low-level adrenaline buzzed through me, and I pulled Lienna past the sleepwalking slots players and into the heartbeat of any casino: the poker tables. The players' attire ranged from formal wear—for those who, like Lienna and I, were imitating wealth—to sweat-stained tracksuits for guys who were probably swimming in capital.

"We should play a game," I said eagerly.

She huffed. "We have a job to do, remember?"

"And step one is reconnaissance. We need to figure out where the mythics mingle and how to get there."

"Which we can't do if we're stuck at a table—"

"But if we wander around too long, we'll have half the security team watching us." I tugged my arm away from her hand, grinning. "You find a table with a good view of the floor, and I'll get some chips."

"But Kit—"

Not waiting around to hear her protest, I zoomed off.

Less than ten minutes later, chips rattled cheerfully in my pocket and two martinis—shaken, not stirred—chilled my fingers. I scoured the poker tables, not seeing Lienna's shimmery red dress. Coming to a halt, I craned my neck—then spotted her.

Grumbling in disappointment, I strode out of the poker area and joined her where she stood beside a different table: blackjack.

"Why not poker?" I muttered, holding out one of the two drinks.

She frowned disapprovingly at the glass. "Because none of the poker tables had a good view of *that*."

She nodded toward the nearest corner, where a curtained-off section was labeled with a simple green sign that read, "Baccarat." I'd never dabbled in that confusing French card game, but based on my previous experience, only the richest of the rich dared to wade in Baccarat's waters.

Pulling out an empty chair at the blackjack table Lienna had chosen, I crooked my finger for her to join me. She reluctantly sank into the chair. I scooped some chips from my pocket and passed them to her.

Dropping a red chip onto the green surface, I leaned toward my partner and murmured, "You think the exclusive mythic fun happens back there? I remember Rigel mentioning an upper level."

"I'm not sure." She laid down a chip of her own. "But that's the only area with a dedicated security guard."

As the dealer started flicking cards down onto the table, I glanced at the Baccarat curtain. She was right. A man in a black suit stood in front of the curtain with his arms folded. If there was something more interesting than Baccarat behind that curtain, we'd have trouble finding out. I could invisi-warp me and Lienna to sneak past him, but there was a security camera pointed right at the doorway.

"Getting back there will be tricky," I told her quietly, adding a touch of psycho warping to ensure no one at the table overheard us. "We need to be sure."

She nodded.

"But first," I added, suavely sipping my martini, "it's your turn."

She looked down at the seven and five in front of her, then at the dealer's up card: an eight. A brief hesitation, then she tapped the table. The dealer hit her with another five, and she waved her hand to hold. A safe move.

My turn was next, and I had a pair of nines. I set another chip on the table.

"Split," I said, making the accompanying gesture.

The dealer split my two cards, turning one hand into two, then dealt a two onto my first nine. Lienna's eyebrows crept up as I added a third chip to the table, doubling down. The dealer obligingly dealt me one more card, and as an eight landed, I grinned.

For my second hand, the dealer hit me with a king, and I held there.

The other five players made their moves—two of them busting—then the dealer flipped his hidden card, revealing a jack. Soft groans whispered around the table as the dealer swept away the players' chips, then placed my three winning chips in front of me. I scooped them off the table.

"Kit." Lienna leaned close, her voice low and stern. "This isn't the time for cheating."

I didn't let my pleased smile falter as I started the next round with a single red chip. "It's just probability, Lienna. You don't need magic to win a bit of cash at Blackjack."

She straightened, and the way her eyes skimmed over me before focusing on the dealer made me wonder if she believed me. It wasn't a good feeling.

We were four rounds in—two wins, a push, and a bust for me, one win and three busts for Lienna—when a glamorous couple approached the Baccarat doorway. The guard asked them something, then he smiled and pulled the left side of the curtain open, holding it for them as they disappeared into the room beyond. That didn't seem right. Unless the guard had memorized the faces of everyone on the mythic invite list, getting through that doorway was way too easy.

I tapped the table for a hit, grimaced at my resulting sixteen—the dealer sitting pretty with an ace for his up card—and waved my hand to hold. As the dealer continued around the table, Lienna poked me in the thigh.

An elderly woman in a crisp white pantsuit had sauntered up to the Baccarat door. She exchanged a few words with the guard, just like the previous couple, then retrieved something about the size of a greeting card from her jacket pocket. The guard examined it, gave her a friendly nod, then pulled back the curtain and ushered her inside.

"He opened the other side," Lienna whispered.

"Huh?"

"He pulled the curtain away from the left side for the first couple. But now, he opened the right side."

My eyes widened. Could there be two doorways hidden behind one curtain? One that led to the Baccarat room, and one for mythic invitees?

"Time for us to get back there," I told her in an undertone. "But we'll need a distraction to get past that guard."

"What sort of distraction?" she asked warily.

With a quick smile, I pushed my chair back and scooped up my chips, leaving one as a tip for the dealer. Lienna followed suit.

"Come, darling," I said in a deep, sultry James-Bond-esque tone—minus the accent. I offered her my arm. "Let's try our luck at the poker tables."

She quirked an eyebrow as she slipped her fingers into the crook of my elbow. "What are you scheming now?"

"Nothing at all," I protested innocently, swirling my half-finished martini in its glass.

With chips rattling in my pocket, I meandered toward the most boisterous poker table in the room. The players were beefy men in their fifties who looked like dockworkers crossed with disillusioned gym teachers—big, loud, strong, full of bravado, and not nearly as good at Texas Hold'em as they thought they were.

Positioning myself behind the biggest, drunkest man, I targeted his mind and waited for him to lift his cards for a peek. His shoulders stiffened as he "saw" his hand. He gawked at the board, then at his cards, then back at the board. Coughing awkwardly, he suppressed his glee and casually bet every single chip he had.

I hung back, Lienna shifting her weight from foot to foot beside me. The other players considered their pal. Two folded, but another went all in too.

Bursting out with a cackling laugh, my victim threw his cards down triumphantly and crowed, "Royal flush!"

Silence followed his declaration. His friends stared at him in confusion.

The dealer cleared his throat. "Sir, that's not a royal flush."

"What?" the man blustered. "Are you blind? That's a perfect—"

I dropped the warp.

He blinked. Confusion twisted his thick features, his drunken brain processing the cards on the table and how they were suddenly completely different. One second passed. Two. Three.

The dealer coughed again. "The winner is the other gentlemen—"

"I had a royal flush!" my victim bellowed at the top of his lungs. "What kinda scam is this casino running? This is bullshit! You're a buncha thieves!"

With each accusation, his voice got louder, and when the dealer tried to slide the piles of chips toward the real winner, the enraged man tore it out of his hands and scooped the chips toward himself.

More shouts broke out as security guards sprinted toward the commotion. The well-dressed dude manning the Baccarat doorways didn't move, but his focus was fixed on the irate Hold'em hooligan.

I grabbed Lienna's hand and pulled her into motion. "Time for the cat's eye."

She whispered the incantation, and I dropped an invisi-bomb over the entire floor, erasing us from everyone's perception. The cameras wouldn't be fooled, but the security guards in the control room could only look one place at a time, and right now, they'd be looking at the screens displaying the enraged gambling monkey wrestling three other men while howling about robbery.

No one would be looking at the quiet Baccarat door, and no one would have any reason to check the footage later.

At least, that's what I was hoping for.

Lienna and I waltzed casually up to the curtain. I layered another warp on for the guard so he wouldn't notice the fabric move, then I guided my partner through the right side and into the mystery beyond.

The mystery, as it turned out, was just a small antechamber with a single elevator. I tapped the call button, and the doors slid silently open. We stepped inside, and the doors closed again. The elevator controls offered only one destination: a button marked with the silhouette of a lily.

Lienna and I studied the button, then glanced at each other, the air between us sizzling with bright anticipation and exhilarating danger.

"Are you ready to mingle with the richest and baddest mythics in the city?" I asked in a hushed voice.

She rolled her eyes. "You're enjoying this too much."

"Hell yeah, I am."

The stakes were high. And I had a feeling they would only get higher.

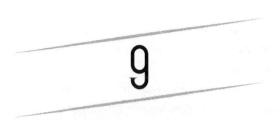

9

AS THE ELEVATOR DOORS slid open, I half expected a freaky *Eyes Wide Shut* style masquerade party or regal banquet with rare and pricey foods that are super gross but everyone pretends to love because they cost more than a yacht.

Instead, we were greeted by a ballroom-sized space with a red and gold carpet significantly more subdued than the one on the main level. Game tables dotted the periphery of the room, each lit by its own dramatic chandelier, and the most glamorous lounge I'd ever seen filled one wall, the marble bar top surrounded by leather seats.

The room's centerpiece was a massive sphere suspended from the ceiling with heavy-duty chains. Thick acrylic panels supported by a steel frame created a transparent ... tank? It seemed to be full of water, but from my vantage point, I could only make out flashes of movement. Was it a big-ass fancy aquarium?

Men in suits and women in slinky dresses with diamonds dripping from their fingers milled around, holding champagne glasses and chatting casually about their millions of dollars—or, more likely, discussing murder and drugs and whatever else mafiosos chat about. This was a Yamada Syndicate operation, after all; they and their associates were the opposite of squeaky-clean businessmen.

Besides, anyone who wasn't an outright criminal was criminally rich, so I didn't feel bad about painting them all with the same brush.

Lienna and I ventured away from the elevator, pretending we belonged. My expensive suit no longer seemed so fancy, and I debated using a warp to add a pound or two of diamonds to Lienna's outfit.

As we moved closer to the spherical aquarium, something inside shot toward the top—a petite, blue-skinned woman with long, bluish-white hair. As she twisted in the water, her crystalline eyes flashed past the mythic observers.

A fae?

No sooner had the realization hit me than her tankmate appeared: an unholy baby kraken with way too many writhing tentacles. And by "baby," I meant it was the size of a couple of dolphins.

The fae woman—a water nymph, I was pretty sure—flung her hands out, and streams of faintly glowing bubbles zoomed at the kraken creature, driving its tentacles away from her. She kicked higher, and the crown of her head broke the surface. She fired more bubbles at the octopus from hell.

A hushed murmur ran through the watching crowd, as though a pro golfer had just landed their ball in a sandpit. A sick, queasy feeling settled in my gut. This was the evening's entertainment for Vancouver's mythic elite.

Lienna tugged on my sleeve, and I wrenched my gaze to her. Her face was pale and lips thin.

"You see anyone with a scepter?" she whispered, nodding across the crowd.

Right. We couldn't get distracted.

"Let's do a loop," I suggested. "If he's not out here, he might be in a private room."

We commenced our circuit around the space, scanning the mingling mythics. I was seeing lots of nice suits and designer shoes, but no royalty impersonators.

"You'd think a guy with a four-foot scepter would be easier to spot," Lienna muttered as we neared the halfway point in our loop, her eyes averted from the aquarium battle.

"I think if your nickname is 'the Ghost,' being difficult to spot is your MO." I, too, was working hard to ignore the suspended tank as the spectators let out a collective gasp in response to a muffled splash.

We ambled among Blythe's wet dream of arrests waiting to happen, careful to keep our distance from anyone giving off an employee vibe. No swoony, villainous kidnappers or bejeweled scepters made an appearance.

Completing our circuit, we headed to the lounge. I leaned against the glossy counter, waiting for the bartender while I scrutinized the nearest game tables.

"Kit," Lienna hissed.

I turned and followed her gaze. My breath caught.

A pair of men had just stepped off the elevator—a slim Asian dude in a simple black tux that marked him as security and a tall guy in a long black coat with the hood pulled up. He'd clearly missed the dress code on his invitation.

And in his hand? A baseball-bat-sized scepter studded with jewels.

"Time to warp," I whispered, then split us, making our real selves invisible while the fake pair—looking damn sexy in their finery—headed away from the lounge and down a hallway, where I let the warp vanish.

Meanwhile, the real us walked casually toward the Ghost and his escort. They headed past the game tables and into a wide corridor lined on one side with private game rooms. The security dude led our target to a closed door twenty feet down the hall, while Lienna and I strolled along, a dozen paces behind, acting innocent in case any cameras were watching us.

At the door, the escort gave the hooded man a somber nod, then turned on his heel and zoomed back the way he'd come, almost colliding with my invisible shoulder.

The Ghost pushed the door open.

"This is our chance!" I hissed, rushing forward.

Lienna and I reached the door right as it closed behind him. I whipped up a fake door so we didn't tip off our criminally inclined specter on the other side, then grasped the door handle, turned it as quietly as possible, and pushed it open just wide enough for Lienna to squeeze through. I slid in after her and shut the door again.

A spacious sitting room with four elegant accent chairs circling a round coffee table greeted us. A chandelier cast soft light over the furniture, leaving the corners of the room in deep shadow. A matching door on the opposite wall provided a second exit to another part of the casino.

The Ghost stood a few steps inside the door, his hooded head turned toward the occupant of the room, an elderly man with a white beard. A slim briefcase, the kind that always held fat stacks of cash in movies, waited on the coffee table.

Our rogue target didn't approach. He didn't even offer a greeting, which would've been rude if the old man in the chair hadn't been dead. His sightless eyes stared at a spot on the ceiling, his head flopped back and limbs limp.

The Ghost surveyed the room, then spoke in a voice as flat and bland as a phone support tech on his sixth back-to-back night shift. "Show yourself."

I started, my wide eyes flashing to Lienna. She yanked her Rubik's Cube from her purse, but before she could use it, the room darkened strangely, the shadows thickening and swirling as though they had turned to black smoke.

The darkness shimmered, and I realized we weren't the only living people in this room.

A dark figure leaned against the wall beside the second door, arms folded. He should've been visible all along, but somehow, I hadn't seen him before this moment.

I looked from our suspect to the other man, then back again. And just to be sure, I performed another doubletake, not trusting my eyes.

"Uh …" I whispered to Lienna. "Are you seeing what I'm seeing?"

The confusion wrinkling her forehead confirmed I wasn't accidentally hallucinating myself.

In front of us was the Ghost, dressed in dark clothing with his hood pulled up and the telltale scepter in his hand.

And across from him was another man dressed all in black, the hood of his long leather coat shadowing his face. Black jeans, black gloves, and black boots that looked custom-made for crushing law-enforcement officers under their gritty black soles completed his ensemble.

What in the name of Ghostly doppelgangers was going on here?

"I wasn't expecting *you*," Scepter Ghost said. "Was it necessary to kill my client?"

"Was there any reason not to?"

Whoa. If our original suspect had the blandest, most forgettable voice in the history of criminal voices, then New Ghost was the exact opposite—and his deep, raspy tone was a way better fit for the chiseled, brooding hunk o' hotness from the Ghost's photo.

I peered into his hood. Though he was only twenty feet away, I couldn't make out even a hint of his face through the deep shadows. Was it just me, or should that over-the-top chandelier have illuminated his face with or without a hood?

Bland Voice pointed at the briefcase on the coffee table. "Is my payment in there?"

"It was."

A moment of displeased silence, then Bland Voice adjusted his grip on the scepter. "That money belongs to me."

"Finders, keepers."

I could hear the smirk in Sexy Voice's tone.

"But that's not why you're here," his doppelganger growled. "What do you want with me, Ghost?"

"Ghost," Sexy Voice repeated in a musing tone. "I thought that was you."

I was so confused.

Bland Voice scoffed. "Are you upset I've added to your reputation? Or are you shedding that alias now that you've been revealed as the Crystal Druid?"

So wait, the new guy was the real Ghost? But then who had we been tracking? Bland Voice had the scepter, which meant he'd sold his victims' belongings to Brad. Or did it? Did both Sexy Voice and Bland Voice sell to Brad, the vendor unaware that *two* scary hooded men were peddling ill-gotten wares?

My head spun with renewed confusion.

"I don't dictate what others call me," Bland Voice continued mockingly, "but if it bothers you, I hereby renounce any claim to the moniker. It's all yours."

Sexy Voice made a rough sound in the back of his throat. "I couldn't care less that you're hiding behind my reputation. I'm more interested in *what* you're hiding."

"The same as you. We're in the same business."

"Really? I don't recall licking Varvara's boots at any point."

Varvara? How did the dead Russian sorceress factor into this brain-boggling equation?

"She talked about you," Bland Voice said with a grating laugh. "Told me how much of a disappointment you were after all the tales she'd heard. How you *rescued* her apprentice, ruining a ten-year investment. That reputation is wasted on you."

"Yet I'm the one who killed her." Sexy Voice's gloved fingers curled into fists. "And now that you've confirmed you worked for her, I'll kill you as well."

Bland Voice snorted. "Are you really—"

"*Impello!*"

At the real Ghost's barked incantation, the other man flew backward and smashed into the wall. Lienna and I dove aside, barely avoiding a collision.

Fake Ghost lurched up as Real Ghost pulled his open jacket aside to reveal a combat belt around his hips, the dark leather lined with vials of potions. He plucked one off his belt, but before he could do anything with it, Lienna flung a stun marble. It missed him by two inches, clanged against the wall, and rolled under a chair.

Both Ghosts looked toward the sound of the marble. I leaped to my feet, unsure which of them I should take on as too many things happened at once.

The chandelier flickered as Fake Ghost swung his scepter at Real Ghost, the room's furniture and its dead occupant between the two men.

Amber light flared over Real Ghost's forearm as he activated a spell.

Lienna raised her Rubik's Cube as she started to call out an incantation.

"*Ori caecus!*" Fake Ghost snarled.

The scepter's bejeweled top flashed, the world went blinding white, and my eyeballs melted.

10

NOT LITERALLY.

My eyeballs didn't actually liquify and stream down my cheeks like molten lava, but it sure as shit felt like it as agonizingly bright light blinded me and I fell to my knees.

I pried my burning eyes open, an anime-worthy stream of tears rushing down my cheeks, and all I could see were light spots and blurry shapes. The blur closest to me groaned with Lienna's voice, and I fumbled for her shoulder.

Another few blinks brought my vision into better focus, but I had to blink again because a pair of black-jeans-clad legs stood alarmingly close, and that made no sense at all.

"Who are you two?"

Ah, Sexy-Voice Ghost. Except he didn't sound so "rumbly audiobook narrator" when I was sure his question translated to, "How mercilessly should I murder these snoopy strangers?"

One more blink brought the Real Ghost into full focus—standing over Lienna and me where we'd crumpled after the blinding attack. Scepter-brandishing Fake Ghost had disappeared. The dead man was still flopped over in his chair, though.

"MPD," I croaked, hoping he might hesitate to butcher agents. I pushed off my knees and into a crouch, wiping my suit jacket's sleeve across my face. "Don't do anything stupid."

As I spoke, Lienna whispered, "*Ori te formo cupolam.*"

Her cube's familiar watery barrier burst to life around us, forming a protective dome. The Ghost stepped back from the shield.

Lienna scrambled to her feet and tugged the hem of her dress down as she faced Vancouver's most wanted rogue. "Zakariya Andrii, we're placing you under arrest."

For a painfully long moment, he was silent—then he laughed. A thrill of fear ran down my spine.

The Ghost raised a gloved hand and pushed his hood back. As it fell onto his shoulders, shadows peeled away from his face. The bastard looked even better in person, dark stubble roughening his strong jaw, his short hair rumpled, and his green eyes iridescent with power—and cold amusement.

"All right," he rumbled. "You two puppies don't look like much, but I'll give you the benefit of the doubt."

Puppies? He couldn't be more than four or five years older than me.

He hooked a finger under his shirt collar, pulling out a tangle of leather ties holding brightly colored crystals, and I forgot to be insulted as alarm pinged through me.

His lips moved, and a red shimmer washed over him. Another incantation, another shimmer.

Holy shit. He was putting on his magical armor. The terrifying, undefeated, never-before-arrested Ghost was preparing to do battle with us.

"Uh," I stammered. "Hold up. My partner was being a little hasty when she said—"

He grasped a third crystal. "*Ori ne fiat.*"

Silver light burst over his fingers. He lifted his hand, the light morphing into a writhing orb, and hurled the magic into Lienna's shield at point-blank range.

The shield dissolved with a sizzling hiss.

Yellow radiance flashed over his hand as he swung his arm out. A glowing whip of amber light slammed into my chest, throwing me hard into the wall. Lienna slammed into it beside me.

As I staggered, lungs locked, I targeted his mind and threw a rudimentary Funhouse warp at it, shattering his perception of the room into a dozen distorted fragments.

He lurched back a step, surprise washing over his features. Lienna spun her cube.

"*Ori te formo cuspides,*" she gasped.

Inky missiles from Lienna's cube fired at him. Amber light bloomed over his arm, and a semi-transparent shield formed in front of him. Her attack blew large holes in the shield but failed to reach his body.

He couldn't see well enough to have known that attack was coming; he'd activated the shield on reflex.

His other hand darted to his belt of alchemy toys. Desperately, I distorted the Funhouse warp further, breaking the mirror-like shards of his perception into smaller and smaller pieces.

He tossed a vial at the floor. Grayish yellow smoke billowed out from the shattered glass, and I clamped my arm over my nose and mouth—but it was too late.

The bitter tang of the gas coated my tongue, and in an instant, dizzying nausea was boiling through my stomach as my world transformed into the worst Six Flags experience of all time. The floor dove under my feet like I was standing on an invisible rollercoaster, and beside me, Lienna dropped to her hands and knees.

A hand grabbed the front of my shirt and slammed me back into the wall. Along with bruising pain, I felt a seam rip open along my back. I gasped, struggling to focus on the Ghost's face as my vision wavered.

"Decent attempt," he said with dry sarcasm. "Maybe with a few years' practice, you'll stand a chance."

His hand opened and I slid down the wall, landing on my ass. A couple of buttons from my shirt fell into my lap. That bastard had ruined my only good shirt. Through the debilitating dizziness, I saw him turning. He was walking away.

Wasn't he going to kill us?

Using a chair to shove up onto her knees, Lienna slurred an incantation and hurled a stun marble. It flew wide and clattered into the corner. I couldn't blame her for missing that throw.

Circling the furniture and the old man he'd murdered, the Ghost strode toward the exit at the far end of the room. He was escaping.

Jaw clenching, I pulled my concentration together and directed a warp at the door. As he reached for the handle, the entire door disappeared, replaced by unbroken gold wallpaper.

He stilled, then his head turned. Green eyes met mine.

"Oh sorry," I said breathlessly, trying not to retch and vowing to never look at a rollercoaster again. "Did you want to leave? Here, have a door."

It reappeared in front of him.

"How about another one? The more, the merrier."

A second door popped up beside the first. Then a third. Then a fourth, fifth, and sixth, until the entire wall was filled with identical doors.

The Ghost stepped back, looking across the newly doored-up wall, then grabbed the handle of the original door and wrenched it open—revealing gold wallpaper.

Knowing what he'd try next, I pressed a hand into the wall behind me, concentrating on the feeling.

The Ghost touched the wall warp, and I projected the feel of solid wood into his mind. Though I could see his hand hovering in front of the hallway beyond the open door, he could *feel* that wall.

Dropping his hand, he swung the door closed, and I hastily suppressed the sound of it slamming shut, further confusing his sense of what was real and what wasn't.

He gave the door one more look, then turned around, his eerily vibrant glare locking on me.

Ah. Shit.

"Cute trick," he growled, striding back around the furniture obstacles. "But stupid."

I focused on the head-spinning, stomach-twisting sensation his potion had inflicted on me and psychically flung it at him. The feel of the floor dropping away hit him, and he lurched sideways, catching himself on a chair. Lienna dug frantically through her purse, probably searching for another stun marble. A stun marble would be ideal right about now—assuming she wasn't too dizzy to hit her mark.

"All right, little agents." The Ghost pulled a vial from his belt and held it up. "You can die by this poison. It'll kill you both in about thirty seconds and make your current discomfort feel like heaven. Or …"

My wavering vision shimmered more weirdly—and a dark shape materialized in front of me. My brain couldn't make sense of the shaggy form with bright ruby eyes until its lips peeled back, revealing wet fangs. Then it snarled and my brain figured it out: a wolf.

A huge, snarling, murdery-looking fae wolf with terrifyingly large teeth lunged at me. I reeled back, barely managing to keep the multi-door warp going. Canine fangs snapped at my chest, catching the front of my shirt. More tearing sounds.

My back hit the wall, and the wolf stood over me, a piece of my expensive dress shirt hanging from its teeth. A second snarl sounded close by, and I glimpsed another real-life dire wolf snarling in Lienna's face. She'd frozen with her hand in her purse, staring into its glaring eyes a foot away.

"Or you can feed my vargs," the Ghost finished coolly. "Unless, *somehow*, you can think of a third alternative."

A third option … like allowing him to escape?

The nauseating effect of the Ghost's last potion was wearing off, which did nothing to mitigate the terror his bloodthirsty pooches were inspiring in me, but I dared to look away from them to the master. Despite all the distractions, I couldn't help but notice he could have already killed us. For a notorious murderer, he was showing a hell of a lot of restraint.

However, judging by the banked but arctic impatience in his eyes, he wouldn't hesitate much longer.

"You have five seconds," he intoned.

Shit.

"Three seconds."

Ignoring the threat of the snarling wolf in my face, I harnessed all my psychic energy.

"Your time is—"

He broke off as I layered something new on the multi-door halluci-bomb. Floating in a semi-circle in front of his face were six blown-up photos from the missing persons cases Lienna and I were investigating. The photos changed, showing six more victims. Then six more, and six more, until I'd shown him all thirty-six. Thirty-two teens, three adults, and the boy who'd been kidnapped outside the Arcana Historia—his photo had been of his bracelet.

The Ghost's eyebrows drew down as his focus swept from face to face, and when I let the warp fade, he turned to me. "What the hell was that?"

"According to the MPD, those are all people the Ghost has kidnapped."

Lienna's wide-eyed look silently asked what I was doing—but even I wasn't sure what I was doing. All I knew was that one word had stuck with me since the Fake Ghost had sneered it. *"You rescued her apprentice."*

Rescued.

"Some of those are your victims," I told him. "Some of them aren't."

"What makes you think that?"

"That Fake Ghost is kidnapping people and letting you take the blame."

He seemed to consider whether to deny it, then rumbled, "You say that like I should care."

"Don't you? You could kill us, but you haven't. Clearly you aren't the complete murdering psycho your bounty paints you as. You have lines you don't like to cross, right? I'm guessing human trafficking is one of them."

The Ghost had accused Fake Ghost of working for Varvara Nikolaev, and one of her big schticks had been human trafficking. The bad blood between them could run deeper than a personal grudge.

"Why would he have a problem with human trafficking?" Lienna hissed at me. "He's a child abductor too."

"He's after that Fake Ghost," I hissed back.

"That doesn't make him the good guy!" She forgot to whisper this time. "He's a criminal!"

"So was I, remember?"

Her mouth snapped shut, the low snarls of the fae wolves filling the room.

I looked back at the Ghost. "Just answer one question. Did you kidnap a teen boy yesterday morning near Arcana Historia?"

He studied me, his vivid green eyes cold and piercing.

"I just want to save the kid," I said quietly. "That's it, man."

His mouth thinned. "I wasn't anywhere near there. I've been busy hunting that bastard and his pals before they scatter too far."

I believed him. I wasn't sure why, but I did. "Then the Fake Ghost is the kidnapper. If you're after him too, we can help each other—"

"I don't 'help' anyone," the Ghost interrupted. "Especially not the MPD."

I glanced at the varg in my face, then back to the rogue.

"So you're a … *lone wolf?*" I was so tempted to use my powers to add a *ba-dum-tss*, and despite the very real danger we were in, I couldn't help but add in my best English accent, "'He's mad that trusts in the tameness of a wolf.'"

"Very funny, Shakespeare," the Ghost growled. "I don't work with comedians either—or fools."

Hold up a hot second. Had the scary rogue man recognized my *King Lear* quote? Was he bantering back at me by referencing the fool? How could this guy be a literal god of manliness *and* well-read?

My pretend crush on his unholy, broody hunkiness might've just shifted closer to reality.

Shaking myself, I quickly countered, "What about working with people who have information you need? Now that this Fake Ghost knows you're after him, he won't be easy to find again. We know stuff about him you don't."

The druid took a deep, silent breath. If he was considering my offer—and, thusly, considering *not* turning us into wolf kibble—his puppy pals weren't aware of that. They remained uncomfortably close.

"We know his victims," I added, receiving another furious warning glare from Lienna that I ignored. "Locations of the crimes, access to the MPD databases, and confidential informants. And a whole apartment full of evidence."

The Ghost's expression was inscrutable, but then without any apparent direction from their master, the two vargs relaxed their snarling muzzles and retreated. Shadows swirled around them, and they faded out of sight as creepily as they'd appeared.

I sucked in my first deep breath since the whole confrontation had begun.

"An exchange of information," the Ghost rumbled. "That's it. Across the bridge, south of Pacific, the large apartment building under construction. Meet me at the west entrance in twenty minutes. If anyone besides you two sets foot on the property, I'll kill you both."

I bobbed my head in a quick nod.

"And if your information is useless," he added as he pulled his hood up and crossed to the door, "I'll feed you to my vargs."

The door swung open, then banged shut behind him, and I sagged back against the wall, finally letting the fake-doors warp go—but my tired brain didn't clue in until Lienna spoke.

"He used the other door."

My exhausted gray matter whirred sluggishly, more focused on the old dead guy the Ghost had abandoned us with. I looked from the far door that I'd been disguising—which led into a narrow hallway—to the nearer door, the one we'd come in. The one that led back into crime-minglers central.

Hadn't the Ghost wanted to go through the other door?

I pushed to my feet. "Why—"

A thunderous crash interrupted me, and screams echoed from the room the Ghost had entered.

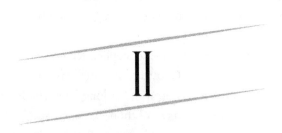

II

THROWING THE DOOR OPEN, I sprinted out of the room. That old dead guy wasn't my problem anyway.

I raced down the wide hallway, suit jacket hanging open and torn shirt flapping with each stride. Two steps into the main room, I came up short. Lienna smacked into my back, then leaned around me for a better view.

The massive, spherical aquarium was shattered on the floor, and several thousand gallons of water were rushing across the carpet. Among the shards of acrylic and twisted metal, the tentacles of the mini-kraken writhed.

The Ghost in his long coat and shadowed hood stood feet away from the creature. The water nymph clung to his arm, her limbs visibly trembling. As the crowd of shocked mythics retreated, he pulled something from his belt, shook it, then tossed it into the air.

It exploded into white mist. The hazy cloud roiled outward, sweeping over the crowd. They all vanished—then a scream rang out.

Suddenly, everyone was screaming, and a handful of white-faced gamblers bolted out of the cloud. A thick tentacle shot through the rolling mist and caught a man's leg. Falling hard, he howled in terror as the tentacle dragged him back into the haze.

Great. We were in a real-life Stephen King novel.

A moment later, the Ghost strode casually from the fog. He carried the nymph with one arm, her long hair dripping water over the carpet in his wake. Without so much as a backward glance at the screaming horde trapped in his potion-fueled smokescreen with the three-hundred-pound kraken toddler he'd unleashed on them, he disappeared through a door marked with a stairwell sign.

I swallowed hard. The MPD file on this guy didn't do him justice.

Lienna grabbed my arm and pulled me along the perimeter of the room, keeping well away from the kraken-infested cloud in the center. "You've done it now."

"Done what? You mean keeping us alive and negotiating a ceasefire with an ultra-powerful druid who can help us save a kidnapped teen?"

"An ultra-powerful druid who's also a murderous rogue and who will probably kill us as soon as he gets all our information!"

"I doubt it. Guys like him have a code. Not a bro code or even a legal one, but some sort of moral code they follow."

"And you're basing this on what, exactly?" she hissed as we ducked through the same stairwell door the Ghost had used.

"The fact he could've killed us twenty times over." I jogged down the stairs. "But he didn't. Not everyone on the wrong side of the law is morally bankrupt."

"Do you hear yourself? First torturing informants, now trying to convince me that a known murderer who *also kidnaps children* isn't a bad person? Did you not see the dead man he'd *just killed* in that room?"

"I'm not proposing we marry the guy!" I jerked to a halt on the stairs and faced her. "I'm using him to get the information we need to save the boy and catch the Fake Ghost!"

She glowered at me from one step up. "And then what, Kit? You going to let this Ghost walk? Let him go on to commit more theft, blackmail, illegal artifact dealing, kidnapping, and murder?"

I hesitated—and got angrier because I was hesitating. "What do you suggest we do?"

"We arrest him and get his info that way."

I scoffed. "He kicked our asses without breaking a sweat. We'd need an entire team to take him down, and Blythe told us we're on our own. The only way we're getting information from him is if he gives it to us."

Her hands clenched and unclenched, then she blew out a furious breath. "Fine! We'll meet with him. But if this backfires …"

I waited a moment. "If this backfires, then what?"

She bit her lower lip, then swept past me, motions sharp with anger and anxiety. I inhaled, searching for calm, then followed. I needed to keep my cool for our second encounter with Vancouver's scariest rogue.

THE GHOST'S chosen meeting point was a half-finished high-rise with curved concrete pillars sweeping up the outside that would look really cool when the building was finished. A chain-link fence wrapped around the property, and the vestiges of a construction crew's supplies were scattered in the mud inside its perimeter. Blue tarps and sheets of plywood covered the windows, shielding the interior from the elements.

I parked the smart car under the friendly glow of a streetlamp across the street. Before setting out, we'd changed from our formalwear—tragically torn-up formalwear, in my case—and back into street clothes, then Lienna had spent the short ride spinning her Rubik's Cube into a new pattern. An anti-druid spell, I'd wager.

"I wonder if he'll show up," she murmured, tucking the cube in her satchel before opening her door. She'd emptied her fancy black purse into her trusty shoulder bag after changing outfits.

"He will. He wants our info."

"Or he wants to kill us in a more private location." Climbing out, she headed for the back of the car. "Come here."

I followed her to the hatch. She opened it and dug into a small fabric case tucked between a large black duffle bag and my garment bag. Maybe I'd get lucky and "tattered" would be the next hot trend in men's business attire.

"Universal antidote," she informed me as she selected two small vials from among the assortment of mythic first-aid supplies in the case. "It won't protect us from his nastier potions, but it'll give us a chance against more common alchemic poisons."

She passed me a vial, then downed the other one. I twisted the cap off mine and dumped the potion onto my tongue. It stung like ice water, even though the vial was only a bit cooler than room temperature. My mouth tingled strangely.

"Are you sure *this* isn't a poison?" I asked dubiously, handing it back.

"Of course." She capped the vial and replaced it, then closed the hatch with a grim expression more appropriate for a funeral. "Let's go."

Together, we circled to the west side of the building—and there, leaning in the shadowy doorway, was a figure in a long black cloak, the hood pulled up.

Lienna frowned. "How did he get here so fast?"

"Magic?" I suggested. That wasn't a joke because, you know, he was very magical.

We squeezed through a handy gap in the fence and approached the doorway. The Ghost pushed the door beside him open. If it'd been locked, he'd already dealt with it.

Lienna and I followed him inside, using our phone flashlights to navigate. Aside from a dizzying forest of concrete pillars, the interior was completely open. A makeshift table with a plywood top was pressed up against the wall near the door, some papers and an ashtray full of cigarette butts on it. A work light rested on the floor, connected to an extension cord that snaked its way under a tarp.

Lienna flicked the light on, illuminating the lobby in a harsh orange glow and stark shadows. I thumbed through a few papers on the table—mostly blueprints, plus a large map of downtown Vancouver showing power, plumbing, and natural gas lines.

"Cozy," I murmured as I faced the druid. "So, uh, Zakariya—"

He pushed his hood off, revealing an irritated scowl. "No."

"No what?"

"Names aren't required." He leaned against the table. "This is a business transaction. Your information for my information."

"Your information first," Lienna jumped in aggressively, one hand tucked in her satchel for a Rubik's Cube quick draw. "Then we'll tell you what we know."

The Ghost's gloved hand hung casually close to the hilt of a big-ass knife strapped to his thigh. "You first."

She widened her stance. "That's not how this works."

And she was right. Withholding information and getting combative with each other was *not* going to work. I stepped between them, wearing my most congenial grin.

"Let's do this right, guys," I said. "We all want the same thing. We're after the Ghost—the Fake Ghost. The not-you Ghost. You realize this no-name brand version of our partnership is going to get really confusing, right?"

"Deal with it."

I shrugged. "I could whip up some brand-spanking-new nicknames for you. That's kind of a specialty of mine. How about 'Fifty Shades'? It goes with your very monochromatic getup and the dark, brooding—"

"Zak, then." He glanced at Lienna. "Is he always this annoying?"

My partner's lips flattened. "Yes."

"All right, Zak," I replied with a chipper bounce in my voice. "I'm Kit."

"Agent Morris," Lienna corrected.

I gestured to her. "And she's Li … Agent Shen."

"Wonderful," Zak said indifferently.

I rubbed my hands together. "Back to business! We're all trying to catch the Fake Ghost."

"I don't *catch* people. I kill them."

"And we want to rescue the people he's kidnapped," I replied. "There's some serious overlap in that Venn diagram. I know nobody here is thrilled with this arrangement, but it can save us all a lot of time. So, what do you have for us?"

Zak pushed away from the table, his eerily bright green eyes uncompromising. "Let me be clear, *Kit*. You aren't calling the shots. I am. I'll decide what I'm sharing after you prove you have something useful for me. And if you don't like that, well …" He swept his hand out at the abandoned construction site. "You won't be leaving until I decide you can leave."

If the situation hadn't been so tense, I was absolutely certain Lienna would've been muttering, "I told you so," at my back.

I faced the Ghost, no longer offering friendly smiles. "You say that, but it's actually the other way around."

Targeting his mind, I Split-Kit myself—twice. Two doppelgangers stepped sideways out of my real body. As the three Kits faced him, his eyes narrowed.

"The reality is, *Zak*," the three of us said, my voice echoing through the space, "you aren't leaving without *my* permission."

I didn't know if I was convincing him of my power because I wasn't really convincing myself. But if I knew how to do anything, it was bluff.

Two more Split-Kits stepped out of the others. Five doppelgangers surrounded him, all of us grinning in challenge. We raised our arms in innocent shrugs.

"Unless you want to test how well you can fight my partner—who's an abjuration prodigy, by the way—when you can't trust anything you see, hear, smell, or even feel."

On the last word, I added the sensation of a hand pressing against Zak's back between his shoulder blades. He jerked away and half turned, finding nothing, not even a Split-Kit, directly behind him.

His gaze slid across the identical Kits on every side as though debating whether one was real or they were all fake—and a slow smile curved his lips. It wasn't friendly. It wasn't even amused. It was a cold acknowledgment.

"Interesting." He arched an eyebrow. "But I'm still not sharing my information first."

I let out an exasperated huff, then let the Split-Kits vanish. "Fine, I'll go first. Lienna and I were given this case: catch the Ghost, who just abducted another teen victim. We started following the evidence but ended up tracking that other shit-wicket instead of you. We have no idea who the hell he is, why he's impersonating you, or which one of you is the scummier scumbag."

Zak snorted with muted amusement. Maybe I was breaking through that rough, chiseled exoskeleton.

"So, cards on the table," I finished. "Tell us who that guy is."

"I don't know."

Lienna rolled her eyes. "Oh, come on!"

"I don't know anything about him," Zak clarified, "except that he worked for Varvara Nikolaev. He was heavily involved in her human trafficking business. I suspect he was in charge of it."

"If he's a big human trafficker, why has he never come across our radar before?" Lienna demanded. "We're the MPD."

"You just answered your own question." Zak folded his arms. "Varvara had loyal lieutenants in every corner of

Vancouver's underbelly, controlling all her operations so she'd never have to show her face or get her hands dirty."

"And you're hunting them," I guessed. "Destroying everything she built and everyone she associated with."

"Yes."

"Because she annihilated your farm?"

A dark, murderous rage flared in his eyes. "In part."

His tone warned me to drop that subject real quick, so I backtracked to our target. "This lieutenant guy, you don't know anything else about him? Name? Class? Favorite restaurant?"

"According to his reputation among Varvara's other men, he could find anyone and make them disappear without a trace."

"Varvara's other men?" Lienna jumped in. "Who are they? Can we question them?"

"I'd show you their graves, but I didn't bother burying them."

Yikes. Avoiding Lienna's accusing glare, I said hastily, "The teen he nabbed yesterday vanished into thin air, according to a witness. All our other case files went cold the moment the victim disappeared too. Was he behind all the abductions?"

"How many case files do you have?"

"Thirty-six."

Lienna frowned. "I thought it was thirty-three."

I shook my head. "Thirty-two teenagers, three adults that don't really fit with the others, and the most recent victim."

"Let me see them," Zak said.

Lienna shifted from her stern crossed-arms stance to a more casual hands-in-pockets position. "We don't have the files with us."

"But that's not a problem," I said, making a grand sweeping gesture. Six of the victim photos appeared in poster form, their names and ages beneath them. Not wanting to attempt to warp thirty-six photos at once, I rotated through all the victims six at a time, like I had back at the casino. Good thing I'd spent so much time studying the profiles.

Zak studied the display. "You're a psychic, obviously, but what kind?"

"Psycho warper," I replied, injecting a bit of pride into my answer.

He pursed his lips in thought but didn't comment. Maybe he didn't want to admit he'd never heard the label before.

"Including our most recent victim, thirty-three are teens. Mostly runaways, street kids, or lost in the foster system, from what I can tell." I brought up photos for the outlying three. "And then we have this trio. Adults established in the mythic community. They have families and jobs."

"What are the dates of their disappearances?"

"The teen abductions span the past six years, but the adults vanished in the last four weeks."

"'Filip Shelton,'" Zak read, the name of the officer of M&L's Vancouver branch. "He and the boy from yesterday disappeared after I killed Varvara five days ago."

"And?" Lienna prompted.

"And that means Varvara's lieutenant wasn't as dedicated to her as she thought. He took a contract on Filip Shelton. There's no other explanation for why he'd target someone after she died, especially an adult."

"He found a paying client two days after his former boss's death?" Lienna murmured. "That's fast."

"Too fast," I agreed. "He was already supplementing his villain income with abductions."

Zak nodded sexily. How did someone nod sexily? Maybe it was the steely gaze. I needed to take notes.

"What about the teens?" Lienna finally pulled her hand out of her satchel. "Were they contract abductions like Filip or convenience kidnappings for Varvara's human trafficking operation?"

"I made a map of the abduction locations," I said as my two compatriots studied the profiles silently. "I thought it might help narrow down where the Fake Ghost lives."

"How would that work?" she asked skeptically.

"It's called geographic profiling." I took out my phone and swiped through my files. "Perps usually want a buffer zone between the crime scenes and their home base, but they also like to hunt in familiar territory. If you have enough data, you should theoretically be able to find a hole in the middle of the crime scenes where the perp lives."

I walked over to the makeshift table and flipped through the huge sheets of paper until I found the map of downtown Vancouver. Comparing it to the map I'd made last night, I floated mini photos of the victims above their respective last known locations. Five of the teenage victims and one adult didn't fit on the map, which only covered a few square kilometers. I placed those around the table, approximating where they'd been taken.

Zak watched me work with a Shania-Twain-esque "that don't impress me much" expression. "They teach you this in MagiPol school?"

"Not where I come from," Lienna muttered.

"I saw it on *Criminal Minds*," I said. "You could learn a thing or two from Dr. Spencer Reid."

We appraised my hallucinatory multimedia presentation. There definitely wasn't a circle anywhere on the map that screamed, "Bad guy sleeps here!"

I sighed. "Unfortunately, I couldn't find a pattern when I put this together."

"Take away the adults," Lienna suggested. "And the boy from yesterday. If this lieutenant was doing two types of kidnappings, the contract abductions and trafficking victims might follow different patterns."

"He wouldn't be able to control the locations of the contract abductions," I realized. I dropped the adult profiles and the kid from yesterday morning, but that left five profiles hanging outside the edge of the map. "We've still got one in New Westminster, two in Surrey, and another two near the university."

"Get rid of them," Zak ordered quietly.

"We can't just toss them off the map for no reason," I pushed back. "The evidence has to make a pattern on its own, not because we sculpt it that way."

"He wasn't responsible for them."

Lienna straightened, righteous fire igniting in her eyes. "Then who was, Zak?"

"You can lose this one too." He pointed at the profile of a girl named Nadine River, last seen at a homeless shelter in the city's core, then indicated three more downtown disappearances. "And those as well."

"You son of a bitch," Lienna snapped. "You took them!"

"I didn't *kidnap* anyone."

His emphasis on "kidnap" grabbed my attention. Just because he hadn't abducted them didn't mean he hadn't done something else to those kids. "Where are they, then? In the bellies of your pooches?"

"Tell you what. When the MPD starts giving a fuck about homeless mythic teens, I'll let you know what happened to them."

My renewed revulsion toward the druid faltered. I stared at him, brow furrowed.

"The MPD has a foster care system," Lienna said sharply. "And—"

Zak barked a sarcastic laugh. "Yeah, sure. And their system, run by an understaffed, underfunded handful of MPD administrators who couldn't keep track of every kid and every foster parent even if they worked a hundred hours a week, isn't an unofficial kid auction for mythic traffickers."

My eyes bulged, and beside me, Lienna's mouth bobbed open and closed.

Zak returned his attention to the map. "Bring back the illusion."

"It's called a warp," I muttered, still reeling. Concentrating, I made the profiles reappear, and as they popped into their proper places, my breath caught. "Do you see …"

He nodded.

"A circle," Lienna murmured, gazing at the ring of remaining profiles.

"More like a wibbly-wobbly amoeba." I pressed my hand roughly in the center of said single-celled organism. "I'm willing to bet our big bad Fake Ghost lives somewhere around here."

"Not lives. Operates." Zak brushed my hand aside and pointed to a building on Dunsmuir Street. "The old CP Rail tunnel."

I peered at the spot. "I think that's a parking garage."

"It is now."

With that, he spun away from the table, his long coat flaring, and strode toward the exit. As he reached back for his hood, he looked over his shoulder at me.

"By the way, Kit …"

The darkness looming beyond the glare of the work light thickened. Shadows writhed to life, oozing upward like smoky tendrils.

The Ghost smiled icily. "The shadows of your 'warps'? They aren't nearly convincing enough."

He pulled his hood up—and a swirl of shadow formed around him. The darkness swept over his body, and when it faded, he was gone without a trace.

Lienna and I stared at the spot he'd vanished in frightened silence.

"Shit," I muttered weakly. "He really is the Ghost."

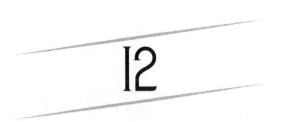

12

THE PARKING GARAGE Zak had pinpointed was only a few blocks away, and we arrived in less than ten minutes.

Was it crazy that we were going to the exact location Zak had indicated? As Lienna feared, it could be a trap. It could also be a decoy to distract us while Zak went after his impersonator.

But it was our only lead.

Dull yellow lights held back the darkness as we pulled into the parking garage. Lienna brought the vehicle to a halt, silently debating which way to go, then turned away from the ramp that would've taken us up a level. She rolled past rows of parking stalls, sparsely populated by old sedans, and as we neared the farthest corner of the garage, our headlights fell on a tall figure in a long coat.

Lienna parked and we climbed out. Zak ignored our approach, his attention on a patch of graffiti decorating the wall. Colorful spray-painted letters and abstract designs were layered over one another in a nonsensical tangle.

"Admiring the artwork?" I asked as we joined him.

He didn't take his eyes off the wall. "This isn't art."

"I think Banksy would have something to say about that. And we could've given you a ride, you know."

"It's a spell."

I guess that was a "no" to the ride, then.

Lienna stepped closer to the wall and brushed her fingers across the rough grooves hidden under the spray paint.

"There's a door here." She traced a thin arch of runes hidden among the gang tags, then glanced at Zak. "How did you know about this?"

"Several of Varvara's lieutenants spilled their guts to me recently." He smirked in a brutally amused way, as though inviting us to ask whether he meant that literally or figuratively. "One of them mentioned a hideout here, but I hadn't gotten around to checking it out yet."

I surveyed the wall. "How do we open the door?"

Turning to Lienna, Zak canted his head toward the graffiti. "See anything that could get nasty if the spell is tampered with?"

"Nothing obvious, though there could be surprises hidden in all that graffiti. Why are you asking me?"

"I don't have 'abjuration prodigy' Arcana skills." He pushed one side of his coat out of the way and pulled a test-tube-shaped vial from his belt. A viscous, sunset-orange liquid filled it halfway. "But I do know my alchemy."

Pulling the cork from the top, he stepped toward the graffiti.

"What are you doing?" Lienna demanded.

He raised the vial. "I suggest you stand back."

"Wait!" Lunging forward, she grabbed his arm.

My stomach flipped as Zak fixed a dark, murderous glare on her—which she returned without flinching. They were about two seconds away from an explosive magical melee in the middle of a public parking garage, which would be less than ideal for a whole host of reasons, not the least of which being that Zak would end our mortal existence and I didn't want to die next to a 1994 maroon Hyundai.

I raised my hands in a "please don't kill us" way. "What's the problem, Lienna? Do you see something dangerous in the spell?"

"Not yet, but I've hardly had a chance to look." She tightened her grip on Zak's arm. "I can break the spell. I'm an abjuration sorceress. That's what I do."

The druid twisted his arm free—and before she could grab him again, he swept the vial in a wide arc. Droplets of syrupy liquid splatted on the graffitied wall, fizzing violently on contact. Smoke oozed up as pockmarks appeared; the potion was eating through not only the paint but the concrete itself.

With a hollow clunk, an arch-shaped section of wall dropped by half an inch, leaving a thin crack outlining the door.

Zak slashed a derisive glance at Lienna. "What you do takes too long."

"Asshole," she growled under her breath.

I winced, seeing no way to diffuse the extra-special hatred budding between her and the rogue.

He pressed his palm against the door and the whole slab of concrete slid backward, opening a gap wide enough for a single person to slip through. Without a glance at us, he stepped into the darkness.

Lienna launched after him, and I squeezed in last, finding myself inside a dark tunnel well over double my height. The air was musty and cracked tiles lined the walls. The floor was in even worse shape, with crumbling pavement, potholes, and a half-buried railroad track turning the terrain into a real ankle-breaker.

Zak shoved the door back into place, sealing us inside and eliminating any source of light. Wonderful. I'd never broken an ankle before and I looked forward to the new experience.

Before I could fish out my phone, Zak's rumbling voice murmured an incantation. The tunnel filled with a soft white light, emanating from one of the crystals hanging on a leather tie around his neck.

"Stay behind me," he said, striding onto the train tracks.

"Do you know where this leads?" I asked.

"It only goes one direction."

"But—"

"Follow me or don't. Just stay out of my way."

Lienna grumbled something under her breath, and I doubted it was complimentary. The two of us followed the mysterious, unsociable rogue into the dark tunnel.

"Maybe he can sense the other Ghost," I whispered to my partner.

"How would he do that? He's not a telethesian."

"Secret druid powers? Maybe his wolf pack is running ahead to check things out."

"Or maybe he can't stand the idea of someone else taking the lead."

I bit my tongue. Pot, meet kettle.

The tunnel bent to the left, and as Zak rounded the curve, his handy glowing crystal illuminated an underground platform about four feet above the tracks. Another set of tracks ran parallel on its other side.

He vaulted onto the platform; Lienna and I followed suit.

A staircase, which connected to the street above, was sealed shut with boards and concrete barricades, and I could hear the din of city life overhead. A small grate in the ceiling revealed slivers of a lone pedestrian's shoes walking past. I tried to calculate how long we'd walked and in which direction.

"That must be ... Beatty Street," I muttered. "Should we keep going? See where these tracks take us?"

"They end at a Costco," Zak replied. "The exit is sealed off like this one."

I smirked as an image of the almighty, hooded Crystal Druid cruising through the wholesale warehouse popped into my mind's eye: grabbing a sixty-four pack of toilet paper, a fifty-pound bag of kibble for his vargs, and a trio of oversized ketchup bottles that would last even the greatest hot dog enthusiast a lifetime.

With a thoughtful expression, Zak jumped off the platform onto the second set of tracks. He looked in both directions, then headed into the tunnel that ran back the way we'd come.

"Where are you going?" I called, leaping off the platform after him. Lienna reluctantly copied me.

"These tracks run parallel," he replied. "They should lead to an unfinished station underneath the garage."

"That's where Varvara's lieutenant is?" my partner prompted in a not-very-nice tone.

He grunted in response.

It was my turn to roll my eyes. A little inter-squad communication would make this whole investigation run so much smoother, guys.

Maybe I should quit the MPD agent business and get into couples' counseling. I could sport some spectacles, hold a notepad, and say, "… and how does that make you *feel*?" a whole bunch. Not that I needed to ask to know how my comrades felt. Lienna was furious we were letting a self-admitted murderer lead our investigation, and Zak was peeved that two rookie MPD agents were tailing him like lost ducklings.

"So," I called out, breaking the combative silence, "assuming we find this guy hanging out in his lair like Lex Luthor, what's our plan?"

"Kill him."

"*Arrest* him."

I sighed. "'Kill' and 'arrest' are fantastic verbs, guys, but neither constitutes a plan."

Zak looked over his shoulder at me and put a quieting finger to his lips. Oh, so no discussion needed, then? Wasn't I silly, wanting to pause for a strategy sesh prior to a potential battle against a criminal who'd easily thwarted our collective magic once already?

The druid pointed ahead, then closed his fist over his flashlight crystal, dimming it. We had arrived at the lair.

"Want me to invisi-warp?" I whispered to Lienna.

She shook her head. "Save your energy. We might need it."

The three of us slunk as quietly as we could through the shadows. As before, the tunnel opened into a wider, higher space with a platform to our left. Unlike the previous spot, however, there were no tracks on the other side—just a concrete wall with a metal door in the middle. Both platform and tunnel ended in a crude stone wall, and the ceiling was similarly natural, the straight walls meeting raw stone in a collision of man's subterranean industry and the stubborn belly of the earth.

Keeping hushed, all three of us hopped up onto the platform and looked around. No runes or mysterious symbols or artifacts. Just some scuff marks in the dust.

Simultaneously, we faced the lone metal door. A shiny padlock, much newer and cleaner than anything else down here, secured a thick steel plate holding the door shut.

Zak pulled out his scary orange syrup and poured a drop onto the lock. It fizzled and dissolved, and he pulled the lock off.

Returning the vial to his belt, he backed several steps away and set his feet, one hand on the hilt of the knife sheathed on his thigh. Lienna pulled her Rubik's Cube out, a stun marble in her other hand. As they faced the door, ready for combat, I silently swung the locking plate open and grasped the handle.

Lienna gave me her "I'm ready" look, and Zak moved his chin in the slightest of nods.

I took a deep breath, then twisted the handle and whipped the door open.

13

INSIDE WAS A SMALL cube-shaped room with strange umber padding on every surface. Soundproofing. The room was insulated to keep any sounds from escaping—like screams for help from abduction victims.

Two such victims were chained to the floor. One was a boy around fourteen with light brown hair and the other was a man in his forties, lying on his back and by all appearances unconscious. His sweat-beaded skin had a sickly pallor.

The boy scuttled fearfully back into his corner, face scrunched in a squint from Zak's light spell.

I hastened through the door ahead of my battle-posed comrades. Dropping into a crouch, I offered the boy my best I-come-in-peace smile. "I'm Agent Morris from the MPD. We're here to help. What's your name?"

Out of the corner of my eye, I saw Lienna kneel beside the other prisoner and put her fingers to his neck to check his pulse.

Zak entered last, ignoring both victims, his attention on the sole piece of furniture in the barren room: a tall wooden cabinet with another heavy-duty padlock sealing it shut. The only other object was a large plastic pail with a lid that could only be the prisoners' bathroom.

"Daniel," the boy answered, his voice unsteady.

"Nice to meet you, Daniel. Would you like to get out of here?"

"Yes," he choked, tears filming his eyes. His gaze darted to Zak, who looked more like a jacked-up Ringwraith than a benevolent rescuer.

The druid studied the cabinet. Skipping his melter potion, he pulled that massive dagger from his thigh sheath, revealing a ten-inch blade with a partially serrated edge like an army knife. He jammed it into the slit between the cabinet doors and pried them open, flinging splinters of wood across the room.

Leaving him to rummage through the cabinet, I turned my attention to the manacle around Daniel's ankle. "How are you feeling? Are you hurt?"

He shook his head. "Just hungry."

A clatter—Zak had pulled a briefcase-like object from the cabinet shelves. It was strangely smooth on all sides and had runes carved into its matte black surface.

"What's that?" I asked.

The druid inspected it. There were no visible locks or hinges—no way to open it. "Something important."

I fully expected him to smash it against a wall to see if he could break it apart like a goddamn coconut, but instead, he crossed over to me and Daniel. Setting the case aside, he pushed his hood back.

Daniel blinked nervously.

"I'm going to get this off you," he rumbled in a softer tone than I'd heard from him yet. Not gentle, really, but definitely on the soothing side. "Do you know anything about the man who brought you here?"

Daniel shook his head. "He barely said anything."

Zak poured a drop of his dissolves-everything potion on the manacle, waited while the metal sizzled, then snapped it off. "When did you last see him?"

"I-I'm not sure. I can't really tell time in here." His forehead scrunched. "What day is it?"

"Saturday," I told him. "You were kidnapped yesterday morning, about thirty-six hours ago. Come on, let's get you up."

Together, Zak and I pulled Daniel to his feet. He wobbled unsteadily, his face pale in the glow of the druid's crystal.

"Kit," Lienna said tersely from her spot beside the other victim. "Something is wrong with this man. He doesn't seem to be injured, but he won't wake up. His pulse is weak, and he's got a hell of a fever."

"Is he sick?" I asked.

"Poisoned," Zak and Daniel said in unison.

In explanation, Zak pointed at the cabinet he'd broken open. The top three shelves were lined with glass bottles and flasks containing liquids of all different colors. The bottom two shelves were nearly empty: a couple of artifacts and a space where the briefcase had been.

"He needs help fast," Lienna said, looking up at us. "Let's break this manacle off him and get back to the surface."

Daniel tapped my shoulder. "There's a light switch."

He nodded toward the door, and I hastened to flip it on. A strip of LEDs embedded in the ceiling lit up, bathing the room in an ugly yellow light that clashed horrifically with the equally ugly orange padding. In the increased illumination, I recognized the unconscious adult victim as Filip Shelton, the second-most recent abductee from our files.

Zak crouched beside Lienna, peering at Filip. He selected a vial from his belt, this one full of purple potion. "Hold his head up."

"What's in that vial?"

"High-potency vitality potion. It'll give him a boost until you get him to a healer."

As Lienna angled Filip's head so Zak could pour the potion into his mouth, I asked Daniel, "Did you see the kidnapper poison him?"

"He forced him to drink one of those." The boy pointed at the cabinet. "But I don't know which one."

There were over a dozen potions in there. How would the healer figure out which one was the poison? And also, why? What did the kidnapper want with a harmless banker? And why abduct Filip only to slowly poison him to death, hidden underground in a soundproofed prison?

Maybe the answers were in that briefcase—assuming Zak could brute-force his way inside it.

"Can we go now?" Daniel whispered. "I want to go home. My mom'll be freaking out."

"We'll be out of here in a few seconds," I reassured him.

Zak used his magic melter potion on Filip's manacle, then heaved the unconscious man up onto his shoulder in a fireman carry. "Kit, grab that briefcase."

I stooped to grab the case's handle, then hesitated as a tingling sensation rippled across the back of my neck. You know that feeling you get when you know you're being watched, even though you can't see who's watching? That shimmer in the corner of your eye?

I'd learned to listen to that paranoid hunch and right now, I was getting it in spades.

"Watch it!" Zak roared.

The lights blinked out, plunging the room into complete darkness—and a blast of white radiance fired into the room in a blinding beam. Zak, holding Filip's unconscious body, took the attack straight to the chest. It hurled him and Filip back into the padded wall.

White spots doubled across my vision as the room went black again. "Lien—"

Something crashed into my ribs like a baseball bat and I crumpled sideways. Footsteps sounded in the pitch black, then I heard Daniel's frightened cry.

"Shit!" I gasped, jumping up. I felt wildly along the wall until I found the light switch, but it was still in the on position. I flicked it down and up with desperate violence, and the lights burst back on.

Daniel's shouts echoed from the platform. I lunged through the door.

There he was: Fake Ghost, aka Varvara's lieutenant, aka the contract kidnapper. Still wearing his Zak-lookalike outfit, the hood of his coat pulled up to shadow his face, he was dragging Daniel across the platform. The boy kicked and thrashed for all he was worth.

"Lienna, Zak!" I bellowed. "Get out here!"

I simultaneously invisified myself and threw a Funhouse warp at the kidnapper. He stumbled, crushing Daniel's chest with one arm. I charged forward.

Amber light flared as heavy steps—Zak's—rushed out the door. His glowing yellow whip snapped toward his impersonator—and caught me in the side, knocking me onto my knees.

"Get him, not me!" I shouted angrily, then remembered I was invisible. Zak could neither see nor hear me. Hence the friendly fire.

Shoving back up, I focused on the kidnapper, who'd reached the edge of the platform with Daniel. The janky lights from the room behind me flickered like strobe lights, making it hell to hold my invisi-warp, but all I had to do was distract this guy long enough for Zak and Lienna to bring him down.

Digging deep in my cerebellum, I conjured up another Funhouse warp and crashed it into Fake Ghost's brain. He swayed to the side as the room fractured and flipped like a VR kaleidoscope—then his lips moved with words I couldn't hear.

Another eye-melting torrent of light screamed out of the scepter and slammed into my retinas like a luminescent missile. I covered my face and doubled over. By the time I could see again, my two compadres were squaring off against the knockoff Ghost—who was no longer ensnared in my Funhouse hallucination because I'd lost it again.

"*Ori vis siderea*," Zak snarled. A shimmering purple glow lit up the platform.

Lienna's voice rang out at the same time. "*Ori te formo sagitta!*"

Crackling menacingly, Zak's melon-sized orb of seething amethyst shot straight for the kidnapper—and a sparking green dart from Lienna's Rubik's Cube rocketed for the same target.

Two feet in front of the kidnapper's face, the sparkle dart pierced the amethyst orb. Both attacks froze for a fraction of a second, then dissolved.

Just like that. A di-mythic druid and an abjuration prodigy in a two-on-one battle against a kidnapping dickweed with a magical baseball bat for a weapon, and they'd canceled each other out.

Half strangling Daniel with one arm, said dickweed swung his scepter around and pointed it not at Lienna or Zak, but at *me*. Invisible me.

He hissed an incantation and a retina-searing flash struck me square in the chest, lifted me off my feet, and sent me sliding across the concrete on my ass. As I collapsed for a second time, more than half blinded, the shadow of the kidnapper leaped off the platform and onto the tracks.

Zak charged after the Fake Ghost, Lienna sprinting right behind him. I started to clamber up and follow, but my chest felt like it was on fire.

Shit, it *was* on fire!

Minuscule blue flames were spreading across my t-shirt, eating away at the material. One edge had jumped onto my jacket and was climbing up my sleeve. I tried to slap it out with my hands, then frantically tore off my jacket and pulled my shirt over my head. I tossed both garments to the ground, where the little inferno flared brighter.

Today was a bad day to be one of my shirts.

With my skin smarting from the fire and my bones aching from getting thrown on my ass, I ran to the platform's edge and leaped down onto the tracks.

A flash of light in the darkness of the tunnel. Lienna appeared, marching back toward the platform, using her phone to illuminate the tracks.

"He disappeared with Daniel." Her mouth thinned furiously. "Zak is looking for them."

"What do you mean, disappeared?" I demanded. "It's a straight tunnel. There's nowhere to hide."

"I know that! But he's gone. Not hiding. *Gone*. I couldn't even hear Daniel struggling. You didn't follow, and I didn't know if you were hurt ..." She glanced back into the tunnel and her shoulders drooped with defeat. "We screwed up, didn't we?"

That, my dear partner, was an understatement of epic proportions.

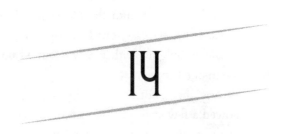

I FOUND FILIP SHELTON, still unconscious, and the black briefcase, still mysteriously unopenable, where we'd abandoned them in the soundproofed room. Lienna hastened to Filip's side and checked his pulse again.

"Is he alive?" I asked, gingerly prodding my singed torso. I hadn't had much chest hair to start with, and it was all gone. Cheaper than waxing, I supposed.

She straightened. "Yes, but his pulse is weaker."

"We need to get him back to a healer at the precinct."

"We can't. Captain Blythe told us—"

"Are you serious?" I blew up. "He is going to *die!* Maybe you won't disobey Blythe to save a man's life, but I will." I bent down and hoisted Filip's body into my arms. "Let's go."

Lienna stiffened at my sudden outburst, then forced a sigh. "I'll be right behind you."

I watched her walk to the cabinet and open her satchel, my teeth gritted. "What are you doing? We don't have time—"

"I'm taking these with us," she snapped. "The healer will need to know which poison is killing him."

Okay, that was smart. I was still pissed, but fine.

I heaved Filip over my shoulder in the same fireman carry Zak had used and headed out onto the platform. Climbing down onto the tracks wasn't easy, but I managed it. Lienna joined me, her satchel bulging with newly acquired potions and the briefcase in one hand.

She led the way, her phone's flashlight chasing off the darkness. I followed a few steps behind, breathing hard from the workout Filip was giving me and half expecting to find Zak and his impersonator locked in mortal combat somewhere along the line.

"What happened to your shirt?" she asked after a moment, slowing until we were walking side by side.

"That shit-wizard set it on fire. And my jacket. But you were probably too busy trying to outdo Zak to notice."

Her jaw locked. "I created a whole new spell back there, and it would've worked if that asshole druid had—"

"If he'd looked six feet to his left at what you were doing, yeah," I growled. "And his spell would've worked if *you'd* looked six feet to your right at what he was doing. But neither of you did, because you both wanted to prove you're better."

"I wasn't—"

"Get your head out of your ass, Lienna."

"*Excuse me?*"

I kept my eyes on the ground ahead—partly because I was still concerned about the ankle-breaking potential of the tracks and partly because I didn't need to look at Lienna to feel the death glare she was shooting my way.

"A druid-alchemist, an abjuration sorceress, and a psycho warper," I said tersely. "Against *one man*. And it's not like he's a goddamn demon mage. But he got away because you refused to make a plan, refused to cooperate with Zak, and refused to pay attention to him in the middle of the fight. And now that bastard has Daniel and we have *nothing*."

My angry words hung over us, and I immediately regretted saying them out loud. I believed every single syllable, but going off on Lienna immediately after a life-and-death fight wasn't my most tactful move.

In a low, controlled voice, she asked, "And what did you do? Other than lose your shirt?"

Ah, the classic "plank in your own eye" comeback.

"I distracted him. What else was I supposed to do? You're the mythical powerhouse with all the scary magic, not me."

She let out a frustrated breath. "Sometimes, Kit Morris, I can't tell if you're playing dumb or if you really are that dumb."

"What does that mean?" I growled.

"Never mind. But you're wrong that we came away with nothing. We have *this*."

She hefted the briefcase. I glanced at it, deciding not to express my doubts that it would prove useful in saving Daniel's life.

We found our way back to the car without encountering Zak, Daniel, or the kidnapper. I loaded Filip into the backseat—thank whatever god that rules over eco-friendly travel that we'd upgraded to Smart Car III—and then we were off, racing back to the precinct through the dark downtown streets.

During the drive, I called ahead to make sure a healer was on standby for our arrival. It was after nine p.m. and I was concerned headquarters would be a ghost town, but the operator informed me the precinct was hopping. Half the staff was still powering through a mountain of investigation, interrogation, charges, processing, and paperwork in the aftermath of Varvara Nikolaev's takeover attempt last week.

Lienna drove us straight into the parking garage, where we were met by the healer on duty—Scooter, a spindly redheaded dude who'd pieced me back together a few times now—and his apprentice. We loaded Filip onto a stretcher, and the apprentice and I carried it into the elevator while Scooter checked his patient's vitals.

Once Filip was safely in the infirmary, Lienna handed over the potions she'd collected from the kidnapper's locked cabinet. Scooter promised to contact us once he had a prognosis for our victim—and hopefully an ETA on his consciousness returning—then Lienna and I retreated into the hallway.

"Look, I know we're not supposed to be here," I said, "but do you think I could run over to my desk real quick for a shirt?"

Another shirt. Would my third one be doomed to a violent demise as well?

Her gaze drifted down to my bare chest, then jolted back up to my face. "Sure. But let's make it quick before we draw too much attention. We need to plan our next move, and we shouldn't do that here."

We hurried to the bullpen. The moment I walked through the door, a wolf-whistle rang out. A dozen heads turned my way.

Well, so much for not drawing attention.

Gina, a middle-aged sorceress, smirked as she retrieved some papers from the photocopier. "I don't think that outfit follows official MPD protocol, Agent Morris." She winked. "But I won't tell."

Lienna rolled her eyes and nudged my bare ribs with the briefcase. "Hurry up."

We scooted down an aisle between cubicles, and I earned three more whistles and one catty, "*Meow*," before reaching my desk. I opened the bottom drawer next to my chair and dug through it. There was definitely a shirt in here somewhere.

"How do you keep track of anything in that disaster?" Lienna wondered aloud.

"I have a system." I pulled out a pair of slippers, which I'd accidentally worn to work one early morning when I'd made the grave mistake of skipping coffee to catch the bus.

"Oh yeah?"

Next out of the drawer was an unopened box set of *Resident Evil* DVDs I'd received from Agent Cutter during the office's Secret Santa exchange. "Yeah."

"Is that why you're *still* searching through a drawer full of random crap?"

My fingers felt the cotton bundle I was looking for and yanked it out. "Aha! Eat your words, Shen!"

I unrolled the balled-up t-shirt and proudly displayed it in front of her. It was stark white and more wrinkled than Larry King, with a blue and green orca design emblazoned on the chest.

"Oh my god," Lienna laughed. "You kept that?"

"Hell yeah, I did." It was a Vancouver Canucks shirt I'd snagged while investigating an anonymous tip about deflated hockey pucks. "That was our first case as official partners."

Her eyes met mine, and for a second, any residual anger I harbored toward her melted.

Then Vincent Park ruined the moment completely.

"Looks like fieldwork is getting the better of you, Morris," my mohawked former cubicle mate snickered as he strode into view wearing a brand-new gray suit.

I was taken aback by his lack of cargo shorts. "Am I dreaming or are those actual pants?"

He squinted ruefully at me. "Are those burns on your chest? Your little hallucinations weren't much help against a pyromage, were they?"

Lienna spun to face him. "Actually—"

"You're totally right," I jumped in with a shrug. I pulled my oversized Canucks shirt on. "Been a rough day."

For all we knew, he could be right. We still hadn't figured out what kind of mythic that ghostly shit-licker was, and while a mage was low on the list of possibilities, it wasn't *off* the list. But more importantly, Lienna and I weren't supposed to divulge the true nature of our investigation to anyone, even someone as annoying as Vincent Park, so letting him believe we'd had a lopsided battle with a mage out on the Vancouver streets was a reasonable cover story.

My nemesis smirked smugly. "If you need actual combat support on your cases, let me know. I can try to fit it into my schedule."

"I wouldn't want to impose."

His smirk widened, then he pointed at the black briefcase in Lienna's hand. "What's in there?"

"Oh, this?" I tugged it from Lienna and held it up, balanced on one hand. "I guarantee you've never seen anything like this."

As his eyebrows quirked skeptically, I drew the top edge of the case up. A crack appeared, and with the hiss of a seal breaking, a whoosh of pale steam rushed out of the gap.

Vinny's eyes widened. He leaned cautiously closer as I lifted the lid. Eddies of cool mist spilled out, hiding whatever lay in its dark interior. Vincent edged closer, squinting. The haze swirled lazily, then burst apart as a terrifyingly huge set of incisor teeth launched from the case like a vampiric Mick Jagger—straight at Vinny's shocked face.

He reeled backward with a high-pitched shout, bounced off the cubicle behind him, and almost fell over.

By the time he straightened, he'd already figured it out. Laughing at his furious glare, I let the warp vanish, returning the briefcase to its unopened state.

"*So* funny, Morris. Real original." Seething, he pointed at the case. "What's actually in there? Or is it something even more embarrassing than your magic?"

"Can you keep a secret?"

He eyed me with suspicion. "I guess."

"Sex toys," I whispered dramatically.

He froze for a second. "What?"

Lienna closed her eyes and tilted her head skyward as though praying to literally any god who would listen to smite me down before I could say another word.

"Sex toys," I repeated, patting the case. "There was a big sale so I picked up a bunch of them after work. If you buy in bulk, they give you this special case. I can make some recommendations, if you like."

Vinny stared at me. "You can't bring sex toys to work."

I snapped my fingers. "Damn, you're right. I'll go turn myself in to HR right now. Lienna, you'd better come too. You'll need to testify against me."

She made a half-coughing, half-choking sound.

Fighting back a snicker at Vinny's expression, I waltzed away with the briefcase in hand. Lienna hurried after me.

"I thought we were *avoiding* drawing attention to ourselves," she muttered as we returned to the elevator. She pushed the call button.

"Everyone around here is used to it," I told her. "I think they'd take more notice if I *didn't* torture him somehow."

"And what about the sex toys?"

I flashed a grin. "Just making sure he'll be too embarrassed to talk about our mysterious briefcase. And if he does, he'll be more focused on my kinky collection than anything suspicious."

She snorted. "Let's get going before you have to tell someone that briefcase contains your hemorrhoid cream or dead gerbil's ashes."

With a cheerful chime, the elevator doors opened—and an angry voice escaped it in a low hiss.

"That may be the case, Söze, but this is *my* precinct and—"

Blythe broke off at the sight of me and Lienna. Her glare snapped from us back to the man in the elevator with her. He was tall and wiry, with bland brown hair and a vulpine face. His dark eyes were cold and flat in a way that raised my hackles; I'd seen that look during my foster-kid days, and it was always bad news.

"Morris, Shen," the captain barked angrily. She hesitated—a very un-Blythe-like thing to do—then gestured at the man. "This is Agent Söze from Internal Affairs. Agent Söze, this is Agent Shen and Agent Morris."

He offered a dead-fish smile and held out his hand. "A pleasure, agents."

I shook his hand. As he released mine to grasp Lienna's, I had to resist the urge to wipe my palm on my pants.

Blythe waited for our greetings to complete, then said, "I'm glad you two are here. I'd like an update on your case."

She was *glad*? She'd *like* an update? Who was this polite woman and what had she done with our captain?

"Which case is that?" Söze asked blandly.

"They're following up on a missing person report."

"Unfortunate. I'm sure all your agents are skilled, captain, but wouldn't it be wise to partner your rookies with more experienced agents for such cases?"

"Agent Shen and Agent Morris are more than capable. Come with me, you two."

She marched down the hall, and Söze smiled at her back. "I'll see you tomorrow, captain."

Blythe kept walking. With a quick look at Lienna, I rushed after her. We caught up to the captain as she swept into her office.

"Close the door," she ordered.

I shut it, then warily turned. Ah. There was the furious blue-eyed laser beam of death I'd been expecting.

"In what way," she growled, dropping into her chair, "was I not clear that you were to keep your investigation *out* of the precinct?"

"We didn't have a choice," I said quickly, sinking into the seat across the desk. "We found one of the kidnapping victims. He was poisoned and on the verge of death, so we brought him to Scooter for healing."

"Is it the boy?"

"No, the previous victim. Filip Shelton, an officer from M&L."

Blythe leaned back with a frown. "Give me a full report."

Taking the chair beside mine, Lienna stole a side-eye look at me. How much of my "unethical" decision-making would my partner reveal? Or, for that matter, how much of our uneasy partnership with a certain sexy, murdery rogue?

She cleared her throat. "We used the evidence from Shane Davila's apartment to track the Ghost to the Red Lily."

Blythe nodded, indicating her familiarity with the crime-family-run casino.

"There we encountered a man who we thought was the Ghost, but it turns out he's actually a former associate of Varvara Nikolaev. He's been impersonating the Ghost to hide his illegal activities, particularly human trafficking for Varvara and what we think are contract kidnappings for other clients."

"A second Ghost?" Blythe's lips thinned. "You're certain?"

"There are definitely two," I said with a confident nod.

"And how do you know which is responsible for the kidnappings?"

"We found the boy who was kidnapped yesterday morning and Filip Shelton," Lienna said. "Then we were attacked by the imposter Ghost. We were only able to save Filip. The kidnapper escaped with the boy."

"His name is Daniel," I added quietly. "I didn't get his last name."

Since Lienna wasn't mentioning how I'd tormented informants and allied with a wanted rogue, I wouldn't mention how she and Zak had royally screwed up our big opportunity to defeat the kidnapper and rescue Daniel.

"And you brought Mr. Shelton back to headquarters," Blythe filled in. "The kidnapper poisoned him?"

Lienna nodded. "It appears so, but we don't know why. He's unconscious. We'll need to talk to him as soon as he's awake."

"I'll ensure no one else speaks to him," the captain said grimly. "And the briefcase you two are carrying?"

"We found it in the kidnapper's hideout," I answered. "It looks like some heavy-duty runes are sealing it shut. No idea what could be inside, but it was the only thing in his hidey-hole with magical protections on it, so it must be important."

"It could be his grimoire," Lienna speculated. "If the kidnapper is a sorcerer. We still don't know his class."

Blythe drummed her fingernails on the desktop. "Can you break it open, Agent Shen?"

"I'm not sure. Lockpicking isn't my area of expertise, and I don't want to damage its contents. But if I could take it down to my lab, I might be able to find a way."

Her lab—meaning her secret room on B3 where she'd been secretly experimenting with highly classified portal magic before losing all her prototypes while rescuing me from a murderous electramage with an illegally contracted demon. Not one of my better days.

Blythe's drumming fingers stilled. "No. You two and that briefcase need to leave the precinct before anyone else sees you."

"Because this investigation is off the books?" I asked more angrily than intended. I smoothed my tone. "How about sending a forensic team to the kidnapper's hideout? That place probably has evidence all over it."

"I won't risk bringing anyone else into this investigation. You two need to get it done yourselves."

"Then what the hell are we supposed to do?" The anger was back in my voice, and tension rose in my chest. "I'm not a crime scene technician!"

Blythe narrowed her eyes warningly. "Then move on to the next lead. And do it quickly."

"When there could be better leads at the suspect's hideout?" I flared, shoving out of my chair. I smacked my palms down on her desk. "You gave us this case and told us it's *so* important, but you've hamstrung us from the start. What's more important, catching this guy or keeping secrets? What are you hiding, Captain?"

Her iron stare bored holes straight through my skull. "Because, Agent Morris, if you don't keep this case a secret, you'll never save that boy or find his kidnapper. There's an information leak in this precinct, and it's connected with the Ghost—or his impersonator."

I stood rock still for a second, then dropped back into my chair. Captain Blythe was no stranger to grandiose ominous statements that made my blood run cold, but this one was on a whole new level.

"An information leak?" Lienna repeated, gripping the edges of her seat. "From our precinct?"

Blythe nodded curtly. "So far, I've only confirmed it exists. I don't know where it's coming from, what the mole has access to, or how many people are involved. But there's a reason we've never come close to catching the Ghost after eight years of felonies."

"No one came close until *Shane*," Lienna gasped. "Because he performs all his investigations in complete secrecy."

"Precisely. Shane pinned the Ghost down with a combat team the day before Varvara's death. It was the first time the Ghost came close to arrest."

I frowned. "I don't remember hearing about that."

"It was never reported." Blythe arched a cool eyebrow. "Reports about the Ghost seem to disappear, but I know it happened outside the Crow and Hammer."

My jaw tightened. Darius, that evasive silver fox. No way he didn't know the Ghost had escaped arrest on his guild's doorstep.

Lienna pressed her fingertips to her temples. "Okay, but the kidnapper—Varvara's lieutenant—has been hiding behind the Ghost's reputation. Is the mole in the precinct protecting the real Ghost, or protecting Varvara's lieutenant by ensuring the Ghost can continue to be his shield?"

"An important question, Agent Shen. One we have no way to answer until you capture one or both of the Ghosts."

"What about the mole?" I asked. "It could be anyone."

Lienna nodded her agreement. I could see the gears turning in her head, and if I knew her half as well as I thought I did, the very notion of someone trying to corrupt the forces of law and order was an unforgivable sin. I was still pretty new to this whole "serve and protect" business and even I was rocked by the revelation that someone here was leaking MagiPol secrets and protecting a child abductor.

"The mole could be anyone," my partner repeated. "Including us. How do you know you can trust us? I mean ..."

She glanced uncomfortably at me.

"I used to work for a criminal organization," I finished for her, reminding myself that she was questioning why Blythe trusted me, not questioning my trustworthiness. "How do you know I'm not—I'm definitely not, for the record—but how do you know I'm not a mole?"

A dry smirk pulled at the corner of the captain's mouth. "Because I got to you first."

"Say what?"

"I'll worry about the mole," she continued, her expression flattening in a way that promised zero mercy for the traitor. "Agent Shen, see if you can get inside that briefcase. Use whatever means necessary, but under no circumstances are either of you to consult another living soul for any reason, is that clear?"

We both nodded, although I knew I'd be breaking that order the instant I heard from our mysterious druid ally again—assuming he hadn't vanished permanently into the ether.

The captain stood up, selected a seemingly random stack of folders from her desk, and hoisted them into her arms. "Go home. Start fresh in the morning. And Agent Morris, change your shirt. You look ridiculous."

15

I DIDN'T WANT TO GO HOME. I wanted to stay up all night, all day, all week if that's what it took to find Daniel and the other kidnapped kids.

But according to Lienna, getting sleep was an order straight from the mouth of our demanding boss, and Blythe's orders were always to be followed and, in Lienna's book, without question. So, we crammed ourselves back into the smart car and headed for my apartment.

"I'll take the briefcase home," she told me as we drove up the ramp out of the parking garage. "I can try some spells there, but there are a lot of runes I don't recognize. Might need to do some research."

I nodded absently, my mind elsewhere. "Who do you think it could be?"

"The mole? I have no idea. Neither of us has worked here long enough to even guess."

"What about that Internal Affairs guy? Söze? Who the hell was he?"

"I don't know much about Internal Affairs. They usually only show up when there's trouble." She wrinkled her nose in distaste. "Maybe someone higher up has caught on to the mole in our precinct, and they sent Söze to sniff them out."

"Then why would Captain Blythe hide our investigation from him?" I slumped back in my seat. "If only we'd caught that kidnapping bastard at his hideout. We'd have all the answers we need."

"Maybe, maybe not."

I canted my head toward her. Streetlamps shone through the car's windows, flashing across her face. "Meaning what?"

She hesitated, her lips thinning. "The information leaks help Zak more than the kidnapper. There's a good chance he's the one who bought or blackmailed an agent."

I scoffed. "Zak's been on the MPD's radar for eight years. Do you think he, all by himself and only eighteen years old at best, bought a mole in the MPD? Compare that to Varvara, who had a whole network of criminal lieutenants running million-dollar businesses for her. Who seems more likely to have bought a mole?"

"Varvara," Lienna admitted. "But we can't be sure. Our safest option—safest for us *and* Daniel—is to avoid Zak and arrest him if we run into him again. He helped us find the kidnapper's lair, but there's nothing more we can get from him."

"You don't know that. Maybe he already caught the kidnapper and saved Daniel."

"Then our suspect is dead." She gripped the steering wheel. "We can't trust anyone, Kit."

"What about our boss? Do you trust her?"

Lienna's eyebrows popped up. "Captain Blythe?"

"Think about it," I said. "No one else has made a peep about information leaks. What if it's a cover story to keep us isolated from the whole department and manipulate us into doing exactly what she wants, totally off the radar? What if she's the mole, and that Internal Affairs agent is here to investigate *her*?"

"Now you're really sounding paranoid, Kit."

"What about Shane Davila?" I plowed on. "You can't tell me that Muppet in human skin didn't give you the heebie-jeebies. He's an unguilded bounty hunter who was given special access to the farm crime scene by none other than Blythe. Then somehow, without explanation, she got access to his entire investigation after he left. Can't you admit there's at least a teensy-weensy possibility that she's corrupt?"

"No, I can't." Lienna pulled the car over to the curb and hit the brake hard enough to jerk me against my seat belt.

I peered out the window at the old, squat brick building beside me. A rusty fire escape clung desperately to its side and crumbling stonework made up its foundation.

Welcome home, Agent Morris.

I opened the car door. "I'll see you in the morning. Keep me posted on how it goes with the briefcase."

"Yeah," she muttered, not looking at me.

I closed the door, and the smart car peeled away. She hadn't even given me a chance to get my garment bag from the back.

Up in my single bedroom, I switched into a t-shirt that actually fit me, dropped onto my bed, and stared at the ceiling. My brain buzzed, exhausted and wired at the same time. How was it not even midnight yet?

Talk about a rollercoaster day. Starting with chasing down Faustus, then confronting Brad at the flea market, then preparing to infiltrate a high-end casino. Finding out there were two Ghosts. Fighting a druid, then teaming up with that same druid. Discovering the abandoned train tunnel, finding our kidnapping victim, then losing him again. And now we'd learned there was a leak in the MPD.

And through it all, my partnership with Lienna had deteriorated faster than the water pipes in my apartment building.

First my interrogation techniques. Then admitting a few sordid details of my past as a con artist. Then my truce with Zak. Then my anger over her refusal to cooperate with him. And the final straw, my questioning our boss's integrity.

I sat up, restless with anger and anxiety. It was like we couldn't understand each other at all. I got that Zak's very existence went against everything she believed in, but we were trying to save a kid's life. Wasn't that more important? Bending—or breaking—a few rules wasn't the end of the world, especially when no one got hurt. We had to rescue Daniel, and—

My mental tirade screeched to a stop, and I replayed my last thought: *breaking a few rules wasn't a big deal if no one got hurt.*

That line of reasoning echoed the philosophy of Lienna's father. Papa Shen had a sporadic habit of letting non-violent criminals escape justice in exchange for substantial bribes, and Lienna had stumbled across that truth less than a year ago. It had destroyed her bond with her dad and driven her two thousand kilometers north to escape it.

Groaning, I flopped back down on my bed. Of course Lienna wouldn't tolerate cutting any corners in an investigation. She was desperate to prove she wasn't like her dad.

But she had to know I wasn't like her dad either, right? I wasn't cheating the system for personal gain.

Time slipped away as I vacillated between guilt for forcing Lienna into an ethically compromising situation reminiscent of her painful past with her father, and resentment that she was painting me with the same brush. She knew me better than that, right?

Oh wait, she didn't. She'd said as much herself.

My aching eyes peered at the alarm clock on my dresser: 1:10 a.m. Oh good, I'd only spent an hour and a half wallowing. My mind was churning too hard to sleep, so I grabbed my laptop, sat up on my bed, and flipped it open. Maybe some good ol' fashioned detective work would straighten my brain out. And by that, I meant creeping through the social media profiles of the Ghost's victims.

I had tried to link the victims to no avail, but since meeting Zak, I now knew we had not one batch of victims, but three: the kids Zak had claimed responsibility for, Varvara's human trafficking targets, and the Fake Ghost's contract abductions.

Of the latter, I knew there were four—Daniel and Filip, who'd been abducted after Varvara's death, and the two other adults, Mercury Tibayan and Soraya Sadeghi. Let's start with Daniel.

I punched his name into Facebook's search bar, hoping beyond hope that a profile picture resembling him would miraculously emerge. Did kids even use Facebook nowadays?

The search results poured in: hundreds of photos from just the Vancouver area. Why did Daniel have such a popular name? Why couldn't he have been named Garfield or Almond or something?

This was going nowhere.

I spent the next half hour scrolling through unhelpful photos, then tried Filip and the other two adults. I found their Facebook pages, but I couldn't glean a hell of a lot. They were just average folks with average jobs living average lives. Their Facebook posts, for obvious reasons, didn't even reveal they were mythics.

Filip was a banker, Mercury was a young mage in the IAE who'd been in Vancouver on a business trip when she'd vanished, and Soraya was the GM of Cantrix, an Arcana guild so small I'd never heard about it until I'd read her victim profile. None of them were powerful politicians or serial killers or celebrities with a sordid past. Who'd pay to have them kidnapped?

Staring at the harsh white light of my laptop screen was giving me a headache. I rubbed my eyes and moaned softly. As I blinked away the dull pain, my bedroom door creaked.

I froze, my heart rate accelerating like Danica Patrick toward the checkered flag.

My door slowly drifted open about a foot and a half, then stopped, as though it'd moved with a change in air pressure or some other innocuous phenomena. Except it'd never once done that before, and I always shut it tightly.

As alarm detonated in my nervous system, I forced myself to take a slow breath. There were no heads peeking into my room, no shadows, no muffled footsteps outside the door. Maybe it was nothing.

But why take chances?

I concocted a Split Kit warp, making my real self invisible. Fake-Kit got up from the bed with a confused frown and approached the door. He swung a warped version of the door wide open, looked around for a reason why it'd moved on its own, then shrugged and headed for the communal bathroom I shared with three other bachelors. On his way out, he swung the warped door back into the same position as the real one.

A moment of silent stillness, then the real door closed of its own accord.

As soon as the latch clicked, the spot in front of it shimmered. A man in a long black coat with the hood drawn up appeared like a highly realistic hallucination.

But I didn't hallucinate. I gave other people hallucinations.

The Ghost lookalike wasn't Zak—I'd spent enough time with the real-deal hunk to tell this dude's shoulders were lacking in muscular breadth—meaning Daniel's kidnapper was paying me a nighttime visit.

He scanned my room, hooded head turning right past me, then reached for the desk where my modest collection of books and movies lived. He dug through them, looking for something, but unless that something was a collector's edition of Christopher Nolan's *Interstellar* or a scratched *Firefly* DVD, he'd be disappointed.

But how the hell had he appeared in my room? Who, other than yours truly, could make themselves entirely invisible? Was this phony phantom also a psycho warper? That would be some *Magnolia*-level coincidence at play.

He moved silently and quickly through the shelf, then turned toward the closet, his hooded face sweeping past the bed where I sat, invisible.

Fake Ghost paused, facing me, silent and unmoving. I could feel his gaze. It was like he somehow suspected I was there—but my Split Kit warps had never failed me before. At least, not until my last confrontation with this same asshole.

Before he could make his move, I dropped my invisibility, revealing myself sitting up on my bed, back to the wall. Only now I was holding a gun and it was pointed straight at his chest.

He recoiled from my sudden appearance, his hood falling off with the motion. For a moment, I glimpsed a bland male face, then his skin brightened like an overexposed photo, washing out his features until I couldn't be sure what I'd seen.

Okay, that was weird.

"Ah," he murmured. "Agent Kit Morris. Nice to see you again."

Not only did he know where I lived, but he also knew my name.

"The pleasure's not mine," I retorted, staring at his mind-bogglingly featureless face. "Back up, turn around, and put your hands against the wall. Quickly. My trigger finger's getting antsy."

The single overhead light in my room flickered.

"You cannot shoot me with a gun that isn't real, Agent Morris."

Son of a bitch.

I remained stone still, trying not to show how flustered I felt. He hadn't been sure I was sitting on the bed, but he sounded really damn sure my gun was a fake. How could he tell it was a psycho warp? My options were to keep pretending, or warp the fake gun into reality. And the latter wasn't an option.

My bedroom light kept flickering, adding annoyance to my already heart-attack-inducing tension levels. This freaky dude seemed to have that effect everywhere he went. The chandelier at the casino, the LEDs in the underground train station, and now the light in my bedroom. What was it with this guy and lights?

As I stared at his overexposed face, the only possible explanation hit me like a slap to the face—and I realized how he was seeing through my warps.

"Why are you creeping around my bedroom, you depraved waste of oxygen?" I sneered, hiding my shocked consternation.

"You have something that belongs to me."

"Your sense of human decency?"

"My briefcase."

"Tell me where Daniel is and I'll tell you where your case is."

He reached under his coat, and his hand reappeared holding a long, thin knife that glowed like white-hot iron. "I suggest you cooperate before I take more drastic measures."

Who brought a knife to a magic fight? What a dick.

I let go of the gun warp since it wasn't fooling him. "I don't have your case. It's evidence in my investigation, so it's sitting pretty under the lock and key of the MPD."

"I'm not inclined to believe you, Agent Morris."

"Where do you think I'd hide it?" I asked rhetorically, gesturing around my room.

He leaned back and took in the totality of my living space. "What a miserable existence. Can I assume your partner lives in better conditions?"

I gritted my teeth. His implication was clear as day: if I didn't have his precious briefcase, maybe Lienna did. And he'd go after her next.

"She doesn't have it either." Keeping my eyes on his knife, I leered like a villain. "By the way, did you check for the *real* Ghost on your way in here?"

Little psycho warper me might not frighten this guy, but the mere threat of Zak had an instant effect—the kidnapper looked sharply at my bedroom door as though it might burst open, an enraged druid on the other side.

I lashed out with my foot. It connected with his wrist, knocking the knife from his grip. As it clattered toward the doorway, I rolled forward and tackled him around the waist.

We crashed against the wall and slammed into the floor—him on top of me. He grabbed my throat with both hands and squeezed with every ounce of finger strength he possessed.

Within a single frantic beat of my heart, my vision dimmed. He wasn't just choking me—his grip was cutting off the blood supply to my brain.

Before I could pass out, I wound up and punched him in the lower ribs. He grunted, but the strangulation didn't relent. So, I punched again. And again. My eyesight was becoming one of those old-timey movies with the overblown vignette shadowing the edges, darkening toward a pinhole.

One more punch and his grip on my throat gave way. I gasped for air and drove my left elbow up under his chin. His head snapped back, and I pushed his weight off me, then rolled over and scrambled for the knife, desperately drawing every molecule of oxygen I could into my lungs.

He pounced on me, dropping his knee into my kidney. A sickening pain roiled through my body, but I shoved it aside and flipped onto my back, throwing another punch into his bruised ribs. He grunted, and I threw him off with a twist of my hips.

The lights in my bedroom continued to flicker, but that didn't matter. I wasn't warping. I wasn't playing mind games.

I was going to pulverize this asshole's face.

But first, I had to get my hands on the only weapon in the room. I lunged toward the door where the knife lay. My fingers wrapped around the hilt—and a blaze of pain exploded through my right leg, just above the knee.

Gasping, I reached instinctively for the spot. My fumbling fingers hit something hard and my vision went white with agony.

A rough hand shoved my back into the wall beside the door. The kidnapper's whited-out face appeared in front of mine as he grabbed the knife I held. His fingers crushed mine.

The muffled sound of a door slamming leaked through the walls. The kidnapper's head jerked up.

"He's here!" I bellowed at the top of my lungs. "Ghost, he's here!"

Hissing, the kidnapper slammed me into the wall again—and darkness plunged over the room, so deep and impenetrable I might have gone blind.

Or had I?

His hands vanished, and a second later, the door beside me clacked, then slammed shut.

My vision popped back in, the overhead light glowing nice and steady.

Panting, I looked down at my leg. Another knife, identical to the one I was holding, was embedded in my thigh. Blood leaked around the wound, staining my jeans.

I swore breathlessly. My hand shook as I reached for the hilt and carefully curled my fingers around it. Even the slight jostling of the blade sent agony tearing through the wound. Scrunching up my whole face, I yanked the blade out.

A strangled cry scraped my throat. Wet blood pooled in the puncture wound and a trickle spilled down the side of my jeans. Next time I saw that bastard, I would give him a few stab wounds of his own.

A sudden hammering on my door made me jump. Fresh torment burned through my leg, and I sagged back against the wall.

"Hey," the nasal voice of a fellow tenant of this shithole called through the thin wood. "Were you shouting?"

"Just stubbed my toe," I called back, straining to sound natural.

"Oh, okay." Quiet footsteps retreated from my door.

I squeezed my eyes shut, concentrating on breathing. Shouting for Zak to rescue me had saved my life. Was that ironic or just pathetic? I hadn't done it because I'd thought he was nearby but because the mere implication that he might be had been enough to spook the Fake Ghost.

Someday, it'd be nice if I could intimidate people like that.

I limped to my bed and found my cell phone on my pillow. Dialing, I put it on speakerphone and grabbed the nearest article of clothing. Lienna picked up as I was tearing my Canucks t-shirt into strips.

"If you're asking about the briefcase," she said in greeting, "I haven't figured anything out yet. I need more time."

"You don't have *any* time," I told her through gritted teeth as I knotted the first strip of fabric around my thigh.

"What do you mean?"

"You need to take the briefcase and get out of your house, right now. He's coming for you."

16

I WOULDN'T RISK LIENNA crossing paths with that stabtastic suck bucket, so instead of asking her to pick me up, I told her I'd be waiting at a park a couple of blocks from my apartment. Unfortunately, that meant I had to walk there.

What was normally a ten-minute trek took me closer to twenty with all the limping and stopping to wallow in pain. I sagged onto a bench, panting and unsteady, and set my backpack next to me. I'd packed some essentials before leaving my apartment, not knowing how long it'd be until I could safely return.

I checked my leg. Blood had soaked through my makeshift bandage, yet somehow my gory state hadn't turned any heads in the post-midnight throng staggering down Granville Street. Tough crowd.

Barely a minute after I'd sat down, Smart Car III squealed to a halt at the curb a dozen yards away. Lienna jumped out and rushed over to me. Concern broke across her eyes when she saw my blood-stained jeans.

"Oh my god, Kit. Are you okay?"

"Yeah, totally." I winced as I stood to greet her. "Well, no. I got stabbed in the leg, so I've been better."

She ducked against my side and pulled my arm over her shoulders to support me. I didn't really need it, but I wasn't about to tell her that.

"We need to get you to a healer," she said, tugging me gently toward the car.

"Backpack," I said, nodding toward it. "And we need to talk to Blythe first."

She reached back and snagged my backpack without leaving my side. "You've been *stabbed*. Blythe can wait."

"I don't think she can. The Fake Ghost knows my name and where I live. I'm pretty sure he knows where you live, too. Or he could find out if he wanted to. You have the briefcase, right?"

"In the car."

She helped me limp to the passenger door and climb in. The black case sat on the floor at my feet.

Lienna got into the driver's seat. "It's possible he could've followed you home, but if he also knows your name, then …"

"He's getting information from inside the MPD," I concluded as the car pulled away from the curb. "And he thought I had his briefcase, which could mean someone at the precinct told him we were carrying it around."

Someone who'd seen me with it a few hours ago. We'd just narrowed our suspect pool by half.

Her lips pressed together. "You're right. Blythe needs to know."

I called Blythe, and she informed me she'd meet us at the precinct. I was a little hurt she didn't ask if I was okay when I told her I'd need a healer as well.

Fifteen minutes later, Lienna and I walked into Blythe's office yet again—or rather, Lienna walked and I limped. Blythe's eyebrows rose at the sight of my bloody thigh. She looked the same as she had when we'd last parted, her blond hair smooth and her crisp white blouse unwrinkled.

"Do you need to see the healer first, Agent Morris?" she asked without preamble.

"I haven't bled out yet." I sank into the chair with a flinch, my leg stretched out in front of me. "I should be good for a few more minutes."

"Then report."

"The Fake Ghost broke into my room to search for the briefcase. He knew my name and that I'm an agent. When I didn't have his case, he implied that Lienna must have it and he knew where to find her. We fought and he escaped."

Blythe's jaw flexed. "He knew your name?"

"Yes, ma'am. I think he got my name and address from someone here who saw me with the briefcase."

Blythe glanced at the briefcase Lienna had carried into the office. "Have you made any progress breaking that open?"

"Not yet."

Leaning forward, Blythe entwined her hands, resting them on the desktop. "Then where are we at, agents?"

"Almost everyone has gone home now," Lienna said quickly. "Let me take the case down to my lab. If I can get it open, we might find out who, or at least what, this guy is. A grimoire would tell us—"

"It won't be a grimoire," I interrupted.

She and Blythe looked at me, one curious and one impatient.

"He uses artifacts and potions, but I don't think he's an Arcana mythic." I exhaled. "He's a luminamage."

The rarest type of Elementaria mythic: a light mage.

Silence settled over the office as my revelation sank in. Lienna's eyes narrowed with thought, while Blythe's whole body locked down like a marble statue, motionless and impenetrable.

"He's sneaky about it," I said quietly. "The first time we encountered him, the room went dark right before he escaped. Second time, the lights went out again when he attacked us, and he vanished with Daniel even though there was nowhere to hide. And when he broke into my room, he was invisible at first. He used light to hide his face, and when he escaped, he blinded me."

Luminamages had the ability to increase, decrease, and bend light at will. They could plunge rooms into darkness, bend all the light away from someone's eyes to blind them, or bend light around people or objects to make them invisible—*real* invisibility, not my hallucinatory version.

"Shit," Lienna muttered. "How did I not guess that?"

"Because he didn't want us to," I said. "It's all part of his subterfuge. He uses potions and artifacts like the Ghost so no one will realize he's a different person. He keeps his real powers hidden."

"They're his secret trump card. You can't defend against his powers if you don't know to expect them."

"Exactly. He's even been using his lumina magic to see through my warps. That's why my abilities have been so ineffective against him."

The flickering lights—that was his anti-Kit technique. I couldn't match my warps to the rapidly changing light conditions, allowing him to see through them. Though that didn't explain how he'd detected me while I was invisible, before messing with the lights.

Lienna sat forward, excitement overtaking her expression. "But now we know one of his secrets! Luminamages are rare. We can look up all the luminamages, registered and rogue, in the Vancouver area, and—"

"That won't be necessary."

Lienna and I swung our attention back to the captain.

"There's only one luminamage in the greater Vancouver area." A strangely manic grin pulled at Blythe's mouth, baring her teeth. "In fact, there's only one in a three-hundred-mile radius."

"Who?" I asked, oddly nervous.

Blythe pulled her desk phone closer, hit a speed-dial button, and lifted the receiver. She pressed it to her ear, still grinning like the Cheshire Cat.

"Agent Harris," she barked into the phone. "Get dressed and get to the precinct. Tonight is the night."

Uh. What?

Her eyes gleamed with exultant victory. "We're taking down Darius King once and for all."

THE MPD'S HEALTH BENEFITS included a dental plan, didn't it? Because the way I was clenching my teeth tonight, I would need one.

On the plus side, my leg was healed. On the downside, the time I'd spent with Scooter getting the wound disinfected, stitched closed, then magically healed had wasted precious time in which I could've been arguing with Blythe.

Not that she would've listened.

"Listen up," she called, striding the length of the bullpen. She'd swapped her usual business slacks and white blouse for fitted leather and a protective vest, and the dozen agents facing her, including me and Lienna, were also decked out in our combat-gear best. The sealed briefcase sat on the floor between me and my partner.

"Our target tonight is Darius King, guild master of the Crow and Hammer." She paced past her line of MagiPol soldiers. "Or as most of you know him, the Mage Assassin."

I started. Did she just say *assassin?* Well, that explained the uneasy feeling he'd inspired in me during our few interactions. He definitely exuded a "you don't wanna turn your back on me" energy, underlined by a "because I might stab you in the kidney if you do" energy.

"He's more than just a thorn in our sides," Blythe continued, a manic fire burning in her blue eyes. "His guild is a haven for rogues and ex-cons. He protects criminals, hides crimes, and abuses every loophole in the system. He has connections in the highest and lowest places, and up until this point, he's proven to be untouchable."

She whipped toward the line of agents. "But not anymore! We have proof that he's responsible for a series of reprehensible capital crimes—crimes which will be revealed in due course, *after* he's in custody and can't weasel out of them yet again."

In the center of the lineup, Agent Harris cracked his knuckles like a mob bruiser about to lay a beatdown on a snitch. His grin had the same rabid mood as Blythe's.

"Darius King is a former assassin and a luminamage. He's highly trained, exceptionally skilled, and unerringly lethal." Blythe smacked her fist against her palm. "So no mistakes tonight! We go in fast and silent and take him down before he knows we're there."

Agent Harris stepped out of the line to face the rest of us. "Agent Tim has already scoped Darius's residence and confirmed he's at home. He should be sleeping. This will be a no-knock, no-warrant raid. We'll be using two points of entry—the front and back doors. Captain Blythe's team will take the front, with Morris covering the door. My team will take the rear, with Shen on the door there."

Leaving the rookies to guard the doors. I was super okay with that. I didn't want to be leading the charge into the home of an assassin who could make himself invisible.

"Our primary objective is to apprehend the target," Blythe revealed, taking over from Agent Harris. "Use whatever force is necessary, but capturing him alive is a priority. Expect resistance. If things get messy, our strategy is to defend and move Agent Cornwall close enough to use a holding spell."

"Are we expecting he'll be asleep in his bedroom?" Agent Nader asked.

"Yes, and that's our first point of attack. Second floor, room at the end of the hall."

My eyebrows shot up so fast they almost launched into orbit. "You know where his bedroom is? *How?*"

If the look she fired at me had been a bullet, it'd have gone right through me, several walls, and knocked the engine out of someone's car in the parking lot.

"This mission is *absconditum esto*," she said without otherwise acknowledging my interjection. Grabbing a canvas bag hanging over a nearby cubicle wall, she held it open in front of the team. "That means no phones, pagers, tablets, or laptops."

I checked the hairlines of each team member, assuming none of them were gray enough to still use a pager—right up until Agent Harris yanked one off his belt and tossed it in with his phone.

As our teammates dumped their devices into the bag, Lienna dutifully slid her cell phone in as well. Blythe swiveled toward me, bag outstretched and her expression uncompromisingly expectant.

I got her reasoning. Someone in this precinct was leaking information to the luminamage kidnapper. She couldn't risk the mole finding out about this sting operation.

"Come on, Kit," Lienna muttered out of the corner of her mouth.

Grimacing, I slid my cell from my pocket and added it to the collection.

"Good," the captain said, closing the bag. "Let's go hunting."

Despite the groupthink bravado and general tough-guy vibe of the team, I wasn't feeling ultra-confident as we headed for the parking garage. Sure, I had a protective vest, a gun that fired sleeping potions, a couple of potion vials on my belt, and a shielding artifact that doubled as a baton, but I'd only ever trained with these things. I'd never used them in a real-world raid.

And frankly, twelve on one weren't the best odds when the "one" in that equation was known as the Mage Assassin.

17

"THIS IS STUPID," I said the moment I shut the door of the smart car. "Like downright imbecilic."

Lienna cranked the ignition. "Blythe called our precinct's best agents. We can take him."

"I don't mean *that*. I mean going after Darius in the first place. He isn't the kidnapper."

"I get that you don't want it to be Darius, but it all fits." She reversed out of the parking spot and maneuvered the car behind the unmarked black van that held most of the team. "He's a luminamage, the only one in the city, *and* an assassin. His height and build are a match. He's an old pro at evading the MPD and his guild is full of problematic mythics just like him. Blythe even said his mage switches are daggers."

"Don't you think if an *assassin* had pulled his daggers on me, I'd have ended up with a blade through my eye socket and not my leg?" I shook my head. "Lots of people use daggers, and we already know our perp likes to copy other mythics to confuse his identity."

"Luminamages are *really* rare."

"That doesn't make it statistically impossible that more than one could live in a city of over two million people."

"But not likely." She clutched the steering wheel as we zoomed along the abandoned downtown streets, dawn still a few hours away. "You said he hid his face. Why do that unless you would recognize him?"

"To make sure I couldn't identify him later? I don't know, but he *wasn't* Darius. I've met Darius. He has a completely different aura."

She puffed out a breath. "We still have to rule him out. Why are you so against this? If Darius is the kidnapper, then we've got him, and we can rescue Daniel tonight."

"And if he isn't, then we've wasted time and resources invading the home of an innocent man."

"Darius King is not an innocent man."

"So Blythe keeps saying, but if she spent half the energy she's wasting on this raid on following a useful lead, our investigation would've been over yesterday."

"A useful lead like what?"

I jerked my thumb over my shoulder, indicating the briefcase on the backseat, sitting beside my backpack. "We could focus on the luminamage's briefcase, which he wants back very badly. Or—and this is crazy, I know—we could focus on the *victims*. You know, the boy named Daniel who's been in that lunatic's care for almost forty-eight hours."

Her scowl deepened at my sarcasm. "What do you want me to do, Kit? Tell Blythe she's dead wrong and wasting her time?"

"Yeah, that's exactly what I think you should do. It's what I did."

"Look how much that accomplished," she snapped. "There's no changing her mind. She's convinced it's Darius."

"And you're just going to go along with it?" I shot back. "Pretend you don't realize this is Blythe's revenge fantasy playing out and she's letting a personal grudge derail our investigation?"

"*You're* just going along with it!"

"Because *you* are! What am I supposed to do without you?"

"You didn't need my support when you were making deals with Zak."

I clenched my jaw. "I can't break into that briefcase. You can."

"And I will as soon as we're done with this."

How long would that be? An hour? Two, three, four before Blythe was done tearing Darius's home apart in search of evidence that wasn't there? Would she even let Lienna take the briefcase down to her lab, or would she toss it in an evidence locker and set us on some other stupid, pointless task?

Our argument petered out as Lienna pulled Smart Car III onto Prior Street, a skinny tree-lined road with single-family homes on both sides. The MPD van pulled over in front of a family-sized SUV, and Lienna parked in the space between them. With any other human-sized vehicle, it would have been a tight squeeze, but since we were driving a car designed for hamsters, it fit in with plenty of room.

She cut the engine. "Look, Kit. I know you think this is the wrong course, but Captain Blythe is our superior. We'll see this through, then we'll focus on the briefcase."

She knew I was right about Darius—and she was still backing this short-sighted shitshow of a raid because Captain Blythe was demanding it.

I stared through the windshield. "I don't like following orders I know are wrong."

"That's part of the job!" She smacked her palms on the steering wheel. "If we don't follow orders, if we don't obey the rules, then we're no better than the criminals we're trying to stop. The law is the law, and no one is above it, even if they don't like it. That includes us."

"But not Blythe?"

Her lips tightened. "Blythe might be partly motivated by her personal opinion of Darius, but she also has a lot of evidence. The only thing she's ignoring is your *equally* personal opinion."

I said nothing. In front of our car, agents in black were unloading from the van.

"It would be irresponsible not to follow up on Darius's possible involvement in this case," she added, a note of desperation in her voice.

"But that doesn't matter," I told her. "Even if Blythe had shit evidence, you'd still do what she says because you follow orders, and you follow rules, and you follow laws, no matter what else is going on."

And I don't.

She turned in her seat, her dark eyes pained as they met mine. "If we pick and choose what orders and rules and laws to follow, then what are we, Kit?"

Pushing her door open, she climbed out. The door closed behind her with a *thunk*.

I stayed where I was, watching through the windshield as she joined the other agents. They milled about, waiting for something before moving on Darius's residence several houses down.

What are we, Kit?

I dug my knuckles in my temples as though that would clear the confused fog from my head—then jolted at a sudden vibration in the vicinity of my ass cheek. My phone was *zng-znging* at me.

Yes, my phone. The one I *hadn't* dropped into Blythe's bag back at the precinct. I'd handed over a fake warp phone instead.

I fished it out, keeping it on my lap so no one would see the glow of the screen through the car's windows. The unfamiliar number gave me pause, but I hit the answer button anyway. "Hello?"

"Where is the briefcase?"

Ah, I'd recognize that delightfully raspy voice anywhere. "Hey, Zak. How'd you get my number?"

I definitely hadn't swapped contact info with him, and the fact that the Ghost could come up with my phone number on short notice concerned me.

"Do you have it?" he asked, ignoring my question. Big surprise.

Twisting in my seat, I grabbed the case and hauled it into the front of the car. "Got it right here."

"Where are you?"

"Ten feet away from an MPD raid team." I put the briefcase on the driver's seat and fished around in my many belt and vest pockets. "I'm surprised you called. I expected you to be more of a short-and-sweet texting guy."

"Texting takes too long," he replied impatiently.

"Hm." With a jangle, I pulled my handcuffs from a pocket. "I like texting. I'm far more eloquent in the written word, like a digital age poet."

"Sure you are, Shakespeare. Now tell me where to find you."

That was the second time he'd called me that. He was tiptoeing dangerously close to official nickname territory. Were we becoming friends?

"Where are *you*?" I asked, flipping the cuffs open. I clipped one side around the handle of the briefcase. "I take it hunting down the luminamage didn't pan out, on account of him stabbing me in my bedroom a couple of hours ago."

"Luminamage?"

So much for stab-wound sympathy from my new bestie. "Yeah, he's a light wizard. Captain Blythe thinks he's Darius King."

"She's wrong."

"Preaching to the choir, bud. But she's got a serious hate-boner for him, so we're about two minutes away from SWAT-teaming through his front door."

"You're wasting your time. Bring me the briefcase so I can end this."

Through the windshield, Blythe was angrily beckoning me to join the team. Beside her, Lienna watched me with a stony expression.

I let out a long breath. The last thing I wanted to do was unite with the no-knock incursion groupies in their self-righteous vigilante roleplay exercise. But stealing an invaluable piece of evidence and handing it over to a rogue druid who was promising to use it to murder a suspect in my kidnapping investigation wasn't appetizing either.

"I don't suppose you've got any information on Daniel," I queried. "Or Filip. Or any of the other victims."

"Bring me the briefcase and I'll tell you what I learned."

My eyes widened—then widened further as Blythe marched toward the car, looking more pissed off with every step.

"Can't right now," I said, trying not to move my mouth. "I'll call you back."

I disconnected the call without waiting for a farewell—unlikely as that'd have been—and stuffed my phone in my pocket just as Blythe yanked the door open.

I gave her a humorless smile. "Was I speeding, officer?"

"You're delaying the operation, Morris," she snapped. "What are you waiting for?"

"Conviction."

Okay, so I probably shouldn't have said that.

Hastily ducking away from her murderous glower, I took hold of the handcuffs I'd attached to the briefcase and clipped the other end around the car's steering wheel. That'd delay any would-be thieves, and from my assigned doorman position, I could keep an eye on the car during the raid.

I climbed out, reluctantly facing Blythe.

"Conviction," she repeated in a tone equivalent to a black mamba's venom. "Let me give you some, then, Agent Morris. Darius King wasn't merely an assassin. He was an MPD-contracted special agent who carried out highly classified, highly sensitive assignments—until he turned rogue, murdered six members of the supreme judiciary court, and walked away like he'd done nothing."

I stared at her. "How did he get away with a crime like that?"

"No evidence. Not even Shane Davila could build a case against him." Her lips curled furiously. "Whatever he pretends to be, he's a rogue and a traitor, and tonight he will face justice. Is *that* enough conviction for you, Agent Morris?"

"Yes, ma'am." Not like I could say anything else.

"Then move your ass," she barked, turning on her heel and marching back toward the van.

Wow, I was even *more* excited now. Time to assault a former assassin who used to work for the MPD. No way this could go wrong.

Falling into line with my team, I followed close behind as we swarmed silently toward a two-story sandstone house on the north side of Prior Street. It looked like it'd been built in the forties but was well taken care of, with a short stone wall lining the perimeter of the property.

So, this was where the most hated guild master in all of Vancouver slept at night.

Captain Blythe made an aggressive beeline for the light wooden door that served as the front entrance, tucked back on a cute little porch. While Agent Harris rushed his team around to the side of the house, Blythe disabled the front door's lock with a potion reminiscent of Zak's melt-everything liquid. She burst inside. The rest of the team followed her up the stairs toward the bedroom that our captain was apparently quite familiar with.

I halted in the doorway, then backed out onto the porch. I stood there for a second, listening to the shuffle of Agent Harris's team reaching the stairs, then swung myself up onto the porch railing. I sat on it, dangling my combat boots over a winter-bare shrub a few feet below.

A former MPD-contracted special agent would have the connections to buy or blackmail an informant in the precinct, but that didn't mean he was the kidnapper. We had zero hard evidence that linked Darius to the kidnappings, the Ghost, Varvara, Daniel's abduction, or anything else. Whatever he'd done in the past was just that: the past.

It didn't take long for the commotion of the raid team to echo back outside. A door slammed and something crashed. Not exactly stealthy.

"This is so stupid," I muttered to myself.

"I'm pleased to hear you say that."

My head jerked to the side as a man faded into view beside me: around fifty years old, tall and trim, with well-groomed salt-and-pepper hair and a short, matching beard.

The Crow and Hammer's wily silver fox leaned back against the railing, arms folded as he gazed through his open front door, listening to the frenetic MPD team tearing his home apart.

18

"YOU DON'T SEEM SURPRISED to see us." I gestured at his tidy forest-green sweater and black slacks. "Or do you keep late hours?"

Darius didn't answer. He was studying me with unusual intensity, a slight crease between his eyebrows.

"Can you tell?" I asked after a moment.

"That something isn't as it seems? Yes." He smiled faintly. "But I'm not sure what, which is rather unusual."

"You aren't the only one with a trick or two up his sleeve," I replied with a smirk, and in the same way he'd faded into sight, I faded out—or rather, the fake-Kit who'd been sitting on the railing faded away.

Slow tension, a readiness to act, slid through the former assassin.

I faded in again, still sitting on the rail but facing the house instead of the front yard. Swinging my feet, I arched an eyebrow in silent question. That little experiment had just confirmed my theory that something about my usual Split Kit warp didn't fool a luminamage's senses.

The very dangerous man a few feet away raised an eyebrow in turn. I was tempted to ask about the whole "MPD-special-agent-turned-traitor" thing Blythe had mentioned, but on second thought, that seemed like a bad idea.

Our tense, silent moment broke with the unmistakable sound of glass shattering from inside the house.

Darius glanced at the open door. "To what do I owe the pleasure of the MPD's late-night visit?"

"They think you're a kidnapper," I replied.

"But you don't?"

"I've met the kidnapper. He's a luminamage, but he isn't you."

"Can I assume Aurelia heard the word 'luminamage' and immediately decided I was to blame?"

Aurelia? Oh yeah, this guy and the captain had a history—a personal one—if he could use her first name that casually.

"Pretty much," I confirmed. A deep bang—probably a piece of furniture being overturned—sounded from the second floor. "I don't suppose you've got a rock-solid alibi for Friday morning and yesterday evening?"

"I was at my guild on Friday morning, and yesterday evening I was part of a dinner meeting with the guild masters of the Pandora Knights, Sea Devils, and Odin's Eye. Our reservation at The Darjeeling Grill was at six and I left around eight."

If Darius was telling the truth, he couldn't have kidnapped Daniel, nor could he have been at the casino or the underground station. That would definitively absolve him in the eyes of anyone who could spare a moment to think objectively.

He glanced at the second-floor window as an especially loud crash echoed down. "That sounded like my antique standing mirror."

I tried not to visibly seethe over the stupidity of the raid. "Bad luck for you that the real perp is also a luminamage."

"It seems so. Do you have a better lead?"

"Maybe, if I could get anyone else to focus on it."

Well, *Zak* was focused on it, but that was a whole other can of worms. Then again, the briefcase wasn't my only lead.

"Say, Darius. What does an officer at M&L, a young mage in the IAE, the GM of a tiny guild called Cantrix, and a teen boy visiting Arcana Historia have in common?"

"Is that a rhetorical question, or am I supposed to guess?"

"Guess, because I don't know the answer either."

He stroked his beard thoughtfully. "Cantrix is an Arcana guild, as is Arcana Historia. An officer and a GM are both part of their guild leadership teams. The mage … hmm. Are these victims of the luminamage kidnapper?"

"Yeah."

"Do they have names?"

"Filip Shelton, Mercury Tibayan, Soraya Sadeghi, and Daniel. I don't know his last name."

Darius nodded, staring at nothing while the demolition of his home serenaded us. The agents inside called to each other, their frustration at not finding their target growing. It wouldn't be long before they came outside to check if he'd escaped.

"I think you may need to look less at who the victims are and more at what they were doing." Pushing off the rail, Darius turned to face me. "I don't know about the other two, but Filip and Soraya have something in common."

"What?"

Agent Harris shouted about checking the basement. They were almost done, and Darius realized it as well.

"Look up the Complexor Bylaw," he said, stepping back. "I'm afraid that's all the help I can offer."

"That's okay. You've been a big help in more ways than one."

"Oh?"

I grinned. "You sure everything is *as it seems?*"

His eyes narrowed at the way I'd echoed his earlier phrasing. He studied me intently, then surprise flickered across his features.

My grin widened as my second fake-Kit faded away. The real me—actually real this time—appeared beside the door I was supposed to be guarding, facing the street so I could keep an eye on the smart car and its invaluable contents.

"So," I said, "the second one was more convincing?"

"Significantly," Darius replied. He seemed amused, but a shiver ran down my spine at the sharp glint in his eyes. "Did you just use me as a luminamage guinea pig to test your technique?"

"Hope you don't mind."

"Not at all, Agent Morris. I'm always pleased to see what my fellow mythics are capable of."

That nervous shiver doubled. "Thanks for the tip on the bylaw. I'll look it up."

"Do that." He offered his hand.

Only after I'd grasped his warm palm did I realize his motive. He wanted to confirm this version of me was real. I'd tested my ability to fool a luminamage, and now he was testing his ability to detect my warps. How much did he know about my magic?

"Ground floor is clear!" Agent Harris yelled from the kitchen.

Another voice called back, "Basement's clear, too!"

"Where the hell is he?" Blythe's voice rang with fury. "Did he escape? Agent Shen! Agent Morris! Get in here!"

Darius raised an eyebrow at me. "You should rejoin your team."

"No one came through the back." Lienna's voice floated out. "Did anyone check for a panic room?"

Why the hell would she suggest that? Did she *want* to spend the next hour scouring the house for hidden doors? Even though she seemed to agree with me that this suspect—and this lead—was a dead end, she was still treating it as legit. Still wasting time.

Well, I was done wasting time.

I pulled my hand from Darius's. "I actually have something else I need to do."

"Morris!" Blythe yelled more loudly. "Agent Harris, find him."

"Good luck, Agent Morris," Darius murmured.

"Yeah, you too."

With that, the luminamage assassin vanished from where he stood—and so did I.

Invisi-bomb in full effect, I waited as Harris burst through the open door. Lienna came out on his heels, and as she passed me, I lifted her car keys from her pocket. She didn't notice. Pickpocketing wasn't a skill I needed all that often, but I'd learned it well.

"Morris!" Agent Harris bellowed, looking around for me.

"Kit?" Lienna called anxiously.

Ignoring a stab of guilt, I slipped past her and hastened down the porch steps. She'd be fine. She wanted to investigate Darius like Blythe had ordered, so she could do that. And I'd borrow the car to pursue a different lead.

As I strode down Prior Street toward the waiting smart car, I pulled out my cell phone, found the last number that had called me, and sent a short text.

```
Meet me in thirty minutes at the same place
as last time.
```

I watched the message pop into the brand-new chat, then typed four more words and hit send again.

```
I'm bringing the briefcase.
```

ABANDONING MY ASSIGNMENT, bailing on my partner, swiping important evidence, and stealing an MPD vehicle.

Yeah, I was gonna be in trouble.

It was after 4:30 a.m. when I parked across from the under-construction apartment building where Lienna and I had met Zak yesterday. Briefcase in one hand and my backpack in the other, I trudged tiredly past the security fence, using the same gap as last time, and pushed through the door.

Though it was unlocked, I didn't see any lurking druids in the shadowy interior. Mind you, with the luminamage hiding in the light and Zak hiding in the dark, this building could be teeming with sketchy mythics and I might never know.

Switching on the work light beside the big planning table, I changed out of my combat gear and into my far comfier civvies, then slid up on top of the flimsy surface, taking the weight off my healed but aching leg. Leaning back against the wall with the briefcase tucked under my arm, I closed my eyes to rest them.

I sank instantly into a dream wherein a handsome, raven-haired man beckoned me into a dark room. He opened a locked cabinet, eerily similar to the one we'd found in the abandoned train station, revealing an astonishing array of bondage equipment. Except, instead of leather and chains, every piece was made of … cheese.

"Fifty shades of gruyere," I whispered in awe.

The man fondled a mozzarella-based whip. "I have some very specific feta-shes."

Good god, between the stress of the investigation, sleep deprivation, lying about sex toys, and the fact I hadn't eaten in far too long, my mind was a swirling mess of strangeness.

A gust of cold wind roused me from the brie-lliant dream, and I opened my eyes as a hooded, black-clad figure strode toward me.

I pulled the potion gun from the holster on my belt and leveled it at him. "Hood off."

He pushed his hood back, revealing Zak's unimpressed but impossibly vivid green eyes. "Can't recognize me?"

"That luminamage bastard has a thing for imitating people." I holstered the gun. "You're late."

"Where's your partner?"

Right on cue, my phone buzzed against my butt cheek.

"Raiding Darius King's house," I replied, pulling out my phone to find Lienna's name filling the screen. Looked like she was in possession of her cell phone again. "Make that 'back at the precinct.'"

The druid cocked an eyebrow. "Does she know you're here?"

I powered down my phone, cutting it off in mid *bzzz*. "No."

Zak moved closer, his attention shifting to the briefcase. "Reconsidering your employment?"

"Also no." Pocketing my phone, I slid off the table and pulled the briefcase with me. "I just want to catch this SOB and save Daniel."

"You should reconsider. The only thing you'll get from following orders is a shitty pension or a death certificate."

Why did he sound so certain about that? How much did he know about the MPD? I didn't think he was responsible for the information leak in my precinct—the luminamage kidnapper showing up at my apartment knowing my name strongly suggested he was the one with an inside contact—but Zak had inexplicably come up with my phone number.

Putting that worry out of my mind to fret about later, I jiggled the unopenable black case. "So what's the plan?"

"You give me the briefcase."

He reached for it, but I scooted backward.

"What are you going to do with it?" I asked.

He took another half step toward me. "Break it open, use whatever is inside to find the luminamage, then kill him."

I took another step back and bumped the table. "Then I'm doing all that with you."

"You're going to give me the briefcase and then you're going to walk away."

"And never see you or the briefcase again? Not happening." I dropped my free hand to the pistol in my holster. "You let me do this with you, or you don't do it at all."

Zak's eyes narrowed. "You can't stop me."

"Maybe not. But I can make things interesting."

He considered my threat, then took a long, deeply annoyed breath. "Fine. But don't expect me to protect you."

I created a Split-Kit warp and let the fake version of myself continue to stand there with an equally fake replica of the briefcase, while the real me sidled out of firing range. I wasn't sure if Zak was making a return threat, but I wasn't taking any chances.

The druid didn't move, watching fake-Kit, and I wondered if I was fooling him.

The last time I'd used my warps on him, he'd said my shadows weren't convincing enough. That warning had stuck with me. Zak had his freaky fae shadow magic going on, and the luminamage had light-manipulation abilities—and my warps hadn't fooled either of them very well.

That was why I'd tested an improved Split Kit on Darius. My first fake-Kit had been the normal one, but my second had involved extra concentration on the play of light and shadow on and around the warp. I was using the new version now, and like Darius, Zak didn't seem to suspect it was fake.

A badass point for Morris, finally.

"What would I need protection from?" I had fake-Kit ask.

The door to the building clattered, then swung open, letting in another rush of cold air.

"You'll see," Zak muttered, turning toward the dark doorway.

A woman swept inside—and she was the most fantastical creature I'd ever seen.

19

"HOW DISAPPOINTING!" the woman announced loudly. "I expected to meet the Ghost alone."

The heels of her knee-height leather boots clicked as she strode toward us. Inside the boots were tucked a pair of brown pants, tapered at the bottom and billowing out into a puffy waistline. The pants were separated from a ruffly white blouse by a thick, tiger-striped belt. A floor-length, electric blue, faux fur coat hung off her shoulders, where a bright orange bob haircut capped off the look. She had a hot pink suitcase on wheels in tow, and a trio of reds completed the ensemble: rosy cheeks, scarlet lips, and crimson-rimmed cat-eye glasses.

She. Was. Fabulous.

She looked like a popstar pirate from another planet making a cameo in an edgy science fiction movie from the nineties.

"Alone!" she said with a click of her tongue at Zak. "I told you I'd meet you *alone*."

The druid crossed his arms. "I know what you said."

"I like to keep a low profile," the popstar pirate complained, then craned her head back in a loud laugh. "*Ha!* Who am I kidding? But meeting strange new men in the middle of the night in an abandoned building is not a thrill I'm interested in."

It looked like Zak had summoned her here, which meant it was in my best interest to reassure her I wasn't a threat. Except for one little problem. I was still warping a fake-Kit for the druid, and since I hadn't realized this woman was about to join us, she wasn't part of said warp. She could see the real me.

With a mental shrug, I let fake-Kit vanish. Zak started slightly, his head whipping toward the real me, then back to where the fake version had disappeared.

"I won't be any trouble," I said quickly, offering my hand to the woman. "My name is—"

"Call him Shakespeare," Zak interrupted. "You can call her Demi."

I perked up. "As in Demi Moore?"

"No," she replied with a cackle. "As in demolition."

I couldn't stop myself. "As in *Demolition Man*? Starring Sylvester Stallone, Wesley Snipes, and America's sweetheart, Sandra Bullock?"

"*No*, as in actual demolition. Do you even know why I'm here?"

I frowned. "Not really, but also, I don't think 'demi' is the root word of—"

"Such a depressing locale." She spun to take in the unfinished lobby. "Couldn't you have picked somewhere with a better mood?"

Zak gestured to me. "Give her the briefcase."

I hesitated as the myriad of ways this situation could backfire rushed through my brain. I didn't know this person from a hole in the ground, and if she was an associate of Zak, then it didn't matter how marvelous her outfit was—she was more than likely dangerous.

She swept over to me with a broad smile. "What briefcase, darling? And what's in it?"

I held it up to show her, the runes etched on it cast into stark relief by the work light. "I don't know. But I need to find out."

"Ooh!" she cooed with a shiver. "This is giving me chills. I love it! Hand it over and I'll bust this baby open."

This was what I'd come here to do, right? I mean, not *this* exactly. I hadn't expected to enlist the services of a cosmic buccaneer, but if she could open the briefcase, I had no reason to be reluctant.

I offered her the briefcase, which she gleefully snatched from my grip and held up to her face.

"Hoo-boy! This is going to be fun. I can't remember the last time I saw runes I didn't recognize."

"But you can open it, right?" I asked.

"The battle is the fun part. Not the victory." She dropped the briefcase onto the table, then lifted her suitcase up beside it. Twisting around, she looked at Zak over the top of her glasses. "My usual fee?"

The druid nodded. "I've already contacted them. You'll receive it as soon as you succeed in opening the case."

Contacted who? Receiving what?

The fur-coated lady unzipped her suitcase. She took off her glasses and replaced them with a pair of safety goggles, then grabbed two more pairs and tossed them to Zak and me. "Protect your peepers, boys."

Zak fastened his around his face and still managed to look hot as hell, while I stared at my pair, confused.

"Aren't you a thief?" I asked.

"Why?" Demi shot back as she dug through the suitcase. "Are you a cop?"

I made sure to keep my voice even as I replied, "No. I mean, aren't you a lock picker or something? What do we need safety goggles for?"

She pulled on a pair of rubber gloves and snapped them into place. "You don't want any shrapnel in those puppy-dog eyes."

"Woah, hold your detonators for a hot second. Just how committed to this demi-lition nickname are you?"

She gave me an impish smirk. Zak shrugged.

"You're not going to blow it up, are you?" I took a frantic step toward the table. "I need whatever's inside there intact."

"Don't worry, darling," she soothed as she selected a flat disc from her suitcase. It resembled a fridge magnet, but I suspected it was actually an arcane artifact. "First, I want to find out what this beauty's made of."

She placed the disc on the top of the briefcase, prodding it into place with her gloved fingers until it was roughly centered over the largest rune.

"*Ori dissolvo!*" she exclaimed with a dramatic finger waggle.

The disc sizzled, eating into the briefcase's exterior in a similar way to Zak's melter potion. Through the spitting steam, the rune beneath the artifact began to erode—then the artifact halted its sizzling as though someone had hit pause on its remote control. A thick red sheen of what could've been light or liquid flowed out from under the disc and coated the briefcase. It glowed for several seconds, then faded.

"Oh my. This is much weirder than I could've hoped for." Demi picked up her disc and looked it over. "That defensive spell disabled mine and restored the original seal at the same time. Never seen anything like it, but I'm thinking it's a form of abjuration. What do you think, Ghost?"

"Your guess is better than mine."

"Abjuration isn't really my style," she mused. "I prefer to jam a bomb inside it and pick through the pieces afterward."

I coughed slightly. "Do you think we could try a more delicate approach before we start chucking dynamite at it?"

Demi went elbow deep into her suitcase again. "Dynamite is lame. If I'm resorting to human tech, I'm using plastics."

Plastic explosives? My god, she really was *Demolition Man.* Or Rocket Raccoon. Or Danny McBride in *Tropic Thunder.*

"What else do you have?" Zak asked.

"Oh, darling," she replied with a condescending lip pout. "So many things."

As she sifted through her bag of explosive tricks, I sat down against a concrete wall a safe distance away. This would take a while.

Zak watched for a moment more—Demi had retrieved a squirt bottle and was covering the briefcase in a fine white mist—then joined me. He shrugged out of his long jacket, revealing a sleeveless black shirt, a collection of crystal artifacts hanging around his neck, and a heavy-duty alchemy combat belt.

Tossing his coat aside, he sank down beside me, all while I stared at him. Okay, yeah, I was slightly distracted by the pattern of black feathers tattooed down his bare arms—seriously, would tattoos make my biceps look that good?

Because our arms were similarly buff and I wasn't opposed to some tasteful ink.

But his godly figure aside, I was more intrigued by the bloodstained bandage wrapped around his right forearm from wrist to elbow. He started unwinding the gauze, and my frown deepened at the mixture of fresh red blood and darker, dried stains.

He peeled the last of the bandage off. The remnants of more tattoo work decorated the underside of his forearm, but it'd been ruined beyond recognition by deep scratches that marred his skin as though he'd been raked with a panther's claws. Messy stitches held the wounds closed.

"Holy shit," I muttered.

Tugging his safety goggles off, Zak examined the fresh blood trickling over his wrist. I, being a coward who didn't want chunks of exploded table in his eyeballs, left my goggles on.

"Sutures tore," he observed, then reached behind his back with his good hand and fumbled with something. A second later, he pulled a black leather pouch off his belt, unzipped it, and retrieved a pair of small, curved medical scissors. Without batting an eye, he poked them into the first scratch and started cutting the stitches.

Swallowing my stomach down, I picked up his pouch and peeked inside, finding an assortment of first aid supplies.

"What happened?" I asked, pulling out a tiny, unlabeled vial of purple liquid. "Did the luminamage do that to you?"

"No." More blood ran down his arm as he snipped the sutures. "This was Varvara's parting gift. She was wearing claw rings. Poisoned, of course."

"Do you need a healer?" I asked uncertainly.

"I need tweezers."

"Huh? Oh." I hastily replaced the potion in his bag and passed him a pair of shiny metal tweezers. "If you're poisoned, though, shouldn't you—"

"I'm an alchemist." He plucked the snipped bits of suture thread from his flesh, and I shuddered at the sight. "I know what poison she used. If it was going to kill me, I'd already be dead."

"But those wounds look bad."

"That's why I'm treating them again," he said in a "duh" tone of voice. "Pass me the dark orange potion."

While I played nurse for Zak, Demi carried on with the briefcase, gaining more excited energy with each new, destructive toy she could play with. As I handed Zak a vial of hot-sauce-colored goop, a series of sharp explosions startled me so badly I dropped it in his lap.

"What the hell was that?" I demanded.

Not even glancing Demi's way, he popped the cap off the vial.

I sagged back against the wall. "This was an awful idea. If I'd just done as I was told, I'd still have a job, and we'd have an equally good chance at opening the damn briefcase."

"Not equally," the druid corrected as he dribbled the potion over his wounds. "The MPD isn't known for innovative thinking."

I watched Demi apply a layer of glue to a pair of triangular pads and set them on either side of the briefcase. "Meaning what?"

Long white wires extended from each triangular pad, which Demi plugged into a handheld device with an enormous dial. Was she going to defibrillate the briefcase?

"Clear!" she yelled, punching a button on the device.

The briefcase hopped a couple of inches off the table and the red shield erupted around it.

Yes. Yes, she was.

Zak wiped the potion off his arm. "You'll find more talented mythics with unique skills hiding from the MPD than joining it. Give me the suture thread and needle."

I passed him both. "Are you going to give me a Darth Vader speech next? 'Give yourself to the power of the dark side. Join me and we can rule the galaxy.'"

Yeah, I was mixing and matching quotations, but I was too tired and frustrated to care. And he just ignored it anyway.

"How were you recruited?" he asked. "Blackmail or a plea bargain?"

My jaw clenched. Captain Blythe giving me the choice between a lifetime in jail or seven years of the MagiPol life probably counted as both. "Is that a common recruitment technique?"

"For powerful mythics they want to control?" He shrugged and threaded the curved suture needle.

Demi called out another warning and pressed the button. The briefcase leaped even higher into the air, but the result was the same.

"That's not me," I told him. "I'm not powerful. My magic is basically hallucinations. I can't blow things up or cast spells or make shields or—"

"Are you an idiot or just a fool?"

I scowled at him, but he was focused on his arm. With nary a flinch, he struck the needle into his wounded flesh.

He tugged the thread through his skin. "Why are you playing the MPD's game? Blackmail, plea bargain, whatever they pulled on you, there's nothing stopping you from breaking away now."

"I ..." My mouth bobbed in a very goldfish way. "I can't," I said lamely.

"You stole evidence and met a wanted rogue without the MPD having a clue where you went. Seems like you can do whatever you want."

My teeth ground against each other. Darth Vader wasn't supposed to be this persuasive. "It's not that simple."

Zak fixed me with a pointed stare. "I hope for your sake you aren't sticking around because of your partner."

"Of course not!"

He resumed stitching his arm. "You'll always be an ex-con to her."

My temper flared. "What would you know?"

"People like her don't know shit about what it takes to survive for people like us."

Like us. Did I have more in common with a murderous rogue like Zak than with my fellow MPD agents? Was that why all my decisions seemed to upset Lienna, even when they seemed so logical to me?

I pressed my lips together. "We aren't *that* similar, because last I checked, I strongly preferred saving kids to abducting them. And you still haven't explained what happened to the teens you *say* you didn't kidnap."

He canted his gaze toward me, then jabbed his arm with the needle again.

"I've been to your farm, Zak. I saw the house, the big kitchen, the bunk beds. You had the teens there, didn't you?" When he didn't reply, I leaned toward him. "I was a foster kid.

I could've been one of those teens you made vanish. I need to know."

With an irritated sigh, he drew the thread through his arm. "They're all fine. Better than they were when they came to me for help, so don't bother looking for them. They don't want to be found."

"You helped them?" I squinted at him. "I didn't realize the ruthless Ghost was a secret softie."

He snorted. "I've been killing since I was seventeen. I'm not soft and I'm no one's savior."

"Except to a bunch of homeless teens you saved."

"For selfish reasons."

"What selfish reasons?"

"None of your fucking business."

Okay, someone was done sharing. I still couldn't help but ask, "Who did you kill when you were seventeen?"

"My master, the druid who trained me. I spent over a year planning it, and the only thing I regret is not killing him sooner."

"Was he an epic shit-stain?"

"Understatement."

"Then I get it. I had a foster dad in that category." I hesitated. "But why keep killing after that?"

His green eyes turned to mine, and there was a brittle resignation in them. "Once he was dead, all the targets on his back shifted to mine. All his enemies wanted to rip me apart and all his former associates wanted to snuff me out. I kept killing to survive."

I let that sink in, feeling the weight of it. Could I have survived something like that? I doubted it.

"So you're right," he added, returning his attention to his gory sewing. "We aren't that alike."

I shrugged. "You can't be sure about that. For all you know, I could also suture my own arm while holding a casual conversation."

Zak let out a short laugh. "The disinfectant was also a numbing agent. I can't feel a thing."

I blinked. "You really aren't as much of a cold bastard as you act, are you?"

"It's all about appearances, Shakespeare. Scaring the shit out of people is one kind of shield. Acting like a harmless, dimwitted jokester is another."

My amusement faded, and our eyes met in mutual understanding. Neither of us was quite what he pretended to be.

He resumed sewing, and I watched him for a few minutes before asking, "Didn't you say you had information for me about the victims?"

"Not the victims. The kidnapper." Zak angled his arm toward the light, checking his work. "Knowing this guy has been doing solo work gave me a better idea on where, who, and how to ask about him."

"And?"

"My sources say his name is Radomir Kozlov. He headed all Varvara's operations in Bucharest before coming with her to North America fifteen years ago. Guess they couldn't bear to be apart."

"How sweet."

"Here, he acted as her righthand man, running things when she was gone and handling whatever issues came up. Someone suggested he was angling to step into her role, and that might be why he was taking jobs on the side—building up his cash reserves for the inevitable takeover."

"Takeover? So not a 'peaceful retirement' sort of leadership change?"

"Not in a business like hers."

Musing over that information, I watched Zak sew up the rest of his arm, then helped him bandage it with fresh gauze. Just as I was knotting it around his wrist, Demi strode over to us, hands on her hips.

"I'm running low on gunpowder, boys," she declared. "I wasn't kidding about those plastics, but they'd take the building down too, so we might be SOL."

No way. We couldn't be shit out of luck, or any other form of non-excrement lucklessness, because I'd risked everything to bring the case here. I'd betrayed Lienna's trust, invited Blythe's wrath, jeopardized my job, and gambled my entire future to open that case.

It couldn't end here. I wouldn't let it.

20

I SHOVED TO MY FEET, wincing at the stiffness in my thigh, and tugged off my safety goggles as I faced Demi. "We can't quit."

Still seated on the floor and surrounded by bloody medical tools, Zak stretched his newly repaired arm out and slowly closed his hand into a fist. "Giving up, Demi? I thought you wanted to get paid."

She ran her fingers through her orange hair. "I did pick up something new that might work, but it'll cost you extra."

Grabbing his coat, Zak pushed to his feet. "I arranged your payment already."

Demi went back to her suitcase and lifted out a weird black orb. "This is a new and expensive artifact and the refills are pricey as hell. If you want me to use it, you're gonna have to pay for the premium package, darling."

He pulled his coat on and tugged it straight. "I'm not asking them for anything beyond your usual fee."

I didn't want to know what—or who—they were talking about. Whatever "fee" Zak had arranged for her services was likely something I, as an MPD agent, was better off not knowing.

Demi blew air noisily through her lips. "Then you'll have to sweeten the pot with something different. What else you got, Ghost?"

"Nothing, which is what you'll get if that case is still sealed when you walk away."

Her eyes narrowed dangerously behind her safety goggles. "I'd rather cut my losses now. We're done."

With that, she turned back to the table and started packing up her supplies. Alarm cut through me, and I whipped toward Zak.

"You're letting her leave?" I hissed. "That briefcase is our best lead!"

"I know other people. I'll try someone else."

"Just pay her more!"

"Not worth it."

Giving up on Zak, I hurried to Demi. "Do you know why we need to get into that briefcase so badly?"

"That's none of her damn business," Zak growled.

"He's right." Demi stuffed the defibrillator back in her suitcase. "People don't pay me to ask questions. In fact, I'm paid *not* to."

That made sense, but I plowed on anyway. "That case belongs to a man who's been kidnapping kids. He snatched a boy named Daniel two days ago. If we don't find him soon—"

She waved her hand as though to shut me up. "That's terrible and all, but I've had my heartstrings tugged on too many times, darling. I don't do charity work."

Turning to her suitcase, she scooped up her squirt bottle. Desperate and furious, I grabbed the sleeve of her fur coat to stop her.

She spun ferociously toward me, and something sliced my hand.

I jerked back, staring in surprise at a long, thin line of blood welling up on my palm—then I saw why. Her soft blue jacket had morphed into an armored trench coat, replete with a thousand spikes in place of the fur. The ends glowed like vicious Christmas lights. She looked like a porcupine-human hybrid from five hundred years in the future. Or Sonic the Hedgehog from an evil parallel universe.

"Don't you *dare* touch me again!" she raged, her voice dropping into a hoarse bellow. She stepped threateningly toward me. "If you think you can coerce me into doing what you want, you've got fewer brain cells between your ears than you have hairs on your prepubescent balls."

Message received.

But also, *not* received, because I needed her to open the briefcase. I held my hands up placatingly. "I'm not trying to force you. I'm trying to save a kid's life, and—"

"And that's your cute little sob story, which I can't verify and wouldn't bother to if I could," she snarled. "I don't care."

She didn't care.

No one cared. Not Blythe. Not Zak. Not Lienna. They didn't care about Daniel or the other kids—at least, not enough. I was the only one fighting with everything I had for this boy.

And I wasn't giving up.

I dropped an invisi-warp on both her and Zak's minds, then retreated behind the druid. If nothing else, he could take a magical porcupine quill to the face for being an unhelpful jackass.

The demolition master looked around wildly at my disappearance.

"Look, Demi," I said, warping my voice into a deep reverberation so she couldn't pinpoint my location. "I don't want to do this, but I need your help, and I'll do whatever it takes to save those kids."

The glowing ends of her spiky coat grew brighter and, unless my mind was playing tricks on me, the spikes grew longer.

"Careful, Kit," Zak muttered.

Did he know I was behind him, using him as a shield?

A spike popped off Demi's left shoulder and fired diagonally like an arrow, embedding into the steel beam overhead. "Give me a good reason, or even a bad one, and I'll rain hell down on this whole room. It won't matter where you're hiding."

Holy exploding sea urchin, Batman.

"Do you think that porcupine coat can stop me?" I boomed. "You have no idea what you're up against."

With my words, shapes began to move in the darkness beyond the reach of the work light. Humanoid forms drifted into view, shadows dripping off them like inky fog. Tattered black clothes fluttered with their movements, their faces drawn and pale, and red eyes glowing in their sunken sockets.

Demi's head jerked side to side as she took in the bloodthirsty creatures circling her. "Those—those aren't real."

"Are you sure?" Fake-Kit reappeared in front of her, in the same spot where I'd vanished. "Are you ... really ... sure?"

As he spoke, he pulled his lips back to show his teeth. His canines elongated into fangs.

Demi clenched her hands into fists. "You have to the count of five before I make you regret the moment you met me."

The other specters opened their mouths, baring matching fangs, and shuffled closer, closing their ring around her.

Fake-Kit continued to give her a horrifying smile. "Just agree to open the case, Demi."

"Five," she snarled.

"Do you think your coat can save you?" Fake-Kit asked, his voice going hoarse and guttural. His skin paled and sank into his face until he was as gaunt as the other creatures.

"Four!"

"Kit," Zak rumbled in an undertone heavy with warning.

I steeled myself. I'd do what I had to. I'd scared Faustus and Brad into cooperating, and I could scare Demi too—even if I felt way shittier about it.

Vampire Kit's eyes glowed red. "You're not leaving until you open the case."

As the softly moaning horde drew close around her, she flung her arms out. A dozen spikes from her coat fired straight through the Creature Feature warp.

"They aren't real!" she shrieked. "They aren't—"

I added the feel of cold, icy hands gripping her arms.

She gasped and jerked away. The vampires reached for her from all sides and a sharp cry escaped her as she spun in a panicked circle. Three more quills shot off her coat, one spearing the ground inches from Zak's feet.

"*Kit*," he growled.

"Two!" Demi yelled shrilly.

"You missed 'three,'" I muttered to myself, then had Vampire Kit hiss, "Last chance, Demi."

The cold hands returned, squeezing her wrists, and when she twisted away, the phantom hands clung to her. Panic flared in her eyes. Her hand plunged into her coat for another weapon. "One, you bastard!"

I sucked in a breath of concentration as the vampire horde crouched to pounce at her—and Zak pivoted on his heel.

His palm hit my sternum hard enough to knock the air from my lungs. I slammed down on my back as all my warps vanished.

Zak half turned toward Demi. "I'll double your fee."

A muscle under her eye twitched. "Triple for not stopping that asshole pal of yours sooner."

"Double," he repeated. "I'll contact them later today."

"*Hmph.*" She puffed out a few breaths, then her spiky jacket collapsed back into a non-glowing fur coat. "Your word better be good, Ghost."

"Have I ever gone back on my word before?"

Demi cocked an eyebrow at me where I lay on the ground, wheezing from the blow to the chest. "No, but I've never seen you work with anyone else either. You might want to find a more respectful partner, darling."

As she returned to the table and the waiting briefcase, Zak reached down and grabbed the front of my jacket. He hauled me onto my feet, then pulled my face close to his.

"I did that for two reasons," he snarled quietly. "First, I wasn't about to die for your idiocy. And second, I asked her here, and I neither assault nor allow my associates to be assaulted in front of me."

I gritted my teeth. "Why didn't you just agree to her price in the first place?"

"Because it's a fucking steep price, you single-minded moron. But you're going to make it worth it. You owe me, and when I come calling, you'll deliver, no questions asked."

"Fine," I snapped, then added, "As long as it's within reason."

"Oh no." His eyes gleamed dangerously. "If you wanted a say, you shouldn't have turned a business transaction into a power play when you weren't the most powerful player in the room."

I wrenched away from his hold and dropped back onto my heels. He swiveled to face Demi, and we watched her set up a metal tripod in terse silence. She kept shooting wary glances my way, as though checking I was still standing there like a normal, nonaggressive psycho.

"Does the MPD know the scope of your abilities?" Zak asked in a low rumble.

"Some of it. Not all."

"A word of advice, then." A green glare slashed toward me. "Never let them find out."

He turned away from me and Demi. While she completed her setup, he cleaned the medical tools he'd used, repacked his first aid pouch, and poured a potion on his bloody bandages that dissolved them into a grayish smear on the concrete floor. Well, that was one way to ensure you didn't leave DNA evidence behind.

Fifteen minutes later, Demi had the briefcase strapped to the top of the tripod, with five black orbs levitating around it. On the face of the briefcase, she had carefully drawn a rune in white marker, copying it from a notebook.

She directed Zak and me to hunker down behind a pillar, flipped to another page in her notebook, then called out an incantation. All five orbs burst, releasing a pitch-black fog that formed a dark sphere around the briefcase. Through the mist, I saw the red shield erupt, but Demi was already chanting a second incantation.

The rune she'd drawn exploded into a hot white flame, igniting the black fog, and the whole thing went up like the pyrotechnics at a Slayer concert.

As the smoke cleared, the three of us cautiously approached the tripod. I half expected there to be nothing left but ash. However, the briefcase looked no worse for wear with two notable exceptions: the runes were gone, and a pair of small latches had appeared on either side of the handle.

I warily tapped a latch with one finger. Rather than being scalding hot from the fireball, it was cool to the touch. I flipped them both up and the inner locks released with a soft click.

"Holy shit," I whispered. "It worked."

And I lifted the top of the briefcase, revealing its well-guarded contents.

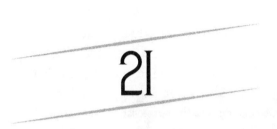

21

ONCE DEMI HAD THREATENED Zak with impalement if he didn't
deliver on her doubled fee, she packed up her suitcase and left,
heels fading away into the early morning light.

And that left the pair of us with the briefcase and its ultra-
precious, extra-protected contents: three books as decipherable
as the Voynich manuscript.

Zak homed in on the biggest, oldest-looking book. The
cover was made of scarlet leather with a gold inscription
written in a language I didn't recognize. He opened it and
hungrily flipped through the pages.

"Can you read that?" I asked, picking up the second book: a
spiral-bound notebook you could get at any office supply store.

"It's a grimoire."

Oh shit. So when I'd told Captain Blythe and Lienna that
there wouldn't be a grimoire in the case because its owner was
a mage, I'd been dead wrong. Whoops.

"*Her* grimoire," he added.

"You mean Varvara? Okay, my new theory is the briefcase belonged to her and Radomir inherited it after you killed her."

Zak nodded distractedly, focused on the book that likely contained every spell and magical secret the evil dark-arts master had known. It was exactly what you'd expect to find in a magic-proof briefcase.

I peered over his shoulder as he turned pages. The lettering was utterly unfamiliar to me, and it was accompanied by some truly baffling illustrations, ranging from impressionistic renderings of plants and fae creatures, to a landscape drawing of a mountain range, to diagrams of the constellations. He stopped on a version of da Vinci's *Vitruvian Man* with a whole bunch of extra circles, the page marked by a torn scrap of paper with incomprehensible notes and several math equations scribbled on it.

The spiral-bound notebook I'd picked up seemed to be a ledger. It was full of numbers and codes, some of which looked like dollar amounts but could have been ISBNs or zip codes for all I knew. The last item in the briefcase was a small flip pad, its contents written in the same incomprehensible code.

"Are you getting anything out of that?" I asked Zak as he continued to peruse the grimoire's pages. "Do you even know what language that is?"

"Something old and Cyrillic."

"You can read it?"

"I can read the notes she wrote in modern Russian, but not the rest."

I tossed the ledger and flip pad in the briefcase and rubbed my eyes, hoping to mash energy back into my skull. "All that and we can't even read anything. This was a massive, stupid waste of time."

Without looking up from the grimoire, Zak said, "We opened the briefcase."

"But we can't do anything with it!"

"I'll find a translator."

"No."

That single syllable of defiance drew his gaze away from the cryptic pages. He fixed a stare on me that warned I should strongly consider retracting my refusal.

"I'm not turning this over to another one of your lunatic associates," I told him. "That eccentric bomb jockey was off her rocker. She could've killed us."

"You shouldn't have threatened her."

"I shouldn't have *had* to threaten her!" I shouted. "A boy's life is on the line. That should be enough for anyone whose moral compass doesn't point straight down into the murky pit of their charcoal soul!"

Maybe it was the sleep deprivation that had shortened my fuse. Or maybe it was because I felt like I was the only person on earth who gave a flying fuck about human life. Either way, I was nearing my boiling point.

"The grimoire is evidence," I said through clenched teeth, reaching for the book. "And I'm not letting you take it and disappear."

He lifted it away from me. "I'm not handing this over to the MPD."

"I'm not either. I'm going to hand it over to Lienna."

"Same thing."

I let out a dramatically exasperated groan. "I'm the MPD too, remember? But we're both working off the books on this case, so none of the evidence is going to the precinct."

"Is that supposed to convince me?"

"Okay, how about this?" I was talking with my hands in a Jack Sparrow kind of way. "Lienna Shen is the smartest, most skilled Arcana mythic I've ever met. She's only twenty-three and she's already a full-fledged abjuration sorceress. So unless you've got an Einsteinian codebreaker who specializes in ancient languages in your Rolodex of rogues, taking this stuff to her is our smartest move."

Zak gazed at me, probably assessing how much of that speech was genuine and how much was exhaustion-fueled mania.

Finally, he gave the slightest nod. "Call her."

Grumbling about how I didn't need his permission, I took out my phone and turned it back on. The device burst into a nonstop seizure of vibrations as all my missed notifications came through. Seven voicemails and twenty-eight unread texts. All from Lienna.

I didn't bother to listen to the handful of voicemails because scrolling through the messages gave me a pretty strong idea of what they would say. Her texted emotions fluctuated between concern for my well-being and homicidal rage, best summed up by her last message:

```
I really hope you're not dead so I CAN KILL
YOU.
```

With a deep, courage-fortifying breath, I composed my reply.

```
I'm alive. We opened the briefcase.
```

I hit send, not expecting an immediate response. She'd been up all night too, so she was likely sleeping—a thought that awoke deep-seated jealousy in my soul. But within twenty seconds, my phone dinged.

WE?!

Not "Thank god you're alive."
Not "You opened the briefcase? That's amazing!"
Not "It's a good thing you followed that lead because I was super wrong about trying to arrest Darius King."
Nope. Just a monosyllabic outburst about the fact I was with Zak and not her.
I wrote back:

I assume you want to see what's inside.
We're at the same place as before.

I assumed correctly. It took her less than half an hour to show up at the under-construction high rise.

She stormed through the entrance, a bright flash of early morning sunlight accompanying her before she slammed the door shut. She was still in her gear, and judging by the bags under her eyes, she'd been on the same sleep schedule as me.

Her burning glower swept the space, searching for a druid—who'd made himself scarce—then stuttered in confusion when she spotted the leftover quills from Demi's deadly coat embedded in various surfaces. Seemingly dismissing that mystery, her attention locked on me like a laser-guided missile.

"*What the hell, Kit?*" she yelled in greeting.

I barely managed not to flinch. "Hi. Do you want to see what we found?"

"Did you help Darius escape?"

"No," I said, not making the slightest attempt to mask my exasperation. "He didn't need any help. He was outside before we arrived."

"But you saw him. Did you have a nice little chat with our suspect while the rest of us were *doing our jobs?*"

"He isn't the kidnapper, and you know it."

She crossed her arms. "No, I don't, and neither do you."

"He has an alibi."

"So you *did* talk to him—then you let him escape," she summarized furiously.

"He was at a meeting with other guild masters when we saw the luminamage in the casino. It's not him—but until Blythe tells you otherwise, you'll think whatever she tells you to think, won't you?"

"Oh, and you're just *full* of independent thought," she shot back, fists clenched at her sides. "Playing into Zak's hands like a naïve fool. Delivering the briefcase right to him."

"I didn't—"

"But he's *so cool,*" she mocked, her voice shaking. "The dark, handsome rebel who does whatever he wants. Tell me, Kit. Which do you want more—to be his loyal little sidekick or to *become* him?"

My temper was scorching me with the urge to shout back at her. I blew out a breath as unsteady as her voice. "The only thing I want is to catch a bad guy and save a kid, Lienna. Why don't you get that?"

"Because that isn't what you're doing, not from where I'm standing."

"What am I doing, then?"

She opened her mouth but changed her mind about whatever she'd planned to say. She waved an arm jerkily. "Where's the briefcase? And where's Zak?"

"Right here."

She jumped half a foot and whirled around to find Zak behind her, looming like a murderous wraith of the night. He held the briefcase in one hand and the three items from inside it in the other.

Lienna glanced at the items, then spun back to me. "You gave our evidence to *him*?"

"Just in case," Zak rumbled, "you decided to bring an MPD team with you."

"Why would I do that?"

I waved at the items. "Lienna, can you please look at what we found?"

"Fine," she said, holding her hand out to Zak.

He passed her the three items.

"The big notebook is a ledger, I think," I told her as she carried them over to the table. "It's written in a shorthand that I haven't figured out yet, but I think it details all the deals the luminamage has made. His name is Radomir Kozlov, by the way."

"How do you know that?"

I glanced at Zak. "Uh …"

She gave me and the druid a deeply suspicious look, then opened the flip pad. "And this one?"

"A list, also in code."

"Hmm." Setting aside the flip pad, she studied the cover of the last book. "A grimoire? But he's a mage."

"It's not his," Zak said. "It's Varvara's."

Lienna opened the leather-bound book. "Varvara was Russian, right? The lettering looks Cyrillic."

"Yes," Zak confirmed. "But it isn't modern Russian."

"Likely the Early Cyrillic alphabet." She flipped some pages and landed on the bookmarked illustration that resembled the Vitruvian Man. She peered at the scribbles on the bookmark. "This looks much newer than the grimoire."

"That I can read," Zak said. "The notes are about lunar cycles for the array construction. Suggests the spell was built somewhat recently."

She moved the bookmark to study the page. "I can see some Latin in here too. The text is in a few different languages, which will make deciphering it that much harder."

"Can you crack it?" I asked. "Or do we need to call Tom Hanks?"

My partner and the druid looked at me blankly.

"*The Da Vinci Code*?" I prompted. "Do *either* of you watch movies?"

Zak shrugged one shoulder. "The only Tom Hanks movie I know is *Splash*."

"*Splash*," I repeated disbelievingly. "Why *Splash*? It was filmed before we were born. Do you have a thing for mermaids?"

"Have you ever seen a real mermaid?"

"Mermaids are real? Also, no."

"Good, because she'd probably be the last thing you ever saw." He looked back at Lienna. "Can you translate it?"

"If I had a few months, sure."

"Then you'd better get started," he suggested in a way that seemed more like a command.

Her nostrils flared with indignation. "Oh, you think so, do you?"

I closed my eyes and leaned against the table. "We don't have time for this."

"Radomir wants that briefcase back for a reason," Zak said. "And I doubt it's for his flip pad."

She shook the leather-bound book at him. "This thing won't lead us to him."

"It's more likely to help than raiding Darius King's house," Zak growled.

"Are you defending him?" she accused. "Is he one of your criminal allies?"

"I'd trust him before I'd trust you."

She squared up to him. "The feeling is mutual."

"How about you both trust me?" I half shouted at them. "I don't have an ulterior motive here. I'm just trying to save a poor kid's life! Isn't that worth trusting?"

Zak remained characteristically silent, but Lienna turned back to me with a deep frown and something pained in her gaze.

"I want to trust you, Kit," she said quietly. "But …"

"But what?" I gave her a hard look. "You don't know what I'm capable of, right?"

Confusion crinkled her forehead. "What are you talking about?"

"Before the casino," I reminded her, "you said you didn't know what I'm capable of."

"Not you. Your *magic*, Kit. The warps—"

"What does my magic have to do with anything?"

She drew herself up as though to unleash hell on me, then glanced at Zak, probably wishing he'd implode on the spot so she and I could talk without an audience.

"Your powers ..." She exhaled in a rush. "Kit, your powers are unlike anything I've ever seen, and I don't know what your limits are. Neither do you. It seems like every week you're doing things I thought were impossible. It's amazing, but it's also terrifying."

Terrifying? Was she talking to the right guy? The muscular, remorseless di-mythic druid with his arms folded watching us—that dude was terrifying. Not me.

"What scares me the most," she continued, struggling to keep her tone even, "is that *you* don't understand how frightening your magic is. *You* don't think it's powerful. You're like a kid running around with a bomb and no idea it might explode."

I shook my head. That didn't compute. "It's not a bomb. It's just a charade."

"That's what I'm talking about! You don't get it! You don't understand what it's like to be unable to trust your own mind. You think mages or sorcerers or"—she gestured at Zak—"are way more powerful, but I can fight them. I know how to defend myself against them. But how do I defend myself when my own mind is betraying me?"

"But I wouldn't ..." I trailed off, scrambling for the right words. I wouldn't what? Wouldn't use my warps on her? I'd manipulated her mind to steal her car keys mere hours ago. "I'm one of the good guys, Lienna. You know that, right?"

Her face twisted as though this conversation was physically painful. My gaze unintentionally darted away and landed on Zak.

I didn't know what I'd expected from him, but somber consideration wasn't it.

"'Good guys' and 'bad guys' is bullshit and you know it," he rumbled. "But she's not wrong about your magic."

An unpleasantly cold wave rippled through my innards. I should've been delighted that ultra-criminal Zak and super-agent Lienna agreed on something, but their consensus didn't fill me with joy.

I was powerful? My magic was frightening? Lienna was scared of me?

Zak crossed his arms. "Are you really just figuring this out now? You don't need firepower if your enemies are helpless against you. I haven't even seen everything you can do, and I can tell you that your old guild severely underutilized your power."

I didn't know how to respond, but Zak didn't seem to have anything else to add. He turned toward the table with the grimoire.

Lienna stepped toward me, searching my face. I had no idea what she was looking for.

"I'm not like him," I told her, unsure why that was the defense I'd uttered first. "I don't do things like him."

Except I'd done worse to Demi, and *he* was the one who'd stopped me.

"But you're starting to," Lienna whispered. "You allied with a murderer, abandoned me in the middle of a raid, stole evidence, and snuck away to join him."

"I only did those things to save—"

"To save Daniel, I know. And your magic keeps getting stronger and keeps getting us another step closer to saving him. But what if you start to see it like Zak does—like a tool to get whatever you want, no matter the cost?"

A gust of wind rustled a tarp on the side of the building. I stared at Lienna, mouth open, searching for a denial that wouldn't come. The ubiquitously feared Ghost used any means necessary to achieve his goals. Was I any different?

Based on the pattern of interrogation and intimidation I'd followed for the past two days, the answer was a definitive *no*.

But my goals were a hell of a lot different. Didn't that matter? He was trying to take a life and I was trying to save one. Couldn't Lienna see that?

"I'm worried about you, Kit," she said softly. "You don't see it, but you're going back—"

"Back to my criminal ways?" The painful uncertainty clogging my lungs flashed into burning anger. "You're right. I haven't changed a bit. This is *exactly* what I did before—risking everything to save a kid's life. Glad you noticed."

She recoiled from my venomous sarcasm.

Turning away, I strode to the table and grabbed my backpack. For a second, I met Zak's questioning gaze, the grimoire open in front of him.

I turned my back on him too. "I'm out of here."

"Where are you going?" Lienna asked, concern sharpening her voice.

"I don't know, but this thing—us—it doesn't work if we don't trust each other."

"You don't trust me either?"

My limbs spasmed oddly as her words cut me like a knife. This whole conversation had been leading to that inevitable point, but hearing her verbalize it stung worse than I'd anticipated.

I slung my backpack onto my shoulders. "Follow your leads. Figure out if the grimoire is important. Check Darius's alibi if you have to. I'm going to do what I have to do."

She followed me toward the exit, practically stepping on my heels. "And what is that?"

"Whatever it takes," I told her, looking over my shoulder as I threw the door open.

Her hand was stretched toward me, hovering in the air as though she was an instant from grabbing me and dragging me back inside—but she didn't. She just stood there, mouth trembling and face pale.

I walked through the door and out into the cold morning light. Alone.

22

"WHATEVER IT TAKES" absolutely needed to involve coffee unless I wanted to pass out on a sidewalk. So, I hopped back into my stolen smart car and drove a few blocks until I found a café brimming with early morning java fiends.

It was eight a.m. on Sunday and somehow these bean addicts were already up, dressed, and ready to seize the day. Trudging through the caffeinated crowd, I felt like a zombie— and not one of those speedy *28 Days Later* zombies, but the original *Dawn of the Dead* ones that moved like centenarians with arthritis in every joint of their bodies.

Reaching the front of the line, I kept my order succinct. "Two of your biggest coffees with a double shot of espresso in each."

"Anything else?" the perky barista asked.

"Whipped cream." I could use the sugar boost. Spotting a breakfast sandwich hiding behind the display next to me, I tapped a finger on the glass. "That bacon-looking thing, too."

The barista retrieved the sandwich for me. "Can I get a name for the coffee?"

"Kit."

"Kip?"

"*Kit.*"

"And for the other one?"

"Huh?" I squinted tiredly at her as she held a marker up to the second empty coffee cup. "Oh. Both for Kit."

The barista mouthed, "Wow," then dutifully scribbled my name on the second cup. "They'll call your name when it's ready."

I paid, collected my many ounces of joe, then found a relatively isolated table in the corner. After relishing the first hot sip sinking down into my chest, I pulled out my laptop, plugged it into an outlet under the table, and connected to the café's free Wi-Fi.

I still had a Facebook tab open on my browser, in which I'd been searching for Radomir's victims and coming up with a whole lot of nothing. But with no new leads, I started scrolling through Filip Shelton's recent posts. If our poisoned accountant woke up, I could question him, but that was assuming Blythe would let me anywhere near HQ. Maybe I'd have to sneak in, because what the hell else did I have at this point?

Filip, according to his limited social media profiles, was a single dude with an extensive pet fish collection. It was honestly a pretty cool aquarium setup, but it wasn't a clue.

I wrote down all his groups and interests, then moved on to Mercury, the IAE up-and-comer whose teardrop necklace we'd found Brad hocking. She mostly posted selfies with her friends and shared inspirational quotes.

Equally determined and desperate, I kept going, cross-referencing every detail I could glean from the victims' online presences, but they had nothing in common.

I leaned my head against the wall and closed my eyes, my hands shaking from the amount of caffeine I'd ingested.

My exhausted thoughts turned to Lienna. Where was she now? Had she rushed the contents of the briefcase straight to Blythe? Or had she stayed in the abandoned building to tackle the grimoire with Zak's help?

I let out a chuff of bitter laughter. Yeah, right. She'd probably bolted out of there the second I'd left so she wouldn't catch criminal cooties from the druid.

Although, that was assuming he would let her leave with the grimoire he wanted. I cracked my eyes open, worried about what had gone down between them without me there to play referee. Lienna might've picked a fight, but Zak wouldn't attack her out of the blue. The guy had standards.

Didn't he?

He'd stopped me from tormenting Demi. A murderous rogue had called *me* out for mistreating his associate. He might have been more motivated by preserving his business relationships than mercy, but it was still a line he didn't cross.

And I had—almost without hesitation.

Was I, as Lienna had implied, morphing into a warped version of the Ghost? Or something worse?

I could've tried harder to play on Demi's compassion. I could've negotiated with her, offered her a deal, promised her an IOU, anything. But I'd jumped straight to using my psycho warping to force her to do what I wanted. Just like with Faustus and Brad. My first instinct was to use "psychological torture," as Lienna had so poetically put it, rather than trying literally anything else first.

Bracing my elbows on the table, I dropped my face into my hands. No wonder she was freaked out. No wonder she was questioning if she really knew me and what I was capable of. What the hell had gotten into me? I wasn't a "force first" guy. With someone like that carnie who'd tried to turn me into Swiss cheese, yeah, I was going to defend myself. But that didn't apply to Faustus, Brad, or Demi.

And in a shock twist of *Sixth Sense* proportions, Zak and Lienna had agreed with each other on one very specific detail: even though I couldn't harm anyone physically, the power I had over people's minds was, allegedly, terrifying.

I slumped back, relaxing into the strange reclining position I'd wedged myself into. I'd promised Gillian, the kindest, humblest, most generous human I'd ever had the joy of knowing, that I wouldn't forget my compassion. I'd let her down again.

My increasingly depressing train of thought lost coherency as exhaustion took over, then derailed entirely into a burning wreckage of REM-induced abstraction. Although this time, my dreams lacked any sexy cheese closets. Thank Gouda.

A loud clatter shook me from my impromptu slumber. My mouth was dry, as it'd been hanging open while I'd dozed. From behind the counter, the barista was staring at me with disdain.

"Sorry," I said, not sure what I was apologizing for.

"You were snoring," she replied, then went back to grinding coffee beans.

The café was noticeably less busy and my laptop had also fallen asleep. I pulled out my phone to check the time. It was after one.

Holy shit. Had I passed out in a public café for four hours? I guess I'd needed that nap.

I shook off the remnants of my drowsiness, made a trip to the bathroom, then resettled in my spot and fired the computer back up, acutely aware that I needed a new approach. Cyber-stalking the victims wasn't working, and at this rate, I would've been better off accompanying Lienna to verify Darius's alibi.

Wait. Darius.

My brain fog vanished like a popped balloon. How could I have forgotten the clue he'd given me? The "Complexor Bylaw."

I logged into the MPD database and typed it into the search. A handful of results hit the screen, quickly informing me that the Complexor Bylaw wasn't actually a law—yet. A special interest group called CORPAC had proposed it, and if the new bylaw passed, it would restructure how guilds voted on mythic laws. Which scrambled my skull noodle for half a minute because guilds didn't vote on bylaws.

Laws were voted into being—or out of existence—by guild masters. Every GM got one vote on every law, and it was part of that "checks and balances" power dynamic between the MPD and guilds.

Bylaws, in contrast, were voted on by special MPD committees. There were global committees for all sorts of things, from magic secrecy to mythic registration to illegal magic to record-keeping for the mythic community.

I rubbed my forehead, then clicked on the second search result, which was an official protest document filed by a Vancouver-based group calling themselves MAC: *Mythics Against Complexor*. It was an open letter stating their belief that the proposed bylaw was undemocratic—not a word I was used to hearing in association with non-human politics.

According to them, this CORPAC group was exploiting a loophole by pushing through a bylaw that would change the GM-voting process without GMs having any say. Instead of each GM having one vote on every new law, GMs would be assigned multiple votes based on their guild's total number of members. More members would equal more votes.

If that happened, the votes of small guilds would cease to matter. A handful of the world's largest guilds would dominate votes and control which laws could be passed.

I skimmed the protest document down to the two hundred and fifty-four signatures that filled the last several pages of the document. And the first name, that of the "Founder of Mythics Against Complexor," jumped off the screen at me.

Filip Shelton.

Holy shit, holy shit, *holy shit*.

I got in one scroll before I screeched to a halt again. Two more familiar names stared back at me: Mercury Tibayan and Soraya Sadeghi. Radomir's two other adult victims.

Filip, Mercury, and Soraya were the driving forces behind the MAC group, the loudest voice opposing the Complexor Bylaw.

My fingers vibrated with excitement as I pieced it all together. I knew someone inside the MPD was feeding Radomir information, and up to this point, I'd assumed the light wizard was bribing or blackmailing his mole. But maybe—and this was the theory I now felt most strongly about—the MPD mole was a corrupt piece-of-shit agent who'd hired Radomir to kidnap specific people involved in fighting the Complexor Bylaw.

Sherlock Morris's deduction game was coming on strong.

But what about Daniel? No one named Daniel was among the long list of signatories, which made sense since it'd be odd for a teenager to sign such a document.

So how did he fit into the puzzle?

I kept digging through the search results, looking for more information about the bylaw. The most important detail I found was the day of the MPD committee's vote: Sunday, January 27. Aka *today*.

It was a global video call based out of New York and scheduled for 11:30 p.m. Eastern Time, which meant it was happening at 8:30 p.m. Vancouver time. Which was less than seven hours from now.

If Radomir's goal—or his employer's goal—was to change the outcome of that vote, he had seven hours to do it. He'd silenced Filip, Mercury, and Soraya, but who else might he target to sway the vote in his employer's favor?

Only one person in the city *really* mattered when it came to that vote: the Vancouver committee member. So, who was that?

Answer: Amy Buchanan.

I pulled up her profile on the MPD database and damn near jumped out of my chair. The only family member listed was a son. And that son's name was Daniel Buchanan.

I found the address of the Buchanan home, packed up my laptop, and darted from the café. As I was dumping my backpack on the smart car's passenger seat, my phone buzzed in my pocket. It was Lienna.

Flip-a-coin time: Was she worried or angry?

Climbing into the driver's seat, I lifted my phone to my ear. "Hey," I said, elaborately casual as I started the engine. "I'm driving right now. Sorry for the noise."

"Where are you going?"

"What are you working on?" I evaded, fairly certain she wouldn't approve of me dropping in unannounced on a victim's family.

"The grimoire," she answered slowly.

"Did you figure out anything?"

"Not yet."

She hadn't called just to give me a goose-egg non-update on the briefcase's contents, had she? A painfully awkward silence filled the line.

I cleared my throat. "What about Darius's alibi?"

"Yeah, it checks out," she admitted.

I swallowed back an "I told you so."

"I ..." She trailed off, then started again in a more businesslike tone. "I got a call from a librarian at Arcana Historia. Someone's been doing research on an abjuration spell and she thought I could help."

"Do you think it has something to do with the kidnappings?"

"No, but it made me think I should take the grimoire to the library and see what I can figure out. Would you ... do you want to meet me there?"

She was inviting me to join her? It felt like an olive branch, but a dried-out one that needed watering.

"I translated that bookmark with notes about lunar cycles," she added, irrigating said olive branch. "The lunar phases and calculations match up with astral positioning from December. I think that spell was recently constructed."

"Did Zak help you with that?" I asked hopefully.

"No. When I wouldn't give him the grimoire, he took off. That was just after you left."

He took off? Just like that? Hmm.

"My meeting's at seven," she continued, "but I'm heading there now to start working on that recently used spell. Meet me there?"

"I'm following up on something else."

"Another lead?" she queried, her voice perking up with interest.

"I'll let you know if it turns into anything."

Another long, awkward silence before she said, "Do that. I'll talk to you soon?"

The way she phrased it as a question made my throat thicken. "Yeah. Bye."

I ended the call, feeling like a huge piece of shit for too many reasons to count. Me doubting her, her doubting me, the revelation that she feared I was backsliding into unlawful rogueism, and the chasm of mistrust I didn't know how to breach—those were just the tip of the iceberg.

Unfortunately for my seven-hour timeline, the Buchanan residence was all the way out in Langley. My GPS estimated a forty-five-minute drive, but between traffic, a vehicle rollover on the highway, and a road closure, it took twice that long.

I parked on a quiet street in front of the Buchanan residence at 3:30 p.m. It was an old rancher with a line of cedar trees forming a privacy screen on one side of the front yard. As I approached the door, two worrisome thoughts hit me.

First—what if no one was home? Had I wasted an hour and a half driving to an empty house? I'd assumed that with her son missing, Amy Buchanan would be staying close to home, but there was no guarantee.

And second—what the hell was I going to say? *Hi there, Ms. Buchanan. Your son was kidnapped by a lunatic luminamage to blackmail you into voting for this new bylaw, right? Cool. I don't suppose you know where he is, do you? Of course, you don't. Otherwise, you'd be out there rescuing your kid.*

I took a breath to steady myself. I'd just wing it, as per my usual.

Seconds after I'd rung the doorbell, the MPD delegate cracked the door open just wide enough to peer out at me. She had a friendly face worn down by stress and fatigue. Her curly, graying hair was pulled back into a loose ponytail, and she was comfortably dressed in a baggy wool sweater and worn jeans.

She gave me a wary look, her gaze flicking from the street to my face and then back again.

"Hello," I said pleasantly. "I'm Agent Morris."

She stepped back from the doorway. "Agent?"

I untucked my badge from my t-shirt, pulled it over my head, and held it out for her to examine. "MPD."

Instead of looking relieved, her alarm increased. "How can I help you, agent?"

"Call me Kit," I told her, flooding my voice with all the warmth I had. "I'm investigating Daniel's disappearance. Can I—"

Her eyes popped wide at the mention of her son, then she grabbed me by the arm and hauled me inside, slamming the door shut behind us.

"You shouldn't be here," she hissed as I caught my balance. Her fingernails dug into my arm. "How do you even know? I didn't report him missing!"

"Why didn't you?"

"Because of the ransom message." She cranked the deadbolt on the door and looked at me with raw fear. "If I talk to the authorities, he'll kill Daniel—and he's always watching."

23

"WHO'S ALWAYS WATCHING?" I asked, though I was confident I knew the answer.

Amy pressed her lips together so hard they turned white, and for a second, I thought she would kick me out. But after two and a half days without her son, she must've been desperate for help, because she took me by the crook of the arm and led me down the hallway and into the kitchen at the back of the house. Large patio doors took up the wall behind a glass-topped dining table, but all the blinds were closed.

"I got the first message two days ago," she said, finding a spot behind the counter peninsula to hover. "He said he had Daniel and if I contacted the authorities, human or MPD, he'd kill him."

"Anything else?"

"That he'd send more instructions later, and I'd better obey them to the letter if I want to see my son again." Her mouth trembled. "He sent a few photos, but I can't tell the time of day. Daniel could be d–dead already."

A shuddering breath racked her body.

"I saw Daniel yesterday," I said quickly, stuffing my badge in my pocket. "I couldn't get him away from the kidnapper, but he was fine. He wanted to get back to you."

Tears welled in her eyes and spilled over. "Y–you saw him?"

"Yes, and my partner and I are working around the clock to get Daniel home safe and sound." I gestured to the dining chair closest to me. "Do you mind if I sit?"

"Go ahead."

"Thanks." I lowered my tired bones onto the seat. "Let's start from the top. Daniel was abducted outside the Arcana Historia library. What was he doing there?"

"He has a free period in the mornings." She wrung her hands with nervous, frenetic energy. "So he went to the library to study until his first class."

I nodded, wondering if I should be taking notes. "Had Daniel been acting strangely? Did he mention anything about being followed?"

"N–no. He seemed completely normal when I dropped him off at the bus station."

"When did you get the first ransom message?"

"Just after ten a.m. on Friday morning." She shivered. "Maybe you should go. If the kidnapper realizes you're here …"

"He won't," I assured her, though I couldn't back that statement up with anything except the doubt that Radomir would travel all the way out here to check on Amy. "Do you know what the kidnapper wants from you?"

"He hasn't said yet …"

I watched her fidget anxiously. "But you can guess. He targeted Daniel because of the vote tonight."

A jerky nod tilted her head. "It's been controversial from the start and—" Her voice cracked and she swallowed to compose herself. "If I don't do as he says, he'll kill my boy."

"I won't let that happen, Ms. Buchanan."

"He said if I brought the MPD into it, he'd know."

That tracked, but even though Radomir had an inside man—or woman—at the precinct, no one knew I was here.

Amy gripped the edge of the counter like a vise. "You said you saw Daniel. What happened?"

What happened? We'd screwed up, that's what happened. *We almost rescued your son, Ms. Buchanan, but our egos got the best of us and we failed.*

"My partner and I found Daniel in an abandoned train tunnel," I told her. "But the kidnapper surprised us and escaped with Daniel."

She turned away, hiding her face, but I could tell by her trembling that she was crying. I got out of the chair, stepped around the counter, and placed a gentle hand on her shoulder.

"We found Daniel once. We can do it again. Can I see the messages the kidnapper sent you?"

Sniffling, Amy pulled her phone from her pocket, tapped on the screen, then handed it to me.

I scrolled through the messages, which had all come from a private number. The first was a photo showing Daniel chained to the floor of the padded room where we'd found him in the subway tunnel. The picture had been swiftly followed by Radomir's first set of orders. Amy had replied, begging him not to hurt her son.

Radomir had sent several photos of Daniel in the padded room. Then, starting early this morning, he'd sent pictures of Daniel at a different location. In them, the boy was bound and gagged and sitting on the floor of a dark room with a tiled floor. The sole source of illumination came from behind the photographer, and judging by the rectangular beam, the light was shining through an open door.

The last message was a reiteration of Radomir's initial orders: Don't contact the MPD, stay home, wait for further instructions.

Sinking back onto the dining chair, I zoomed in on the most recent photo, but it was a featureless room. No furniture, no architectural details, no windows. The only thing that hinted at where Daniel might be was the tile floor, which displayed three gaudy gold stars in the center of each charcoal tile.

One possible clue stood out to me. Radomir had sent four photos of Daniel, all about an hour apart—likely to keep Amy as frantic as possible—and in all of them, there were two shadows on the floor—Radomir's man-shaped shadow as he took the photo, and another object. But no matter how I tilted my head or squinted, I couldn't figure out what the strange object was.

Frustration seethed in my gut. If I had a few weeks to learn how to use 3D modeling software, I could reconstruct the object casting that shadow, but—

Wait. I didn't need 3D software for that.

Standing with the phone in my hand, I faced Amy, who was nervously chewing her nails. "I'm going to try something. And it's going to be weird."

She removed her fingers from her mouth. "What do you mean?"

Not bothering with an explanation of psycho warping, I targeted Amy's mind so she could see what I was doing and created a simple warp. It wasn't too far removed from the Redecorator, but this time, I created four dark walls around the dining room.

Amy gasped. "What did you do?"

"This is my magic," I assured her. "It's a hallucination I'm using to recreate the room in these photos."

She wrapped her arms around herself. "All right."

I erased the table and chairs but didn't add the ugly three-starred floor tiles. With my back to the patio doors—my stand-in for the actual doorway that was the source of all the light in the photos—I added a dark shadow of myself on the floor. Squinting at the most recent photo, I added the weirdly shaped shadow beside mine.

Okay … now what?

I created a vertical version of the shadow shape in front of the patio doors, like a cardboard cut-out. It still didn't look like anything recognizable.

"Is that right?" Amy whispered.

"Huh?"

She leaned closer to point at the photo on the phone. "If light was shining into that room like through the patio doors in here, the whole place would be better lit. The lightbulb is probably right on the other side of the door, above the jamb."

Which completely changed how the light was hitting the object casting that shadow.

I frowned. To do this right, I needed to drastically change the lighting of this room, which was easier said than done. I'd toyed with brightness before, but warping light changed everything and in different ways, depending on where the target of my warp was looking. If I just made everything "dark," the warp would look completely fake.

I looked at Amy's eyes—the size of her pupils, the reflection of the room in her irises—and thought through the diffused illumination of the simple chandelier, the streaks of sunlight through the blinds, and reflected light bouncing off the kitchen surfaces.

It was too much to grasp.

Then I remembered how I had struggled with invisibility on anyone other than me. I'd first tried it with Vera when we'd robbed Faustus Trivium last year, failing miserably until I'd learned to regard Vera as a whole entity—an individual with a specific aura and personality. Then I'd been able to make her invisible.

Maybe that was the key; when we perceive light, we don't break it down into bits and pieces—the shadows and refractions and reflections. We see it as a holistic effect on our world. It was like color. Not the individual, blended pigments, but the final painted product.

So, if I could change color, I could change light.

I looked back at the photos on Amy's phone and absorbed the feeling of the light. The cold, concealing shadows and stark, revealing beam of light from the unseen doorway.

Then I morphed the current light of the room until it matched.

"Oh," Amy breathed.

I couldn't hold back a smile. Learning a new warping skill always made me giddy. It needed a name. How about the Illuminator? Or the Gaffer?

Bah, I'd come up with a cool name later.

Refocusing, I added my shadow and the strange object's shadow. It was easier than usual since I'd been practicing my shadow realism to fool certain luminamages and druids.

"Okay," I muttered under my breath as I added a dark blob that represented the unknown object casting the second shadow. "Let's do this."

Precious minutes ticked away as I flipped between studying the four photos, which revealed the shadow at slightly different angles, and reshaping the blob into something that might've cast the shadow.

I tweaked it. Tweaked it more. Changed the angle of the light and tried again. A headache built behind my mind. The minutes crept toward an hour, stretching my mental endurance into dangerous territory.

"Wait!" Amy exclaimed from her spot in the corner of my fake room. She stepped sideways. "Make those two taller bits round instead."

"Round?"

"Flat and round, like dinner plates."

I changed the bulky protrusions at the top of the mystery object into round discs—and gasped. "That's a film projector!"

"Yes!" she exclaimed. "I almost didn't see it, but at this angle, I realized those top shapes might not be rectangles but something thin viewed from the side."

"You're a genius!" I let the warp go and dropped wearily into a chair. "Okay. Okay, so Daniel is in a movie theater. Probably an old one if it's using a film projector."

"But *which* theater?"

"Let's figure it out."

Amy rushed out of the room and returned with a laptop and tablet. She set up the former for me, then started rapid-Googling on her tablet.

In seconds, I had a map of downtown Vancouver with all the theaters flagged—but would Radomir hide Daniel in a building where someone might discover him? His last hideout had been an abandoned subway station. Keyword: abandoned.

Opening a new tab, I searched for *closed* theaters. There were more than I'd expected, and urgency pounded through me as the search ate up time. It took an aggravating thirty minutes, but we narrowed down the list to one theater that wasn't sold, under construction, or being renovated into something new.

"The Filmic Rouge," I announced. "It went out of business less than a year ago. The building is still up for sale."

I brought it up on street view. The theater was a small venue, sandwiched between a clothing boutique and a pizza joint. A classic marquee advertised a "one-night only" viewing of the Hitchcock masterpiece *Vertigo*. I clicked on the selection of interior photos shared by visitors in years past.

"Look!" Amy exclaimed. "The floor!"

The tiles in the lobby had the same pattern of three stars.

"This is it," I said excitedly. "This is where—"

Amy's phone, sitting in the middle of the table, chimed loudly. Her face went white as she snatched it up and unlocked the screen.

"Oh god," she whispered, clasping a hand over her mouth, her bulging eyes wet with tears. "No, no, no."

I pushed to my feet. "Is it him? The kidnapper?"

Unable to speak, she turned her phone toward me.

Radomir had sent a new photo. In it, Daniel floated a foot off the floor, his limbs outstretched in an X-shape. Blobs of light, too bright for the camera to capture properly, encircled his wrists and ankles, and beneath him was a complex, disc-shaped spell circle.

A new text message accompanied the photo.

```
With one incantation, Daniel will die a
horrific death. You have five minutes to
make Agent Morris leave.
```

My heart drummed a fast, painful beat against my ribs. Radomir knew I was here.

24

I STOOD FROZEN, my mind spinning through possible scenarios. Was Radomir following me? Had he seen me come into the house? Was that slithery lumina-prick in here with us right now?

No, the timing didn't add up. He'd put Daniel into that spell, which couldn't have been a quick process, and I was over an hour away from the movie theater where he was holding his victim. Plus, the background of the new photo looked like a huge white screen—also part of the movie theater—so he hadn't moved Daniel very far.

But if Radomir wasn't here, how did he know *I* was here?

I turned to Amy. "I'm going to get Daniel back."

Her face went even paler. "How?"

"With help, don't worry. You need to stay here and keep following the kidnapper's instructions until Daniel is safe."

She rushed over to her kitchen counter, scribbled something on a scrap of paper, then thrust it at me. "Call me as soon as Daniel is safe. But if I haven't heard from you by eight thirty and he tells me to vote yes, I will. My son's life is more important than a bylaw."

"I understand." I headed for the door. "But I'll call before then, I promise."

Outside, I strode as casually as possible back to Smart Car III, my gaze skimming across the cars parked along the street. They all appeared to be empty, but I suspected a well-paid Radomir goon was nearby, watching Amy's house to ensure she didn't take any drastic measures to save her son.

Just as I was climbing in, a leggy lady in her sixties with dark clothing sauntered past on the far sidewalk. I watched her stroll toward her car—an older black sedan—but she didn't so much as glance at me or Amy's house.

I started the engine and pulled away, following traffic laws as I drove out of the neighborhood like I knew nothing about a kidnapping, ransom, or blackmail.

And the black sedan followed me.

I pulled onto Fraser Highway and punched the accelerator, but the dark car kept pace with me, even as I blew past the speed limit. Not that it was hard for the sedan to keep up—its engine was quadruple the size of the one this oversized bumper car was working with.

Nearing a shopping center, I veered hard to the right, careening into the parking lot. The long-legged driver tailing me didn't have time to react and shot past me.

I'd lost my tail, but that didn't offer me much comfort.

I pulled into a parking spot and kept the engine running as I dug out my phone. It was time to bring Lienna in on everything I'd discovered, and it couldn't wait while I drove back into downtown.

I tapped her number. The phone rang in my ear, then went to voicemail. Swearing under my breath, I left a quick voicemail for her to call me ASAP. Switching to text, I sent her a message saying the same thing, then shot one off to Zak, giving him a heads-up that I knew where Daniel was.

My phone pinged with an instant reply. Why was the druid plugged into his phone and not my partner?

"Where?" was his eloquent response. I texted back that I was driving and would call him later, then shifted gear, launched the smart car back onto the road, and put the pedal to the metal.

I'd spent over two hours at Amy's house figuring out that Daniel was at a movie theater, and then figuring out which movie theater. The long drive—again compounded by stupid delays, even though I took a different route—ate up over an hour, and though I called Lienna six more times, she didn't answer. She must've turned her phone to silent.

While her library manners were impeccable, they were also highly inconvenient.

By the time I found a parking spot two blocks from Arcana Historia, it was after seven p.m. I trotted along the sidewalk, double-checking the shadows for any sign of the old lady who'd followed me from Amy's house, but I seemed to have successfully shaken her.

The scholarly guild masqueraded as a private tutoring service, with a street-level entrance that visitors could use to access the blocky three-story office building. I hastened up the steps where Daniel had been abducted three mornings ago and into a small reception area lined with posters for mathlete competitions, SAT prep courses, and continuing education programs for adults.

Behind the desk, a middle-aged woman looked up from a massive textbook.

I flashed my badge. "Library?"

"First door on the left."

With a wave of thanks, I pushed through a frosted glass door and into a wide hallway. Barely glancing at a locked display case of ancient grimoires, I swerved toward the door on the left and into the paper-scented hush that only libraries possessed. Dark wood shelves gave it a classic "law school library" look broken up by modern touches like a shelf of guild favorites and a table of random books with a sign that read, "101 Magical Things You Never Knew You Needed to Know."

Moving quietly—because you had to do everything quietly in a library—I speed-walked through the stacks of tomes, ignoring the strange looks I got from bookworm sorcerers. I skimmed the aisle labels, and spotting *Arcana – Abjuration*, I zipped into the aisle.

And there was Lienna, standing at the far end with a piece of paper in her hand, her satchel hanging off her shoulder, and her hair pulled back in a ponytail. But she wasn't alone. She was talking to a dark-haired woman who looked short and petite even next to my slender partner.

That must be the researcher Lienna had mentioned she was meeting with. But whatever their meeting was about, it'd have to wait, because Lienna and I had a kid to save and a luminamage to beat down.

I marched through the aisle, and Lienna's gaze darted my way, her eyebrows streaking upward. But the researcher, with her back to me, had no idea I was approaching until I spoke.

"MPD," I growled. "Put your hands in the air!"

The woman stiffened and her hands shot up.

Surprise flickered through me. "Oh. She actually did it."

Lienna rolled her eyes. "Kit, stop tormenting civilians."

I hadn't meant to freak this lady out. I'd been trying to interrupt the conversation and get her to bail.

Stepping around her to stand beside Lienna, I flashed a smile. The researcher was a couple years my junior, with dark-rimmed glasses that only enhanced the shocked wideness of her blue eyes.

I waved my empty hands. "You do know MPD agents don't carry guns, right? Seriously, I was only kidding. You aren't under arrest."

And you can also leave now, please and thank you.

Unfortunately, the woman didn't move, not even to lower her arms. I poked the palm of her upraised hand, and she dropped it so fast her elbow hit the bookshelf next to her. Chill out, tiny lady. I knew the police made people uncomfortable, but what was she hiding that made her so transparently terrified?

"Though ..." I squinted at her face, her cheeks reddening with an embarrassed blush, and recognition pinged through me. "Wow, you're Robin Page, aren't you?"

Robin Page, as in the highly mysterious and evasive demon contractor who fit no demon contractor profile I'd ever seen. We'd run across her name while investigating the Grand Grimoire's GM, Rocco Thorn, but despite our best attempts, we'd never laid eyes on her before now.

"Robin *Page*?" Lienna gawked.

Crossing my arms, I gave my partner one of her own eye rolls. "Really, Lienna? We carried her photo around for, like, two weeks."

"My photo?" the pint-sized contractor stammered in a small voice.

I shrugged. "Well, you know, you showed up out of nowhere, joined the Grand Grimoire, went all John Wick on an unbound demon a few days later, then switched guilds and disappeared. You didn't think MagiPol might notice that, just a little bit?"

Her eyes, which I didn't think could get any wider, expanded to a saucer-like circumference. "Wait ... you're actually an MPD agent?"

I pulled my badge out of my pocket. "Kit Morris. Nice to finally meet you."

"*Agent* Morris," my partner corrected, always the stickler for our proper titles. She showed off her badge as well. "I'm Agent Shen."

"You're an agent too?" Robin squeaked.

Lienna raised an eyebrow. "You didn't know?"

The bookworm shook her head. How was this nervous wreck of a human a power-hungry contractor? I held a hand above her head to confirm I wasn't losing all sense of size from exhaustion. Nope. She didn't even come up to my shoulder. "You're shorter than I expected."

"What are you even doing in here?" Lienna demanded, digging her elbow into my ribs pointedly.

Oh right. As intrigued as I was to finally lay eyes on Robin Page, I had more urgent things on my mind.

"You were supposed to wait in the car," she added.

Was that some sort of code that I was too braindead to figure out? Or was she actually telling me to go wait in the dinky smart car? I'd just spent an hour and a half in its cramped quarters. "So you *want* me to lose both legs to a double amputation after my joints fuse from—"

"*Kit.*"

I changed tracks. "The captain called," I lied. "We've been summoned."

Hint, hint, wink, wink, nudge, nudge. Time to bid your abjuration buddy adieu, Lienna.

"Oh." My partner handed the paper she was holding to the diminutive contractor. "Sorry, Robin. We need to leave."

"S-sure," the girl muttered.

I gave Robin one last smile, still bemused over how a demon contractor had managed to camouflage herself as the most introverted member of a Jane Austen book club, then followed Lienna toward the exit.

"Don't worry," I called over my shoulder. "I'll arrest you next time."

"Kit!" Lienna scolded, opening the library door. As it shut behind us, she seemed to forget her exasperation—in fact, she seemed to forget all about Robin Page as she stared at me uncertainly. "I didn't think you would come."

"You'd have known I was coming if you'd looked at your phone," I told her impatiently. "I know where Daniel is, and we have less than an hour to save him."

AS SOON AS WE SET FOOT on the sidewalk outside the guild, I regaled Lienna with my findings in the café and my visit to Amy Buchanan—not only to bring her up to speed but also in the hope that all my shocking revelations would keep the unresolved conflict from our last face-to-face conversation at bay.

"So," I concluded as we turned into an alley that led back to Smart Car III, "we have fifty-four minutes to get Daniel away from Radomir before the Complexor Bylaw vote."

"Fifty-four minutes," she repeated bleakly. "But we can't just barge into the theater, not with Daniel in that spell. Radomir could trigger it before we free him." She fished Varvara's red grimoire out of her satchel and opened it to the bookmarked page with a detailed illustration. "Are you sure this is the spell Daniel is trapped in?"

Looking down at the Vitruvian Man knockoff, I nodded. The moment I'd seen the photo of Daniel in a spell, I'd known it was the same one from Varvara's grimoire. Radomir, being a mage, couldn't create spells—but he *could* use his dead boss's spells for his new line of dirty work. All he needed was the incantation, which was in this book.

"Can you break it?" I asked.

She handed me the grimoire, then dug into her satchel again. I glimpsed a small hardcover entitled *Early Cyrillic to Modern English* and a leather-bound behemoth with the same strange lettering on it as Varvara's grimoire, then she pulled out a simple notebook.

"I was already working on translating the spell components." She flipped open her notebook. "It combines a holding spell, a levitation spell, and a lethal attack to kill the person trapped in it. If I can bypass the levitation part and break the holding spell, I can get Daniel away from the ..."

"The murder spell?" I surmised. "What kind of murder are we talking here?"

"I didn't get that far, but it'll be something fast and deadly."

Fast and deadly were not the adjectives I wanted attributed to an enemy's weapon. Slow and docile would have been better.

"How long will it take you to figure out how to break the holding spell?" I asked.

"I think I have enough time." She stopped near the end of the alley and looked up at me. Our eyes met, the painful argument from that morning hanging between us. "Are we doing this together?"

I'd spent my hours driving to and from the Buchanan household with no company but my own reeling thoughts. And those thoughts were stubbornly focused on all the things Lienna—and Zak—had said to me.

"We have to," I told her, unsure how to articulate the conclusions I'd drawn in the solitary confinement of the smart car. "That's the only way we can save Daniel."

"Okay," she replied slowly, waiting for more.

I leaned back against the brick wall of the narrow alley, holding the grimoire across my chest. "I've been thinking about what you said. A lot. I didn't realize what I was doing—I mean, yes, I knew what I was doing, but I wasn't seeing it the way you were. It was just another prank, like the ones I pull on Vincent all the time. No one was getting hurt, not for real."

Lienna remained silent, her dark eyes studying me.

"And even when you called me out on it," I went on, "I didn't want to listen because there's a kid in danger, and what if holding back costs him his life? No one else seems to care about him except me."

"I care, Kit," she said quietly. "I've cared all along. But caring about a victim's safety doesn't mean we can go off the rails."

My eyebrows lifted. "You saved my life by going off the rails."

"That—" Her lips turned down. "That was an extreme situation."

"You were saving a life, and Daniel's should be worth as much as mine."

She let out a slow breath. "Kit, this isn't an 'obedience equals failure' and 'rebellion equals success' equation. I don't follow the rules because I can't think for myself or because I don't care enough to break them. I follow them because when I do, I get results. I save lives and stop criminals, and the system helps me do that. It's not perfect, but it works."

I opened my mouth, but she cut me off before I could jump in.

"Not *always*. But most of the time."

Shifting the grimoire to my left hand, I pushed off the wall. "Every system I've ever been thrown into has failed me. So the rules—I have trouble trusting them. I go with my gut and that's what's always worked for *me*."

She parted her lips to speak, a worried crease in her forehead.

"But," I added before she could say anything, "shirking rules doesn't mean I'm reverting to the rogue life or turning into a violent criminal. I was never that kind of guy, and a few hours of Zak exposure won't change me."

"You're right," she whispered. "You were never that guy, not even when we first met."

I wasn't a budding ultra-rogue like Zak, whose morals were more flexible than mine could ever be. But neither was I about to develop a Lienna-like respect for laws, orders, and rules. I fell somewhere between the two.

Where I fell, I wasn't sure yet, but I was okay with walking down the middle of this nebulous road between order and chaos.

"I need you, Lienna." My voice was soft as I extended a hand toward her. "I can't do this without you. What do you say, partner?"

A wavering smile lifted the corner of her mouth. She tucked her notebook under her arm and put her hand in mine. "I say let's do this—let's get Daniel away from that bastard."

I curled my fingers around hers. We held each other's hands for a moment longer, then let go at the same time and resumed walking, our pace quickening with urgency.

"Stopping Radomir won't be easy," she murmured, opening her notebook again. "Especially if I need to break this spell."

"Let's hope my psycho warping is as strong as you think it is."

"It is. And don't forget your trump card."

We stepped out of the alley and onto a sidewalk, and I spied Smart Car III ahead of us, obscured by a bus stop shelter. "About that trump card, there's something I haven't told you."

She cast a frown at me. "What's that?"

"Reality warping causes me to lose all my magic." I pulled out the car keys as we passed the bus stop. "Last time it took forty-eight hours for my abilities to recover, so I can't …"

I stopped dead, all thought of what I'd been saying vanishing in a wave of surprise.

Three feet away, leaning against the side of the smart car with his arms folded, was a familiar figure in a long black coat. As I gawked at him, he pushed his hood back and fixed sharp green eyes on me.

"Reality warping?" he repeated in a mild tone that made me regret opening my big mouth.

"Hey there, Zak," I managed.

"What are you doing here?" Lienna ground out, gripping her notebook like a weapon.

He turned his piercing gaze toward me.

"Right," I muttered. "I may have sent him a text message saying I knew where Daniel was. But I didn't tell him where we were."

"You didn't need to. Do you really think I'd let her walk off with that grimoire?"

Lienna's eyes popped with indignation. "You've been *following* me?" She took a threatening step toward him. "You asshole. You—"

A low snarl interrupted her. A pair of red eyes gleamed as a shadowy canine shape prowled past her to Zak's side, then faded out of sight. Lienna stepped back toward me.

Zak pushed off the car, his focus turning my way again. I expected him to press me for an explanation of reality warping, but instead, he said, "You found Radomir."

"I found Daniel," I corrected.

"And there's a reason you didn't tell me where he is two hours ago?"

"I didn't want you charging in without us. This is a rescue mission, not a revenge rampage." I peered at his face. "Hey, are your eyes different? They seem more … normal."

"It's your imagination. So, where's the kid?"

I hesitated, unsure whether to answer.

"You want Daniel alive, and I want Radomir dead." A slight smirk curved his lips. "There's a lot of overlap in that Venn diagram."

Recognizing my own argument from yesterday, I started to smile, then caught myself. I turned to Lienna, standing silently beside me. "Like you said, Radomir won't go down easily. And he's got at least one helper, which means he could have backup. We could use Zak's help."

Her lips pressed together as she glanced at the druid, then back to me. "Our priority is Daniel. His isn't."

Lienna on my left, Zak on my right, and yours truly smack dab in the middle.

"Quit wasting time," Zak growled, his impatience overtaking our brief comradery. "Either tell me where the kid is or get your asses moving so I can follow you."

Lienna planted her feet and crossed her arms. "We're not leading you there so you can storm in and get Daniel killed!"

"And I'm not waiting around while Radomir disappears again."

I stepped between them. "We'll work together, as a team, the three of us."

"Kit—" Lienna protested.

"We need all the firepower we can get." I looked at Zak. "But we can't be reckless either. A boy's life is in our hands, and we aren't screwing it up again."

My two tenuous allies eyed each other warily.

"We need a strategy where we actually work together. And this time," I added, giving my partner and the druid a stark smile, "*I'm* taking the lead."

25

THE STREETLIGHTS SHONE on the damp pavement as Zak and I approached the Filmic Rouge, Lienna walking a step behind us. The theater was a long, skinny two-story building with a single auditorium and a marquee sign above the ticket booth that read, "Permanently closed. Thank you for 71 years of patronage."

Nerves churned through me. Everything hinged on my plan, and if I'd miscalculated, not only would Daniel die, but probably all three of us as well. To complicate matters, I couldn't rely on my usual warp arsenal. Radomir had already figured out how to see through my warps: by flickering the lights around me. I couldn't keep up a warp's realism in rapidly changing light conditions.

"Remember," I muttered. "The murder spell is triggered by a four-word incantation, so if Radomir starts to—"

"I know," Zak cut in. "But he won't unless he's backed into a corner."

"What makes you think that?"

"Killing hostages before your demands are met is bad for business."

I bobbed my head and nervously adjusted my combat vest. Lugging around all my gear since that dumb raid on Darius's house had paid off. "And we can't dawdle, because the vote is in twenty minutes, and—"

"I *know*. If you keep babbling, I'm leaving you out here."

I squinted at him. "The lone ranger thing works for you. It's cool as shit, and you've got the jawline to pull off the whole roguish badass look, but this time is different."

He quirked a cool eyebrow at me, and I was again weirded out by the normalness of his eyes. They were a deep, dreamy green, but they didn't have that inhuman vibrancy anymore.

"You're on *our* team for this," I continued, speaking fast and quiet as we ascended the theater's wide steps. "And if we don't trust each other, at least one of us isn't walking out of here alive." My gaze flicked to Lienna's terse, focused expression. "She's putting her life in our hands, man. I need to know you've got our backs."

We stopped in front of the wide double doors, the handles bound together with a heavy chain and a thick padlock that'd already been cut. Zak rolled his shoulders, then pulled the broken padlock off and tossed it away.

"I've got your backs," he rumbled. "Worry about *your* part of this grand plan."

I grinned tightly. "Have a little faith."

In answer, he slid the chain off the handles and pitched it off the steps.

I swung the door open and we crept inside. A red-carpeted lobby met us, a small concession stand on the left and the entrances to the bathrooms on the right. Beside the little boys' room was a single door with a "Staff Only" sign, and based on its location, I knew it led to the projector room; with only one auditorium in the building, it wasn't difficult to figure out.

Zak slowly scanned the empty space. "Clear."

"It *looks* clear," I corrected, unholstering my potion gun. The luminamage could be hiding in plain sight, using his fancy light magic to remain invisible.

"My vargs can't smell him nearby," the druid replied. "But he's been through here recently, along with several other people."

Radomir must have brought in backup, then. I'd hoped he'd be too arrogant for that.

We crossed to the double auditorium doors. Lienna hung back several paces, gripping her satchel tightly.

"Ready?" I asked, reaching for the handle.

Zak nodded.

"And the vargs? Teeth sharpened and tummies grumbling for some luminamage flesh?"

"They'll sniff him out. Now quit stalling."

I took a deep breath, raised my pistol, and pulled the door open with my free hand.

A muscular woman stood on the other side of the threshold, dressed in a black tank top that showed off her boulder shoulders and carrying a broad, curved cutlass. She looked like she belonged in the WWE, not in the auditorium of the Filmic Rouge.

"Welcome," she said with a mean, toothy grin—and slashed at my chest with her blade.

Moisture exploded against my torso, the force throwing me onto my ass. My first thought was that her cutlass was so sharp that every liter of blood in my body had erupted from my heart, but when I looked down, I realized I was lying in a puddle of water.

She was a hydromage. I hated hydromages.

She lunged at me, her cutlass shooting toward my face. With a flash of amber light, Zak used the glowing shield that had appeared on his arm to knock her blade away. Stepping into her guard, he slammed his fist into her stomach like the total badass he was.

As she staggered backward through the doorway, green light lit the room beyond, then exploded outward.

In the second before the magical detonation hit, Zak dropped into a crouch in front of me, tucking his entire body behind his shield. The open doors blew right off their hinges and the concussive force threw him back into me, his weight crushing the air from my lungs.

He rolled off me and we sprang to our feet, retreating several steps. Lienna hunkered behind us in a defensive stance, her gaze fixed straight ahead at our enemies.

In the door-less entrance to the auditorium, a lanky man with long, braided hair and leather clothes held a gnarled walking stick with a forest green jewel at its top. He was flanked by the She-Hulk and another woman—the leggy lady who'd followed me from Amy's house. The three rogues formed a line in front of the demolished doors.

Beside me, Zak bared his teeth in a dark grin.

His amber shield melted into a glowing whip, and as he raised his arm, the air on either side of him shimmered. Low snarls rolled through the lobby as a pair of shaggy black wolves appeared beside the druid.

The old lady grinned too, and another weird glimmer disturbed the air, the distortion appearing between her and the druid. A shape materialized in the space—and it wasn't a fae wolf.

An ultramarine scorpion the size of a motorcycle solidified three feet away, black streaks embossing its polished shell-like exterior. Its thick tail curled over its insectile body, the pointed stinger dripping with poison. It opened massive pincers, the serrated edges ragged and deadly.

So we had a witch and her monster-bug familiar, a scarily buff hydromage, and a staff-wielding sorcerer to get through—and that didn't include Radomir himself, wherever he was.

I pulled my eyes off the scorpion to throw a pointed glance at Zak. "The plan doesn't change."

His chin dipped slightly.

I sucked in a breath—and Lienna vanished.

As though that were a signal, the scorpion attacked. Zak's whip snapped out, looping around the bug's giant stinger. His vargs launched at its pincer arms, distracting it.

Darting sideways, I fired my pistol at the hydromage. She whipped up a blob of water to shield herself from the sleeping potions. As expected, I wasn't much use in direct combat. That wasn't my strength.

As Zak's two vargs herded the scorpion toward the concession stand in a chaotic blur of pincers, stinger, and white wolfy fangs, I dove clear of the danger, cast a quick glance around, and Split Kit myself—trying to ignore the sacrilegious demolition of the popcorn machine caused by the fae battle.

Fake-Kit sprinted past Zak as he snapped his whip at the sorcerer, the hydromage blocking it with another water shield. Firing more sleep potions wildly at the rogues, fake-Kit shoved through the door to the projector room and slammed it behind him.

"The boy ran upstairs!" the hydromage yelled over her shoulder. "And the girl disappeared!"

The girl and the boy—how descriptive, what eloquence. But she had conveniently revealed where I should look for Radomir. He was in the auditorium.

With a loud crack, Zak's whip knocked the hydromage's cutlass from her hands and sent it flying. As she rushed after it, the druid grabbed a crystal around his neck, snarled an incantation, and flung a sizzling purple orb into the sorcerer's chest. The man fell on his ass, purple magic splattered all over him, and Zak thrust his other palm at the witch, ten feet away.

"*Impello!*"

The air rippled and the witch flew backward through the open door.

With my path cleared, I sprinted past the distracted rogues and into the auditorium. One hundred and fifty seats faced the stage, which had been converted into a screen.

In front of said screen was Daniel. Just like in the photo Radomir had sent the boy's mother, a creepy yellow spell glowed on the stage floor, and Daniel floated above it, his limbs stretched into an X like a crude imitation of da Vinci's famous drawing.

Even from the back of the auditorium, I could see his eyes were stretched wide with fear and his mouth was gaping. But if he was making any sound, I couldn't hear it.

Radomir was nowhere in sight, but I knew he was here. All he had to do was use his lumina magic to flicker the lights and the invisibility warp I was using to hide Lienna and myself would fail.

But that's where the projector came in. Or rather, my specialized warp version of a projector.

I drew in a deep, focused breath—and the aquamarine scorpion slammed through the doorway and into the auditorium, interrupting me. I leaped into a row of seats as the fae scorpion spun violently in the aisle, legs moving in a dizzying wave. One varg had its jaws clamped down on the scorpion's left pincer while the other dodged the poison-tipped stinger as it tried to get at the insect's soft underbelly.

The witch rushed in after them with a panicked expression—only for the bearded sorcerer to fly through the door as though thrown by a giant hand and crash into her back. They tumbled down the slanted aisle.

The hydromage dove into the auditorium after her comrades—and a crackling purple orb shot out of the lobby after her. It missed her head by inches as she fell to her knees.

Zak strode in last, his amber whip glowing and long coat billowing out behind him. He casually plucked a vial off his belt, pulled the cork with his teeth, and tossed it into the middle of his trio of enemies. The potion exploded into a gray mist, and the three rogues doubled over in violent coughing fits.

And that's why we'd brought the Ghost, aka the Crystal Druid, aka Vancouver's most notorious rogue, who kicked ass and looked good doing it.

Except as soon as I thought that, Zak faltered. His hand flew up to his face, pressing over one eye, the other wide and blinking rapidly.

Blinded. Radomir was here, and he was bending the light away from Zak's eyes to blind him.

Now it was my turn.

Focusing on the halluci-bomb keeping me and Lienna hidden, I layered on an entirely new warp: the Projectionist.

Light streamed from the projection booth, illuminating Daniel and the large white screen behind him. My delightful face popped up, greeting the combatants in the auditorium with bombastic gravitas.

"I am the great and powerful Kit!" my floating, projected head bellowed in homage to the Oz. "Lay down your weapons or I will instruct my servant, the undefeated Crystal Druid, to remove your jugulars and use them to jump rope!"

The three fae, still locked in battle, didn't pay my warp any heed, but Radomir's goons, still hacking up their lungs from Zak's poison attack, looked around to see what the hell kind of impromptu movie screening they were being subjected to.

I brightened the Projectionist warp, concentrating on how the flickering glow scattered around the auditorium. The flickering was the linchpin of the whole plan.

Radomir had exploited my weakness at handling hallucinatory light to see through my warps, but now I was turning that weakness into a strength. Time to see how well a luminamage could control his magic when he couldn't distinguish real light from fake light.

As the erratic flickering of the Projectionist filled the auditorium, Zak dropped his hand from his face and swiveled toward the trio of rogues. He could see again. Success!

But his returned vision had come a second too late.

The hydromage whipped her cutlass through the air, creating a crescent-shaped blade of water that launched at Zak. He dove behind a row of seats, water crashing over him. As he launched up, the sorcerer fired a spell at him. His whip morphed into a shield just in time, but the force knocked him backward.

I kept the Projectionist going full force, knowing Zak's life depended on my ability to stave off Radomir's blindness attack.

But where was the cowardly luminamage? I couldn't see him, even with my crazy light warp.

"Show yourself, you sniveling weasel!" Projected Kit commanded. "Quit hiding like the spineless, subservient troglodyte you are and face me like the strapping young lad you wish you were!"

Was there some irony in my insults? Hell yeah. I was hiding behind a warp and calling him out for hiding behind his light magic. Did I give a shit? Not even the tiniest mouse dropping.

Zak ran along the armrests of the chairs, dodging attacks from both the sorcerer and hydromage. His vargs were busy wrestling with the scorpion, and I couldn't help him either; all my focus was going into my warps, which were taxing my psychic energy something fierce. A widespread invisi-warp plus the Projectionist was a lot to handle.

Familiar fogginess gathered in the corners of my consciousness, and I shot a worried glance at the stage, watching Lienna.

The overhead lighting in the auditorium rippled in a strange pattern. That was Radomir. He was using his light trick to break through my invisi-warp. He was searching for Lienna.

And he found her.

26

AS THE FLICKERING of the real lights competed with my flickering projection, Lienna paused at the top of the short staircase that ascended to stage right and looked up, her face bleached by the harsh glow of the Projectionist's light.

Radomir's triumphant laugh echoed across the stage.

A streak of hot white light erupted from somewhere near the spell holding Daniel, blasted toward the stairs, and slammed into her. She fell off the stairs and landed hard on the floor.

I boosted the flickering of the Projectionist until the erratic flashing resembled a disco club on steroids. My fake light competed with Radomir's real light, and Lienna blurred out of view.

The fogginess in my mind was growing, clouding my senses. The world around me was becoming dull, forcing me to concentrate harder to maintain the multilayered warp.

"You fool!" Projected Kit boomed with a cackling laugh. "Do you really believe, in the few dusty brain cells you have left, that you can defeat me?"

Another light blast from Radomir's scepter flashed toward the auditorium's back wall. He thought I was in the projector booth and was trying to break my warp—but he'd given away his position. He was standing near the front of the stage, almost dead center.

"You are minutes away from annihilation, you insolent pion!" Projected Kit chortled. "Bend the knee or face your inevitable doom!"

"Quit fucking around, Shakespeare!" Zak shouted.

Projected Kit snarled his oversized lip as my real self turned toward the druid. "Does my verbosity annoy y—"

Oh, shit.

No, that wasn't the problem.

A glowing spell was tangled around Zak's torso, pinning his shield/whip arm to his side. The pink haze of a potion hung in the air and the sorcerer appeared to be unconscious in the middle of it.

But the hydromage was still moving, and as I watched in horror, she twirled her cutlass in a figure-eight pattern. Water droplets formed out of nothing and coalesced around Zak's head and shoulders.

He jerked backward, unable to escape the water orb.

His vargs leaped away from the scorpion, rushing to the druid's aid, but the insectile fae scuttled after them. Its pincers caught one by the back leg with a horrible crunch, and the second wolf barely dodged a deadly thrust of its stinger.

Zak fumbled for a potion on his belt, selected a vial blindly, and flung it in the general direction of the hydromage. She danced backward as it hit the ground and exploded five feet in front of her.

In the burning flash, the water dropped away and Zak gasped in a rough breath—then the water whooshed back over his head. The hydromage was still on her feet, and the scorpion was shaking a yelping varg while the other leaped on its back, snarling furiously.

For a heartbeat, I waited for Zak to pull another trick from his bag—but instead, he staggered and went down on one knee, struggling to dislodge the watery sphere drowning him, one arm still bound to his side with magic.

I had no choice. Stepping out from behind the back row of seats, I raised my pistol and fired. A yellow potion burst across the hydromage's upper chest. Surprise flashed over her face, then she toppled, unconscious.

The liquid drowning Zak splashed onto the floor, and he bent over, coughing up water with violent heaves of his shoulders.

I fired a shot into the unmoving sorcerer to ensure he wouldn't get back up, then turned, searching for the witch—but I'd made the same mistake as Radomir: I'd given away my position.

And the witch had noticed.

When I turned, she was behind me, the sorcerer's heavy wooden staff in her hands. She swung it like a baseball bat, aiming at the spot where the potion-loaded shots had originated.

Which, of course, was right where I stood.

The staff slammed into my chest, knocking me off my feet. I crashed down in the aisle, my potion gun tumbling out of my hand. As pain ricocheted through my body, I bent all my focus on keeping my warps going.

The witch raised the staff, preparing to swing it down on me like a battle axe. I flung my arms up to shield my head as she whipped it down.

She jerked, then pitched over backward. Her spasming body collapsed a few feet away, the hilt of a heavy knife protruding from her throat.

I sat up. Halfway along a row of seats, Zak was still on one knee, his free arm half stretched toward me from the throw that had saved my life.

Three minions down. One giant scorpion and a luminamage left.

A dizzying ripple of luminescence rolled through the overhead lighting, and an unsettling laugh cascaded from Radomir's hidden position at center stage.

"You think you've won?" his bland voice called. "Does this seem like a victory to you?"

A small glimmer hovered in the air on the stage, then ballooned into a fiery red orb. The faint outline of his scepter gleamed below it, not fully hidden by his light tricks.

The seething orb swelled to the size of a basketball, then launched stage right with a shrieking roar. It slammed into the staircase where invisible Lienna was still taking refuge and exploded into a massive fireball.

Everything in a ten-foot radius disappeared in the inferno, consumed in an instant. No one could have survived that.

Not even Lienna.

A violent animal howl erupted through the auditorium. The scorpion had flung a varg into the wall, and the other was limping badly as it circled the creature's other side.

Zak pulled a new knife from a hidden sheath in his boot, then shoved to his feet, one arm still trapped by the glowing rope. His eyes met mine.

"He's yours," he called.

Then he whirled, and giving zero shits about the danger or the explosion that had incinerated my partner, he sprinted toward the raging scorpion and his vargs.

I wasted one precious second looking for my pistol, but it'd slid beneath the seats and I couldn't see it. I had a few artifacts in my belt pockets, but with the strain of the warps, I couldn't remember what they were, let alone their incantations.

It was just me and my powers. And they were taking a real toll on my brain.

I launched down the ramp toward the stage. The overhead lights danced with Radomir's magic, and a spark formed on the stage—his scepter was gearing up for round two of the super incinerator spell. No wonder his client had been willing to pay an entire briefcase's worth of hundred-dollar bills for that artifact. The damn thing was lethal.

The fiery orb swelled, then rocketed toward me. I flung myself through the air, doing my best Bruce-Willis-jumps-out-of-the-way-of-an-exploding-helicopter impression. Except my limbs were roughly the consistency of wet noodles and I didn't have CGI or a stunt double to save me.

I landed hard between two rows of seats, the searing explosion burning my back. As the seats disintegrated, all I could think was, *Don't drop the warp, don't drop the warp, don't drop the warp.*

When I popped my head up from behind the seats, I was relieved to see they were still functioning. Projected Kit was making an ugly grimace that reflected my own pain, but otherwise, I'd held on to it all.

A dangerous six paces away, the scorpion was writhing. Zak had freed his spell-bound arm and his whip was wrapped around the insect's tail, holding the stinger away from his vargs as they harried it from the front.

Scrambling over the backs of seats toward the stage, I dug deep into my psyche, scratching the bottom of my energy barrel, and set the flickering of the Projectionist into strobe-light mode. The whole auditorium danced in the pulsating glow.

But the luminamage remained hidden.

He had to be compensating with his own magic. He'd seen enough of my tricks to know how to handle them, and he also knew he only had to buy a little more time to succeed in swaying the vote. If I hadn't been running a hippy convention's worth of hallucinations all at the same time, I could've targeted his mind and forced him into the open. But I didn't have the spare brainpower to do that.

Another canine howl rang out—and Zak's shout. I whirled around as a loud scuffing noise erupted.

The scorpion flailed madly, its head half torn off and gore gooping out from the gaping wound. The insect spun, twitching and spasming, and its long tail swung my way.

I couldn't duck in time. The tail caught me in the gut and hurled me over three rows of seats. I crumpled to the floor in front of the stage, and a silent stillness fell across the auditorium.

The insect's body was sprawled across the seats, its lethal tail limp. Zak and his two injured vargs were six rows up on its other side, the druid panting for air, a bloody knife in his hand, and his eyes wide with alarm.

Alarm not because of the scorpion, but because of me. The fae insect was dead, but I'd lost my warps.

All of them.

Every piece of the multilayered hallucination had died. The Projectionist vanished. My invisibility lifted. And up at center stage, Lienna appeared.

Unburnt and unexploded, she was kneeling in the center of the spell holding Daniel prisoner, her Rubik's Cube pressed to the centermost rune of the elaborate array. Her lips were moving with a chant that would free the teenager.

Lienna had never been with Zak and me. The satchel-carrying abjuration sorceress that the three goons had witnessed had been a warp I'd created right from the start. I'd even created a fake *invisible* Lienna for the luminamage to find and murder as a distraction.

Great job, asshole. You blew up a hallucination. Top-notch battle strategy.

The real Lienna had used one of Zak's melting potions to break in through the Filmic Rouge's rear door and sneak backstage. Even the screen had been altered. As soon as I'd created the Projectionist, I'd layered on a Redecorator warp to inch the screen forward gradually, using the flickering light to mask my deception. That'd hidden about half of the spell array behind the fake screen, which had given Lienna enough room to work her abjuration skills.

She'd spent the last ten minutes breaking the holding spell and was moments away from freeing Daniel.

But that was a few moments too long, because I'd exposed her.

A low, ominous laugh trickled from Radomir's invisible mouth. "Clever. Very clever, Agent Morris."

Hell yeah, it was clever. And every molecule in my drained body was paying the price for that cleverness.

"But not clever enough. And you will die regretting it."

Lienna's lips were still moving, rushing through her incantation, but her wide eyes shot toward me as she realized my warps had failed.

Radomir's voice boomed out. "*Ori—*"

He was beginning the incantation that would trigger the lethal spell. With four words, Daniel would die—and so would Lienna, who was inside the array with him.

"*—morte—*"

The Latin syllables fell from Radomir's mouth, and everything wound down into Zack Snyder-esque slow motion as my mind scrambled to come up with one more life-saving solution.

I was way beyond the parameters of my plan. Radomir was invisible, I had no weapons left, and none of my usual warp tricks were enough to silence him. The last time I'd been this desperate, I'd reality warped a grappling hook into a boat anchor to drown a demon.

But even if I could miraculously summon another physics-bending reality warp, what would I do? I couldn't see Radomir. His light magic had defeated my warps, and I had nothing left.

Except—

"*—moriendum—*"

Radomir's strength was light. Every iota of his power came from it. So, what was his weakness? *The dark.*

I couldn't see him, but I'd always had the ability to vaguely sense minds—and I could feel his now.

"*—cinerescen—*"

As he roared out the final word, I mined the deepest recesses of my gray matter for every last shard of psychic energy, targeted Radomir's mind, and projected a warp of pure, unfiltered nothingness into his brain.

Sight, sound, touch, taste, smell—I stole them all. Every microscopic scrap of feeling he possessed I replaced with a horrifying, empty abyss.

For the first time since we'd entered the theater, the luminamage appeared.

He stood on the stage, just right of center, barely three paces from Daniel, Lienna, and the lethal spell. His entire body had seized up, his mouth gaping on the final syllable of the incantation.

My lungs were burning, my muscles ached, and the blood pumping through my head was louder than a goddamn jet engine, but I refused to relent.

Radomir collapsed onto the stage floor as though every joint in his body had been transformed into cookie dough. His arms flailed around his head and his legs kicked wildly. It looked like he was trying to swim in shark-infested waters.

A pained wail throttled his throat, piercing the air. "Stop! What is this? *Stop it!*"

Lienna gasped the final words of her incantation. The glowing bindings on Daniel's wrists and ankles vanished, and he dropped on top of Lienna. She caught the limp boy and dragged him out of the deadly spell still glowing on the floor.

A rough sob shook the teen's narrow shoulders, a haggard sound that spoke of pain and terror. But the bastard who'd hurt him was experiencing far worse right now.

Radomir writhed and screamed, slamming his body haphazardly against the wooden floorboards without feeling anything. He was trapped, utterly helpless, unable to break free of the nightmare I'd plunged him into. He had no defense and no escape from my power, from the weapon I'd turned against him: his own mind.

And I finally understood, *really* understood, why my powers scared Lienna.

A shadow brushed past me—Zak. He grabbed the edge of the stage and swung up onto it.

My whole world was spinning, my urge to throw up was almost too much to bear, and the tension in my body was so extreme I thought my bones would disintegrate under the pressure. I let the warp die and slumped back into the welcoming cushions of the chair behind me.

My vision continued to swirl, but I heard Radomir's scream cut off. I squinted, bringing him into focus as he shakily pushed up onto his elbows—just as Zak stopped beside him, towering over the righthand minion of his hated nemesis.

The druid grabbed Radomir by the front of his jacket, hauled him up, and threw him backward. He slammed down on the floor again—in the center of the lethal spell, still alight with power.

"*Ori*," Zak began in a low rumble.

Radomir's eyes widened with panic. He lunged forward with frenzied limbs, but Zak kicked him back into the spell.

"*Morte moriendum*," the druid intoned, his merciless stare holding Radomir's petrified eyes, "*cinerescendum*."

"*No!*" Radomir screamed, his piercing cry overlapping Zak's low rumble.

The luminamage's voice cut off as his body seized. A translucent ripple overwhelmed him, clinging to his body like cellophane. His skin stretched and wrinkled as though someone was vacuum sealing him in a clear plastic bag. His flesh pulled tighter and tighter, taking on the appearance of a desiccated mummy. The pallor of his skin went gray, then pieces of it crumbled away until his entire body disintegrated.

A heap of soft gray dust sifted across the stage, all that was left of the luminamage.

27

I PULLED OUT MY PHONE. The time glowed on the screen as I slid it across the stage toward Lienna and Daniel.

8:21. Nine minutes until the Complexor Bylaw vote.

"Call your mom," I said hoarsely. "Tell her you're safe."

Tears streaking his face, Daniel picked up the phone with shaking hands and dialed his mother. I held my breath.

"Mom." Daniel's face crumpled with a sob. "I'm okay. I'm safe ... He's d–dead."

The faint sound of Amy's voice reached my ears, and I let out my held breath in an explosive exhale. My rubbery legs were trembling. I turned around and sank down, my back propped against the stage. I let my head fall against it, dizziness spinning the auditorium in slow circles. Was it nap time yet? I couldn't wait for the sweet release of sleep.

Daniel's slowly steadying voice drifted through my ears as he talked to his mom, and across the auditorium, Zak was crouched over his injured varg. He seemed to be splinting its leg with a broken piece of chair.

A shoe scuffed against the stage behind me. A pair of feet swung over the edge beside my head, then dropped down next to me.

Lienna gave me a hesitant smile as she reclined against the stage too. "You okay?"

"Yeah. That last warp kicked my ass, though."

"What did you do to him? I've never seen anyone react to one of your warps like that."

I pressed my lips together, not wanting to give her another reason to fear my powers. "I erased all of his senses and plunged him into an empty void."

Her eyes widened. I couldn't tell if she was wowed or horrified.

"I know that amounts to torture in the MPD rulebook, but I'd call this an 'extreme situation.'"

"Yeah, it qualifies." She turned to face me more directly, sitting cross-legged on the auditorium floor. "You get it now though, don't you? How powerful you are?"

I let my weary brain flashback to Radomir thrashing about on the stage like an electrocuted break dancer—something I'd done with nothing but my mind.

"Yeah, I get it. Does that worry you?"

She didn't respond, but the look on her face spoke volumes: of course it did.

My gut tightened with nausea, but I forced myself to meet her eyes. "I can't say I'll never do it again. I can't promise I won't cross lines when someone's life is in danger."

She nodded slowly.

"But I *can* promise," I added, "that I'll only do it when it's absolutely necessary. You know, when we inevitably wind up in another life or death situation."

"That means no torturing informants," she pointed out sternly. "Or suspects."

"What if the suspect is Faustus Trivium?" I raised my hands placatingly. "That was a joke. I won't torture Faustus … again."

Her eyes narrowed at me. Okay, not a good joke. Maybe it was hard to find anything I said amusing when she saw me as some ungodly terror who could turn grown men into useless puddles of shivering nonsense with a single thought.

"Look." I raked my hands through my hair. "I can't change the fact I have these powers, but they don't make me a monster. Now that I understand them better, I can use them properly—responsibly."

Her eyes softened. "I hope so."

That wasn't a ringing endorsement, but it was a start.

Across the auditorium, Zak murmured to his injured varg as he checked its wounds. Unconscious goons—or in the witch's case, a very dead goon—were scattered around like ugly rag dolls. "When we work together—like, *really* together—we're a hell of a team."

"This was all you, Kit," she murmured. "Your plan, your powers."

"Oh, don't sell yourself short, partner," I countered. "Your powers are plenty special."

"Kit—"

"Fine. The druid is special too. We're all snowflakes."

A beautiful ripple of laughter burst from her lips. Thank god, I was funny again.

"What are you going to call it?" she asked. "Your new warp?"

I thought about it. "What do you think of 'Curtain Call'? Since we're in a movie theater. It sounds cool, right?"

She tilted her head back and forth as though weighing the name in her head. "How about 'The Blackout'?"

I groaned. "Damn it."

"What?"

"That is a way better name." I leaned in closer to her. "I'm serious, Lienna. I couldn't have done this without you."

I wasn't exaggerating. If she hadn't pushed back, I wouldn't have figured out any of this—not my powers, not Radomir's plan or Daniel's whereabouts. It'd been painful and ugly, and neither of us had done a fantastic job communicating how we felt. But if it hadn't happened, our partnership would've never gotten this chance to recover.

But if I said any of that, it'd come out all wrong. So I didn't try. Instead, I silently wrapped my hand around hers. Her fingers curled, holding on tight, and a painful notch in my chest eased slightly.

"Agent Morris?" Daniel leaned over the edge of the stage, still holding my phone to his ear. "My mom wants to know if she can come get me."

I reluctantly released Lienna's hand. "Uh—"

"You'll have to wait for a healer to check you over," Lienna said. "But as soon as they've cleared you, she can take you home."

Nodding, Daniel repeated that into the phone.

"There's a healer on the way?" I murmured to Lienna in an undertone.

"Not yet." She fished her phone from her pocket. "I should call this in and get a team here."

"In that case, we need to give our ghostly rogue ally a heads-up."

"And we need to get our stories straight on what happened, because we can't mention him in our report." She pushed to her feet, brushed off her knees, then stretched her hand toward me. "Shall we, partner?"

Grinning, I grabbed her offered hand and let her pull me to my feet.

It took my exhausted, jellified muscles a moment to agree to support my weight, then I turned to face the auditorium. Daniel was still talking to his mom on my phone. The knocked-out forms of the hydromage and sorcerer were still immobile, and the dead witch had, for obvious reasons, not moved. Radomir's dusty remains were still on the stage, and the scorpion fae's corpse was defiling three rows of seating.

But otherwise, the auditorium was conspicuously empty.

"Where the hell is Zak?" Lienna growled.

I leaned back against the stage and shook my head. "The Ghost ghosted us."

"WE WERE A TEAM," I complained to Lienna as she closed the theater doors, still smarting over Zak's vanishing act three hours earlier. "We kicked ass together and everything. I think that at least warranted a goodbye."

She slapped the end of a roll of MPD-issued "DO NOT ENTER" police tape against the door frame and stretched it across the entrance. "Did you expect him to stick around and bond with us? He must've suspected more agents would be on the way."

I grumbled under my breath as she taped the second half of an oversized X across the doors.

"At least we're rid of him now," she added. "He has no reason to show up again."

No reason except I owed him an unspecified favor, and I had no doubt he'd come to collect. That would be fun.

On the plus side, we'd managed to process the crime scene, supervise the clean-up crew, and fill out the preliminary paperwork without giving away that we'd had an ally—an extremely violence-happy one. Lienna had gotten credit for the scorpion kill, and I was getting credit for defeating the hydromage and sorcerer. The witch, we'd decided, had tragically tripped and stabbed herself in the throat.

Radomir's death was harder to explain, so we'd agreed he'd also caused his own demise. Such a clumsy bunch of rogues, am I right?

Daniel had gotten a clean bill of health from Scooter, and his reunion with his mom had been tearful and heart-wrenching. She'd thanked Lienna and me about twenty times before ushering her son to her car.

After checking Daniel, Scooter had also quietly let me know that Filip Shelton, the poisoned banker, had briefly recovered consciousness, and his health was improving.

Daniel was with his mom, safe and sound, and Filip was recovering. But with Radomir dead, the odds we'd ever find Mercury Tibayan, Soraya Sadeghi, and the other teen victims were tragically slim. Not that Lienna and I wouldn't do everything we could to find them.

Next time I saw Zak, I would give him a piece of my mind for killing Radomir before we could get the answers we needed.

"Do you think he makes all those dramatic exits because they add to his scary reputation," I mused, thinking back on my interactions with the mysterious rogue, "or is it just a personality quirk?"

"Both?" Lienna guessed, dropping the roll of police tape in her satchel. Together, we descended the steps and headed up the dark sidewalk toward the smart car. It was closing in on midnight and the street was abandoned.

I tapped my chin thoughtfully. "Maybe I should've taken notes on his technique. Do you think the 'dark and brooding' thing would work for me?"

She rolled her eyes. "I don't think it'd suit you, Kit. Besides, you're a psycho warper. You can make whatever dramatic exit you want."

"Oh. Hell *yeah*, I could." My brain was suddenly consumed by all the different warps I could utilize to disappear in front of people and leave them awed by my powers. "I could make a black mist swirl around me and then explode into a hundred bats like Dracula, or I could melt into a puddle and flow away into the sewer—actually, that's terrible. Scratch that one. Ooh! I could transform into a *clown* and—"

"Kit!"

"Right. Sorry. No clowns because … why was that again?"

She sighed. "When I was nine, my cousin took me into a clown-themed haunted house on Halloween. I had nightmares for months."

"Oh," I replied, fighting a grin. "That's—"

"If you say 'hilarious,' I'll—"

"Tragic," I interrupted hastily. "It was tragic. So how about *Poltergeist* for our next movie night?"

She shot me a death glare.

"Does this mean all Batman movies with the Joker are off the table too?"

She heaved another aggrieved sigh.

We reached the car and stopped. Lienna rubbed her forehead tiredly. I could empathize, seeing as I was maybe ten minutes away from keeling over from fatigue.

"It's been three hours since you called Captain Blythe," I pointed out in a hopeful tone. "She's probably sleeping, right?"

"I doubt it." Lienna pulled out her phone. "She'll want a full report."

She lifted the device to her ear, its faint ringing filling the quiet. One, two, three—then Blythe's voice snapped down the line.

"It's Agent Shen," Lienna said quickly. "Agent Morris and I are—" She broke off, listening. "Now? But—" Another pause. "Yes, ma'am." Disconnecting the call, she grimaced at me. "She wants us to meet her."

"Meet her where?"

"At a crime scene."

This late? If I'd been feeling more energetic than a hibernating bear, I might have been intrigued. The captain didn't personally show up for just any crime scene.

Lienna and I climbed into Smart Car III and headed north through downtown. The harbor peeked out from between bland rectangular buildings as Lienna navigated into a commercial area. A minute later, she turned the smart car off the road and into a parking lot. I recognized two MPD vehicles, plus a pair of heavy-duty pickup trucks with matching company logos on their sides.

The scene was brightly illuminated with work lights that cast harsh shadows across the burnt remains of a building, but that wasn't the interesting part of this supposed crime scene.

The lot backed onto the Vancouver harbor, and forty feet out in the water was a medium-sized fishing boat. At least, I thought it was a fishing boat since it had long cranes jutting off the side, presumably for hauling in nets. I could be wrong, though. The only nautical expertise I had involved sinking cargo ships with RPGs.

Lienna parked beside a big black SUV that belonged to our esteemed captain, and we climbed out. The rumble of the vessel's engine drowned out the shouts of the crew and the nearer calls of the people bustling around on the shore. Glowing lights aboard the boat were aimed at the dark water, and thick lines hung from the crane arms, running to something beneath the surface.

"There," Lienna said, pointing to a tall blond figure at the far end of the wharf. We hurried toward her, my head swiveling as I took in the organized chaos all around us.

Blythe looked up as we approached, her usual armload of folders replaced by a single clipboard. She was standing in front of two long, person-sized lumps on the ground covered with black tarps.

"Cap," I said with a jaunty salute, my exhaustion temporarily forgotten. "What's going on here?"

"Agent Morris, Agent Shen. Are you finished with your case?"

"Bad guy dead, evil minions captured, and kidnapped teen rescued," I summarized succinctly, though she already knew that much. "Daniel is fine and reunited with his mom. She let us know that the Complexor Bylaw vote has been postponed pending an investigation."

Her eyebrows lifted slightly. "An investigation?"

"Ms. Buchanan told the committee what happened to Daniel," Lienna revealed, taking over. "She suspects other committee members were being coerced as well."

Blythe's gaze shifted between us. "Did you find out who hired Radomir Kozlov?"

"No," Lienna admitted. "But we'll need to keep searching for his other victims, and we may learn more when we find them."

"Did you learn anything about—"

"Captain!" Vincent Park hurried over, his black leather jacket hanging open to reveal a crisp suit and white collared shirt beneath it. "The crew is about to pull it up."

I squinted at him. "Doesn't Agent Harris wear a jacket just like that?"

Vincent scowled.

"Thank you, Agent Park," Blythe said, ignoring me.

He held out a dripping wet camera. "The divers are done taking photos."

Claiming the camera, Blythe waved him away. As he hastened back toward a group of crew members and agents, she turned on the camera.

"So?" I prompted, vibrating with curiosity. "What is all this?"

"A bounty hunter called in an incident on the helipad involving rogue sorcerers who were attempting an illegal spell. There was an altercation. The sorcerers were killed."

I looked down at the tarp-covered bodies—the sorcerers, I was guessing—then peered around the concrete lot. "What helipad?"

Blythe nodded toward the harbor. "The one that is now twenty feet under water."

"Oh." That explained the boat. And the divers.

Blythe handed the camera to Lienna. "What does that look like to you, Agent Shen?"

I leaned close to Lienna to peer at the camera's small display screen. It showed a murky underwater photo of a slab of concrete etched with runes. Lienna scrolled through the images, her lips pressing thinner and thinner with each photo of the broken helipad and what must've been a ginormous-sized spell array carved into it.

"Well?" Blythe prompted impatiently.

"There are abjuration elements," Lienna replied. "But I can't tell what the spell does."

"Find out. I'll have copies of those photos waiting for you in my office by morning."

"Yes, ma'am."

From the water's edge, Vincent called out something I couldn't pick up over the noise of the ship. Several crew members rotated the work lights to point across the water at the fishing boat.

The three of us turned to watch the boat as its winches whined and the lines retracted, hauling something up from the water.

Lienna's fingers gripped my arm, and she pulled me several steps away from Blythe, who was watching the operation on the water with a steely gaze.

"Kit," my partner hissed, pulling my head down so she could put her mouth right to my ear. "The spell carved into that helipad isn't abjuration. *It's a portal.*"

My eyes widened.

"A *huge* portal," she continued in a rapid whisper. "And do you know who asked me about a portal spell? *Robin Page.*"

"No way!" I gasped.

She yanked on my arm to silence me before Blythe noticed us whispering. "Robin wanted to meet me at the library for advice about a spell she was researching. She thought it was abjuration, but it was a portal like that broken one."

"Holy shit. But why would a demon contractor be researching portals?"

"I don't know."

The winches whined loudly as the fishing vessel hauled up its catch. The water's surface frothed and surged, displaced by something large.

"Hey, Captain Blythe," I said, pulling away from Lienna. "The bounty hunter that reported this, which guild are they from?"

She turned her blue laser-beam stare on me. "The Crow and Hammer."

I opened my mouth, but whatever I'd been about to say disappeared from my head as the object beneath the water broke the surface. The fishing boat rocked in the waves as the cranes hauled the thing out of the ocean.

My jaw hung open, my stomach crawling like I'd swallowed a bucketful of millipedes. "What in the name of unholy kaiju is *that*?"

Neither Blythe nor Lienna answered me.

Hanging from the lines, water streaming off it, was a monster. Not a comic-book monster. Not a mythical beast. Not a movie prop. It was a flesh and fang incarnation of nightmare.

Pale, slimy flesh covered a vaguely reptilian body as long as a bus. Huge talons protruded from its long toes, and a thick tail hung down into the water. Bulbous yellow eyes stuck out from its salamander-ish head, staring blankly, and its wide, slack jaw bristled with curved teeth.

"What ..." Lienna's voice shook. "What is it?"

Whatever it was, it was dead. I gulped my stomach down. "It looks like someone crossbred an anglerfish with Godzilla and raised the offspring in a meth lab."

Blythe's hand, resting on her clipboard as though she were about to jot notes on a new scientific discovery, gripped her pen so hard the plastic bent. "According to the incident report, it's likely a fae."

"That's no fae," a raspy male voice countered.

"No shit," I muttered—then jumped half a foot in the air and spun around as recognition of that voice hit my exhausted brain.

From ten long feet away, Zak stood with his arms folded and his hood drawn up to shadow his face. I gawked at him, legit wondering if he'd suffered a concussion. I had no other explanation for why he was here, in the middle of an active crime scene, and *right in front of the Vancouver precinct's captain.*

Luckily—or maybe unluckily—no one else was nearby. They were all at the water's edge, their horrified gazes locked on the slimy nightmare beast that'd been hauled from the harbor.

"That thing isn't a fae," Zak repeated in a low rumble. "I doubt it's any more native to this world than a demon is."

A demon. Plus a giant portal. Plus a demon contractor who'd been asking about a portal spell.

I did *not* like where this was going.

"Do you know who I am?" Zak asked, his face in complete shadow.

Blythe's blue eyes gleamed in a terrifying way. "Your reputation precedes you, druid, but I never expected you to turn yourself in. Overwhelmed by guilt?"

"Hardly." He uncrossed his arms and held one gloved hand in the air. A small object dangled from a lanyard wrapped around his wrist. "You want this."

"Do I?" Blythe growled softly.

"And you have something I want. I'm here to trade."

Lienna stiffened, one hand stuffed in her satchel, ready to pull out an artifact. "The MPD doesn't trade with rogues!"

"Give me Varvara's grimoire."

"Her grimoire?" Lienna repeated in scathing disbelief. "Why would we hand over a book of deadly dark magic to a known dark-arts practitioner?"

He swung the object, and as it caught the light, I realized it was a memory stick. "Someone hired Radomir. Someone was leaking information to him from inside the MPD. Someone's been leaking information to me."

Zak knew who the mole in our precinct was?

"Give me the grimoire, and I'll give you answers."

"No way," Lienna snarled, yanking out a stun marble. "And you made a big mistake coming here. You're—"

Blythe raised her hand, never taking her eyes off Zak. "Make the trade, Agent Shen."

Lienna sucked in a sharp breath. "Captain—"

"Do it."

What the hell? Had Blythe lost her mind?

Lienna seemed to feel the same way. She stared at her superior for a long moment, then reached slowly into her satchel. She pulled out the red leather-bound grimoire.

Zak tugged the lanyard off his wrist and strode forward. Stopping a dangerous three feet away from Blythe, he held a hand out to Lienna. With a final glance at her superior, she placed it in his waiting palm.

He held up the memory stick. "Careful what you do with this, captain."

"Careful who you cross, druid," she replied, her voice sharp as a blade. "Next time I lay eyes on you will be in my lockup."

His head tilted, the light brushing over his jaw as he gave her a cold, challenging smile. "We'll see."

Grimoire in hand, he turned and strode away, his dark coat billowing out behind him. The darkness around him shimmered, and his two vargs appeared, trotting at his sides. He lay a gloved hand on the larger one's shoulders.

With another shimmer, he and the fae beasts faded out of sight, vanishing before our eyes.

I rubbed my forehead, confused and a bit stunned. Had I passed out? Was this all a dream?

Blythe swung her arm out and her fist smacked me in the chest. I winced. That hurt too much to be a dream.

"Take it, Agent Morris."

I obediently grasped the lanyard and its memory stick of unknown secrets.

"Why did you agree to his deal?" Lienna demanded.

"Why did he *offer* a deal?" I asked. "He could've stolen the grimoire from us instead."

"Because some secrets are too dangerous." Blythe gazed icily at the spot where the druid had disappeared. "And he didn't want them anymore. Now they're ours to unmask and destroy."

"But why?" Lienna asked again, stepping toward the captain. "You could've gotten that memory stick from him without letting him walk."

"Keep friends close." She tucked her clipboard under her arm. "Keep enemies closer. And keep pawns where you can use them. Agent Shen, Agent Morris, protect that memory stick with your lives—and ensure no one else ever lays eyes on it. Do I make myself clear?"

"Yes, ma'am," Lienna and I chorused.

Across the wharf, Vincent called for Blythe. With a short nod to us, she marched away.

Alone, Lienna and I looked at the memory stick I held. What secrets did it contain about the mole inside the MPD— and why did I get the feeling it was much bigger than any of us suspected?

My worried gaze met Lienna's, and I was glad my abilities were growing stronger. We would need all the wits, magic, and luck we both could muster to get through whatever was coming.

KIT WILL RETURN IN
THE FOURTH INSTALLMENT OF

THE
GUILD CODEX
WARPED

www.guildcodex.ca

ABOUT THE AUTHORS

ANNETTE MARIE is the best-selling author of The Guild Codex, an expansive collection of interwoven urban fantasy series ranging from thrilling adventure to hilarious hijinks to heartrending romance. Her other works include YA urban fantasy series Steel & Stone, its prequel trilogy Spell Weaver, and romantic fantasy trilogy Red Winter.

Her first love is fantasy, but fast-paced adventures, bold heroines, and tantalizing forbidden romances are her guilty pleasures. She proudly admits she has a thing for dragons and aspires to include them in every book.

Annette lives in the frozen winter wasteland of Alberta, Canada (okay, it's not quite that bad) and shares her life with her husband and their furry minion of darkness—sorry, cat—Caesar. When not writing, she can be found elbow-deep in one art project or another while blissfully ignoring all adult responsibilities.

www.annettemarie.ca

ROB JACOBSEN is a Canadian writer, actor, and director, who has been in a few TV shows you might watch, had a few films in festivals you might have attended, and authored some stories you might have come across. He's hoping to accomplish plenty more by the time he inevitably dies surrounded by cats while watching reruns of Mr. Robot.

Currently, he is the Creative Director of Cave Puppet Films, as well as the co-author of the Guild Codex: Warped series with Annette Marie.

www.robjacobsen.ca

SPECIAL THANKS

Our thanks to Erich Merkel for sharing your exceptional expertise in Latin and Ancient Greek.

Any errors are the authors'.

THE
GUILD CODEX
WARPED

The MPD has three roles: keep magic hidden, keep mythics under control, and don't screw up the first two.

Kit Morris is the wrong guy for the job on all counts—but for better or worse, this mind-warping psychic is the MPD's newest and most unlikely agent.

THE
GUILD CODEX
UNVEILED

A failed witch with a murder conviction, a switchblade for a best friend, and a dangerous lack of restraint. A notorious druid mired in secrets, shadowed by deadly fae, and haunted by his past.

They might be exactly what the other needs—if they don't destroy each other first.

THE
GUILD CODEX
SPELLBOUND

Meet Tori. She's feisty. She's broke. She has a bit of an issue with running her mouth off. And she just landed a job at the local magic guild. Problem is, she's also 100% human. Oops.

Welcome to the Crow and Hammer.

DISCOVER MORE BOOKS AT
www.guildcodex.ca

THE
GUILD CODEX
DEMONIZED

Robin Page: outcast sorceress, mythic history buff, unapologetic
bookworm, and the last person you'd expect to command the rarest
demon in the long history of summoning. Though she holds his
leash, this demon can't be controlled.

But can he be tamed?

STEEL & STONE

When everyone wants you dead, good help is hard to find.

The first rule for an apprentice Consul is *don't trust daemons*. But when Piper is framed for the theft of the deadly Sahar Stone, she ends up with two troublesome daemons as her only allies: Lyre, a hotter-than-hell incubus who isn't as harmless as he seems, and Ash, a draconian mercenary with a seriously bad reputation. Trusting them might be her biggest mistake yet.

GET THE COMPLETE SERIES
www.annettemarie.ca/steelandstone

A destiny written by the gods. A fate forged by lies.

If Emi is sure of anything, it's that *kami*—the gods—are good, and *yokai*—the earth spirits—are evil. But when she saves the life of a fox shapeshifter, the truths of her world start to crumble. And the treachery of the gods runs deep.

This stunning trilogy features 30 full-page illustrations.

GET THE COMPLETE TRILOGY
www.annettemarie.ca/redwinter

CPSIA information can be obtained
at www.ICGtesting.com
Printed in the USA
FSHW012002050821
83867FS